The Uninvited

A novel by Dianne J. Beale

Back Cover Art by L.V. Jobs

Cover Design by Dianne J. Beale

Formatted and Edited by Dianne J. Beale

The Uninvited is a work of fiction written by Dianne J. Beale. Any similarities to actual persons, either living or dead, are merely coincidental. People, events, names, places, and all other content are products of the author's imagination and are not to be mistaken or perceived as real.

© Copyright 2007, 2009 by Dianne J. Beale. All rights reserved. No part of this book may be reproduced, except for brief quotations in articles or reviews, without written permission from the author.

Acknowledgments

Thank you, Michael, for your continued friendship that has only grown as we have journeyed together in marriage. Thank you for your support and encouragement. I truly appreciate all you are, have been, and will continue to be. Thank you.

I also wish to thank my son, Micah, for his patience whenever my writing would interfere with his carefully set plans. Thank you for the use of your computer and for the many times you set aside a question and worked on something else until I was available. I appreciate your understanding.

Thank you also to Robin Knapp and Tabi Boyce for taking the time to not only read my manuscript, but also to submit your many suggestions. I hope my final effort will make you proud.

And many thanks to those others who took the time to read my manuscript. Knowing you made it through to the end was an encouragement in itself.

I thank Joe Sroufe for his willingness to offer suggestions to a new author and I also thank the authors who took the time to acknowledge my emails even when they were pressed for time. I appreciate that you took the time to encourage a new writer even though you were not able to read my manuscript.

Many thanks to CreateSpace, as well. Thank you for believing in new authors and for making self-publishing an affordable option.

You smile with pomp and rigor, you talk of benevolence and virtue; I act with benevolence and virtue and get murdered time after time. —William Blake

Chapter 1

The week commenced with dark clouds streaming down water as if it were being squeezed from a gigantic sponge. And throughout the week, as the sponge emptied and refilled, clouds continued to cry down on the small town of Mayhaw. Even now, though the week was at its end, a steady, humid drizzle continued to fall.

But Margaret Zeiler, in her sincere elegance, had always enjoyed the rain—especially the rhythmic sounds it shared whenever she'd been given the gift of sitting beneath a metal roof. It had served her often; the musical drum would release peace to conquer the growing turmoil that fed upon her unobserved days of rest.

As she walked across the cracking, neglected, parking lot, she greedily absorbed the falling teardrops, allowing them to infiltrate each thirsting crevice within her soul. She imagined herself as a goblet, ready to receive the combined blessings that the rain would represent.

Then she reached the door. In a matter of seconds, the rich harmony disappeared as if struck by fire, released as steam, and lost to the morning fog.

2

"How is it that I can work at a church and yet feel so utterly alone?" she wondered aloud. But there was not time enough to ponder. Instead, she opened the out-dated, gray, lead-lined, metal door and went inside to the echoing corridor.

Once in her office, Margaret removed her jacket, changed from her sneakers to a pair of basic black pumps, and then headed down the pasty, white hall for the weekly staff meeting. Realizing she had forgotten her notebook, she was glad she'd been trained in the art of punctuality; there were still a good ten minutes left before it would be time to start. She returned to her office, grabbed her notebook and pen, and then retraced her steps back toward the designated room.

While waiting for the others, she began to list reasons as to why she liked the rain. *The rain gives life. It reminds me of rainbows. It encourages me as a symbol of God's faithfulness. It represents God's mercy. It cleanses the air. It refreshes me.*

As subtle, faint music began to fill the room, the list colored to a more negative hue. *It can be monotonous. It hides the sun. It can lead to floods. It sometimes makes me tired. It's not always convenient to carry an umbrella. It is rarely acceptable for clothes to be wet. It can bring dangerous storms.*

The music, slow and familiar, grew louder. Soon it had bathed the room. Without missing a beat, Margaret stopped writing — the pastor had arrived. It would not be long before she was joined by the others.

The Uninvited

It was unsettling how this slight piece of information affected her. She smoothed her hands over her already neatly-placed hair and pulled at her practical, cotton blouse. Then, as if no more than a schoolgirl, she straightened in her seat, as well.

Words and music repeated softly; once again, a phrase from her childhood invaded her thoughts. She missed the variety of compositions that had once filled this church. And it was becoming more and more difficult for her to set aside these feelings. Shouldn't prayer and song—worship of God—mirror life? She couldn't shake off the feeling that maybe she'd been pulled into a mere existence of *meaningless repetition*.

Suddenly she became aware of the complete flatness of her life—a life that now imitated the unrelenting office music: eat, work; eat, work; eat, work; sleep, and repeat. It did carry a smidgen of rhythm, but mostly it seemed rather pointless.

She closed her notebook and looked up at the clock. And just as the others joined her, she let out a sigh that, unfortunately, evolved into a yawn. Thankfully, it seemed that no one had noticed. Instead, the meeting was called to order and she was asked to relate the events from the assembly of the week before.

As she began to read from her neatly organized list, she found herself carefully monitoring her speed. She felt stifled and tense—almost unnatural as she read.

By Dianne J. Beale

"Garnet, were you even *here* last meeting?"

Startled, Margaret looked up from her notes to scan the faces of those around her. But all eyes were turned toward the man at the head of the table — the man who had impatiently interrupted her reading of the minutes. Wearily, she met his gaze. "Sir?" she questioned.

Pastor Andres Loukatos, although average in height, possessed an intimidating frame of muscles. Long, dark lashes hooded his pine-green eyes as they burned into her. His dark hair accentuated the creases of frustration that now marked his typically charming features. With an overstated sigh, he turned to the woman who sat next to her. "Trish, be a good girl and fill your friend in," he sneered.

Trish pushed a lock of her amber hair back up her cheek and stuffed it behind her ear. Her honey-brown eyes held confusion as she spoke. "I'm sorry, Pastor," she stuttered, "I wasn't here for that meeting."

Andres' eyes darkened, revealing tawny flecks. "Neither was Garnet, apparently. Her body may have been present, but that's about all, if I go by her notes. Anyone?" he queried.

Heads moved as people began shifting in their seats to avoid Trish's fate. Not one person dared to speak. "Fine group you are," he offered. "Last meeting it was decided that since Garnet forgot to mention her ambitious preparations to the rest of us, the children's performance cannot take place. Hymns might be adequate for an old folks' home, but they're a little antiquated for an actual church service. We want our music to be fresh—sung *to* God, not *about* Him." Andres accented his speech with a mild shaking of his head.

The room filled with affirmations: *that's right; oh, yeah, we did decide that; if it's not on the calendar, then it's never a sure thing.* Margaret looked down at her notes and then over at the white eraser board that served as a calendar. What was she going to tell the children? They'd been practicing for months. "Sir," she began, but was cut off.

"You know the rules, Garnet. Must you always try to undermine God's plans?"

"I just thought," Margaret trailed off, pleading for the help of a youthful figure that sat to Andres' right.

But Anthony disregarded her attempt to involve him and instead pushed forward to another topic of discussion. "Are we still planning to sell those town homes that the church owns?"

The meeting went on without her. Defeated, she closed her notebook and sat silently until it was time for her to prepare the coffee and doughnuts. Then she got up and quietly slipped out the door.

Once in the café, she busied herself with this menial task. She'd not been aware that she'd been singing until a soft, kind voice broke in. It was Paco, the church janitor. He had offered to help carry the trays. Margaret thanked him, but declined.

By Dianne J. Beale

6

As soon as she was back in the meeting, a hush fell over the room. She awkwardly surmised that she had been the newest topic of discussion. A quick prayer was said, and the meeting ended.

It had never previously occurred to her, but they rarely opened the meetings with prayer. The prayer was more often an after-thought that solidified the pastor's wishes. She decided to grab a sugared jelly doughnut and leave the oppressive room.

"Hey, can we talk?" It was Anthony.

"What are we doing now if we're not talking?" she sulked.

Anthony ignored her tone and ushered her into her tea-scented, nearby office. Once she had set down her notebook and doughnut, he handed her a strangely masculine envelope that smelled of musk—it reminded her of Andres.

"What's this?" she asked.

"Just read it, okay? You know I express things better in writing."

Actually, she knew no such thing. As was demonstrated in the meeting, there was little regard for the written language. The staff members were mighty advocates of body language and eye contact. Too often she had heard how easily any form of literature could be misunderstood. She had dared to joke about it, once, before she knew better: she had challenged Andres by saying that she guessed she

The Uninvited

might as well go and burn her Bible then… after all, she wouldn't want to risk misunderstanding God.

Reluctantly, Margaret remembered Anthony. "You want me to read it now? With you standing here?"

"Yes. That's the idea."

"Why can't you just tell me what it says?" she argued. "This seems a bit odd, with you here and all."

Anthony sounded like a raspy snake when he responded. "Just stop fussing and submit for once!"

"Oh, are we married, then? Did you marry by proxy and not tell me?"

"Always ready with an answer. Never ready to listen."

Margaret's voice became almost a whisper. "Is that what *you* think? Do you even know *how* to think? Or are those Andres' words?"

"Just read the letter, *Margaret*," he commanded. "I'm going now. Andres and I have an appointment for lunch." Then he was gone.

Pulling her Bible down from a shelf, she sat down at her desk, moved the doughnut to the side, and began to work on Sunday's lesson for the children. As she read in Psalms, she finally stopped to open the envelope. She read the letter, jotted down a note to herself, stuck the letter into her Bible, tossed the envelope, and then returned the Bible to the shelf. "Coward," she mumbled, softly, almost under her breath. "I suppose this means you'll soon be spawning a church of

By Dianne J. Beale

your own." Then she rose to finish out her day in the children's building.

Chapter 2

As Margaret pushed open the door to head outside, she realized she'd have to change her planned route. Rain was now hitting the ground so forcefully that it was forming miniature fountains that came and went as if they were timed geysers. Closing the door, she turned back toward her office to grab an umbrella.

Once there, she noticed her sneakers and jacket and decided to put these on, as well. She would walk as far as she could through the building and then make a run for it. Although she had been promised a covered walkway years ago, the collected money had long since been spent. Most of it had gone to obtaining Andres.

Once in the café, Margaret had to face what she had hoped to avoid — people. Immediately she was approached by Trish.

"Oh, are you going to eat here today?" she asked.

Margaret wanted to inquire if it *looked* like she planned to stay. Here she was: standing in a jacket, wearing sneakers, and carrying an umbrella. Yet this was the question that Trish chose to ask?

By Dianne J. Beale

Instead of unleashing her sarcasm, she did her best not to show her agitation since she realized her mood actually had little to do with Trish. Lifting the hand that carried the umbrella, she revealed a small brown sack to show she was also toting her lunch. "No. I can't, really. Sorry. Since I'm not coming in tomorrow, I'll need to get as much done today as I can. For Sunday, you know?" She gave Trish an encouraging smile.

Trish paled. "Oh, no, I knew I forgot something. I'm not sure I'll be able to make tomorrow's brunch. I'll have to check. And I know I can't make it for…" She paused to look around and then lowered her voice. "…for the party." She added these last three words in not much more than a whisper, as if the event was secret. Then she told Margaret to wish Mitch the very best and to party hard enough for all of them.

This last statement reminded her of last week's staff meeting. They had all enthusiastically refused her invitation, adding that she and Mitch should enjoy themselves anyway and toast their beers for them. Margaret found herself puzzling over Trish's last statement. "Aren't you going to at least call him?" she posed.

Trish seemed embarrassed and unsure of herself. "Oh, yeah, of course I will. Um, never mind then. Sorry."

As Trish walked away, Margaret couldn't help but question what her brother saw in that woman. She did have a classic, porcelain doll-like beauty, but she seemed so unaware and helpless.

Opening her umbrella, she then braved the outside gale. The wind had picked up and already she could feel that her lunch was soaked.

When she made it inside the children's building, she removed her sneakers so that her socks could dry out. Then she hung up her jacket and set down her open umbrella. Depositing her book bag and lunch onto the nearby counter, she headed for the one place where she knew she would not be disturbed — a small, windowless, one-room bathroom with a changing table riveted to the wall where the mirror should have been.

Once inside, Margaret moved to the corner farthest from the toilet and dropped to her knees. Tears streamed down her face as she pleaded with God, emptying herself just as the clouds had done the entire week. She cried, agonized, and often just fell silent, allowing her tears to speak.

She remembered when Andres was voted in as the new head pastor. The congregation had been thrown into confusion at the loss of her parents. They had requested that Mitch take their Dad's place.

Thankfully, Mr. Bradley was still alive then. He recognized the need for Mitch, and her, to remain sheep and be nurtured. He had been a close confidant of their Dad, so the church was all too happy to accept his offer to fill in until a new pastor could be found. Besides, he was willing to do it for free.

Mrs. Bradley was one of the sweetest souls that Margaret had ever known. When she passed away a year later, it was as if a part of Mr. Bradley died with her. He aged rapidly after her death.

It didn't help that Janet Townsend was pushing to have her nephew, Jack, appointed as the new head pastor. He had spoken a few times, but the congregation felt he would better fill the position of associate pastor, since he was so very young. And the church had never had an associate pastor — they'd never seen a need for one. Truth be told, they also feared that a pastor, too young, would become "prideful and unteachable."

And then there was Marion Meadows-Jackson. She had worn Mr. Bradley down.

Mrs. Bradley had organized a yearly Live Nativity Scene that Ms. Meadows-Jackson felt should be replaced by something more "meaningful and contemporary." Margaret and Mitch had fought to have the manger scene one last year. They had hoped to usher out this tradition in remembrance of Mrs. Bradley. They wanted to honor the Bradley family — to express their gratitude and love for them.

But Ms. Meadows-Jackson had just remarried, and her husband was not only a strong presence at the church, but also in the treasury. So, at the meeting of decision, she had fumed an ungrateful tirade and managed to pull Janet Townsend onto her side. Janet, indignant that she couldn't guarantee her nephew a pastorship upon graduation, did all she could to then sabotage Mitch and Margaret.

But the one comment that had worked like a poison dart to Mr. Bradley's already ailing heart was from Ms. Marion Meadows-Jackson: "People," she had insisted, "the idea of a live manger scene has long since been dreaded. Each year, we bring a smelly donkey into our church, along with someone's overzealous, diapered baby, and a herd of rambunctious kids. Yet we continued with this tradition because *Louise Bradley* insisted. Let's bury Louise's love-child with her. Okay? If y'all choose to do this, you'll do it on your own. My husband's annual, ever-generous gift will not be available this year."

Mrs. Bradley had requested that her husband continue the nativity scene for just one last time. She had made a promise to each kid who had participated and wanted to be sure that the church would honor her words. Each child had wanted to be either Mary or Joseph, and Louise had only two children left who had not had their turns.

But the elders lacked the funds, and Mr. Bradley and the Zeilers were still pooling their resources to pay for the recent funerals. So Mr. Bradley's health had taken a turn for the worse and Mrs. Townsend's nephew was hired on as the new pastor, after all. Things went downhill from there.

By Dianne J. Beale

The church split. Hard feelings forced division. Margaret and Mitch were drowning in grief; first they had lost their parents, and then the Bradleys (who had served as surrogate grandparents since they were not able to have children of their own).

And somewhere along the line, Andres Loukatos was voted in as head pastor, the nephew was demoted to music minister (and later replaced), and the congregational democracy was handed over to the church staff. The idea sounded good at the time—it seemed to imply a reinstatement of unity.

But, with Andres, it soon became a dictatorship. He fired old staff, forcing them to sign papers of resignation and any board or staff member who dared to voice an opinion (or challenge his interpretations of the Scripture) also suddenly resigned. And now Mitch had chosen to change employers, reducing his status to that of harmless member, as well.

However, Margaret could not let go. This was where she had accepted Jesus as her Lord. And this was her *parent's* church. And right now, it was all she had. It gave her the strength to go forward. She needed to hold onto even the slightest hope that she could resuscitate her parents' dream. She just couldn't let it die with them. So Margaret stayed, in spite of the many sacrifices.

Finally, she stood to wash her face with cold water at the sink. Then she dried with the rough, brown, unattractive towels that only the children and their parents were expected to use.

Returning to where she had left her lunch, she tossed the soggy mess into the trash and began to work toward creating the atmosphere that she had envisioned for the lesson on Sunday. Soon she had lost track of time; it was dark when she finally decided to call it a day.

By Dianne J. Beale

Chapter 3

As Margaret stepped out from the church, a chill climbed her spine. The sky glowed an eerie oyster gray while the fog moved to enclose her in a dank blanket of mildew. The rain had stopped for the moment, but still each street light seemed to be merely a dim shadow of haze; the sky was completely hidden.

Scanning for her Volkswagen Beetle, Margaret was suddenly glad that she had purchased the *salsa red*. She had been drawn to the *harvest moon*. But while she imagined herself a princess, driving about in her carriage of gold, her brother had been more practical. He had insisted that red was the only available color that would remain visible in all kinds of weather.

As she rushed to reach her car, she did not see the figure at her feet. Books went sprawling onto the parking lot, and the bag of Sunday School supplies split. With crafting items spread all about her, she still managed to catch herself before she could fall. But this was not without consequence; a twinge of pain jetted upward from her foot and into the base of her back.

What had she tripped over? Lowering herself toward the pavement, she began lifting the books. She planned to drop them into the trunk where she'd grab a new bag.

"Can I help you, Garnet?" asked a familiar, sultry voice. The church staff had given Margaret this title; they felt that nicknames endeared a person, drawing them close, like family. Startled, she rose with the collected books and pasted a smile on her face.

"Oh, I'll be okay, Sir," she stammered. "You know me; I tend to be an accident waiting to happen. It was some type of animal—a cat—I think."

Pastor Andres, having materialized out of the darkness, began to search the parking lot in an exaggerated manner. "Are you sure?" he asked. "Well, I suppose it is difficult to see just what's out there tonight." He seemed to be patronizing her, as if he knew there had been a cat, but wanted to imply that she had tripped all on her own. "Here, let me help you."

Knowing it would do little good to protest, she handed him the books. She felt silly carrying the remains of a broken bag while he carried such a load, but she was grateful since she did need to get her keys out from her pack.

As she dug through the numerous papers and other obstructive items, she tried to recall why they had chosen Garnet as her nickname. She remembered when she had naively believed it was the color of her hair—a deep, burnished auburn.

By Dianne J. Beale

But then she had overheard the others: "She's such a dramatist, always wearing her heart upon her sleeve." People had laughed, walking away, never even noticing her. Margaret had often wondered why Andres didn't have an affectionate moniker. Now she knew the truth—Andres didn't want equality; he wanted control. Just as children are taught to use *mom* or *dad* with their parents, the church staff had learned to use "Pastor Andres."

Her ever-smiling eyes dulled. When she turned to open the trunk, Andres caught her off guard with his compliment. "I've not ever seen your eyes this color," he commented. "It's almost as if someone could get lost in a misty sea. They're very becoming."

Margaret dropped her gaze to the lock and mumbled a thank you. At times it seemed he was completely absorbed, almost obsessed, with her. At others, it was as if she didn't even exist. She crushed the bag into the corner of the trunk and pulled out a new one for collection of the Sunday School materials.

Andres dropped the books into the trunk and followed to help. Soon they had gathered all that could be recovered. Smiling in satisfaction, the pastor then walked her to the car. Once he had her tucked safely inside, he turned toward the building. By the time she had maneuvered the vehicle, he was gone.

She started at the sound of her cell phone, but instinctively tapped at the edge of her ear. It was her

The Uninvited

brother, Mitch. "Hey, Mar, you okay? Weren't we supposed to meet at six? It's almost eight, ya know."

"Eight? Oh, Mitch, I'm sorry. I guess I got lost at sea again." Mitch had called her Mar for as long as she could remember. He had incessantly joked about how it was Spanish for *the sea*.

Before their parents had died, it was a source of many arguments. She had hated being called Mar. He would tease her and then tell everyone how his sister could cry a sea. He would run from her in mock fear and then say her anger was like a raging sea.

But then it had all changed. Mitch took his new role as guardian very seriously. When her prom date dumped her for a more popular girl, Mitch was there to tell her that she was beautiful—like a calm, reflective sea. His analogies would go on forever. She had come to treasure the name as an endearment. She soon found herself smiling, reminiscing.

Mitch's voice interrupted her thoughts. "Never mind then. I'll just meet you at the house. When'll you get there?"

"I'm pullin' in the drive now. Hey, are those your lights at the end of the street?"

"You betcha, Sis," he said with a chuckle. "I'm right behind you."

Once both cars were parked in the garage, Margaret closed the door. She then climbed out to turn on the overhead light before the automatic one could dim. Mitch,

By Dianne J. Beale

often mistaken as her twin, soon joined her and they entered the house.

"Do you work again this Saturday?" Mitch sighed. "Or are you actually going to have a day off?"

"I'm all yours, Bro. I told them it's your birthday and said we'd be a celebratin'. They want us to toast our beers for them."

Mitch frowned, his wholesome face wrinkling with contempt. "Why would they say that? They know we don't like beer. You'd think they didn't know our story."

Margaret sighed and lowered her eyes. Then she yawned. "That's exactly the point though, isn't it? They do know. I would think that you'd realize this by now. I mean *you're* the one who majored in counseling, not me. Anyhow, I'm sorry I mentioned it. I should have thought... but they're not interested in people — not really. They use things like that, ya know? And I'm just the children's administrator..."

Mitch interrupted, "...and secretary, and receptionist, and substitute–all rolled into one."

"Mitch," she chided, "It doesn't matter. I don't work for them; I work for God. I merely meant that they don't consider me to be that important, at least not like the others."

"Yeah, I hear you. You're not important at all." Mitch ran his fingers through his ginger-flecked hair. "That's why you never get sick days and carry a cell phone and laptop on every vacation you take. What they call benefits, I call business trips. Now, don't you wish you was workin' for me?"

"I thought I *did* work for you," she teased. "I keep house, pay the bills, write the letters, and hire the yard workers. When did you say you're gonna find yourself a wife?"

Mitch laughed a hardy laugh; his gray eyes lit up, exposing flecks of blue. "Just as soon as you find yourself a decent man who will defend you and take care of you. I can't let my only living relative throw away her life, you know. Someone's gotta hold you accountable–protect you from yourself. Besides, there's not a woman who'll put up with me besides you."

"Now I know you've lost it! Every free woman in that church has her eyes set on you. Even Pastor Andres talks as if you are just one step away from perfect. He once called you the male version of *Mary Poppins*. And all the staff agreed!"

"Maybe that was true while I worked there, but now I'm nothing more than a man who is living 'outside the will of God.' Besides, didn't that bother you? Come on; tell me the truth."

Mar smiled. "No, not really. Well, I didn't think it was fair that I got labeled while you got to remain just plain old Mitch. But I brag on my big brother all the time, don't you know? *I*, at least, think you're perfect." She laughed.

By Dianne J. Beale

Mitch rolled his eyes. "Oh, okay. Do you remember what Dad used to say? 'He who flatters is laying a trap.' Proverbs 29:5, I believe. This is me, Mar… you remember, right? Me? Mitch? Why do you let them call you Garnet if you don't like it? I just didn't answer if they didn't use my name."

"I remember. I was just saying that you don't seem to realize how special you really are. And do you really think they'd care about what I think? You need to remember that I'm 'just a woman.' I'd be seen as rebellious where you were seen as assertive. Besides, I can think of quite a few less desirable things they could call me. Garnet wouldn't be bad if I hadn't overheard their reasoning. I had thought it was a compliment to the color of our hair." Mar sighed. "I can't believe you'll be thirty tomorrow. And in just over six months, I'll be twenty-eight. You've invested an entire decade of your life in me."

Mar paused, not wanting to hurt his feelings. "You don't need to protect me anymore, Mitch. I'm not the little girl you had to watch out for when Mom and Dad died. I just want you to be happy. I think maybe it's time for me to let go… to let you live. I mean, I might be flawed," she smiled, rushing on, "but you could have a great family! I know Trish would have you in a second… with or without me. You love her, right?"

"Oh, Mar, nothing's so simple as you like to make it. But let's not argue right now. I think we're both too tired to continue this conversation. Let's watch a movie or something instead, okay?"

"Sure. A movie's fine. And tomorrow we'll celebrate your birthday. I'll get the eats ready and you can set up the movie, okay?"

As she readied the root beers and microwaved the popcorn, she could not help but feel deflated. Something about tonight's encounter was troubling her; she just couldn't put her finger on it. When the tray was prepared, she walked it to the family room, and sat down. Just then she realized she had left the kitchen light on, so dragged herself back to her feet and went to hit the switch.

When she shifted to return to the couch, she thought she spotted a black cat through the nearby window, so she moved back into the kitchen to peer out into the thick, foggy void of the yard. Greenish-yellow eyes stared back for merely a second. Had she imagined it?

Flipping on the outside light, she soon was reminded that this would only impede her senses. She shut it off again, straining to see out the window. And she was still standing, staring outward, when her brother broke into her trance.

"Mar... earth to Mar... hey, what's wrong?"

"Oh. Mitch. Sorry. Nothing, I guess. Yes, nothing." She shook her head to add punctuation, hoping to shake away her silly concerns. "My eyes must just be tired, that's all." She forced a smile and went back to the couch to sit.

By Dianne J. Beale

As the movie rolled on, the cat was forgotten. When they each headed off to bed, they were laughing and relaxed. But her dreams would soon engulf her in a renewed state of unrest.

Chapter 4

Mar awoke to numbers flashing on her nearby alarm clock and a feeling of apprehension. "It must be storming again," she reasoned. But the state of her stomach chased away any notion of sleep, so she rolled off the bed and began to pray.

"God, I don't remember what I dreamed. I thank you for that. I appreciate that You've granted my request to remember names and to feel need without revealing further details."

"And Lord, I now pray for Trish. I'm not aware of any danger or need in her life right now, but I know that You woke me to pray for her."

"Father, place your angels to guard her. Keep her safe. Reveal to her that You are with her right now. Comfort her. You know her every need. Show her that You are with her. Take away her fears."

"Heal her if she needs healing. Give her strength to… to face whatever it is she is facing."

"Lead people to her if she needs help or has not yet been found. Tell her we're here for her. I believe You and

By Dianne J. Beale

have faith in the promises that You have made. In Jesus' holy and mighty name, I pray. Amen."

Mar rose to her feet and was headed toward the kitchen when she recalled the cat. Although she wanted some aspirin from the cupboard, she instead returned to her room. She reproached herself for this spineless decision but chose to crawl back into her bed, nevertheless. Just as she was about to cut the light, her cell phone chimed.

Knowing this signaled either a message or an email, she reached for the phone. "That's odd," she said out loud. "Why would it have chimed then? Is it also malfunctioning because of this nasty storm?"

She was about to unplug it from the wall, and return to the idea of sleep, when its power went off. She disconnected the phone from the plug and it blinked, went off, and then came on again.

Once it had rebooted, Mar noticed that her personal settings were no longer in place. She opened her messaging center's inbox to find that all the messages were gone. Her phone book was empty, as well. Only her smart card remained intact. Puzzled, she called the 24-hour assistance.

"TransMarket, may I have your cellular number and name, please? How can I help you this fine morning?"

Mar responded by slowly stating her number, "601-555-0128."

"And your name and address, please?"

"Oh, sorry. Margaret Zeiler, 2143 Locket Avenue. Mayhaw, Mississippi, 39214."

"Thank you, Margaret. May I call you Margaret?"

"Sure, and your name?"

"Teresa, Ma'am. How can I help you?"

"Well, it's storming here, and my phone appears to have returned to its original settings. Is there any way you could recover my data?"

"No, Ma'am. I don't think so. At least, I'm not aware of any. Are you sure you didn't accidentally tell it to reset?"

"Mostly sure. It was plugged in for the night. I heard it chime, and when I unplugged it, it kinda blinked off, and then on again, on its own."

"Well then, let me connect you to tech support, just in case."

After a brief silence, a voice came over the line. "Tech support, Mark speaking."

"Yes. My phone appears to have returned to factory settings. Can you help me recover any of my lost information?"

"Sorry Ma'am. That's just not possible. Would you like me to check your phone records in case you missed any calls or messages? I'm afraid that's the best I can offer."

"Okay, then. Sure. I guess that's better than nothing."

"The last text message was at 3:22 a.m. It was from 601-555-0197. Did you receive that message, Ma'am?"

By Dianne J. Beale

"No, sir. My phone chirped like it received a message, but there was none. Then I got what's happening now. I've lost everything not saved to the SIM card."

"Coulda been a virus. Turn it off for the night and bring it to one of our stores in the morning. The rest of the messages were all from before 8:00 p.m. yesterday, so you prob'ly didn't miss much."

"Okay, then. Can you tell me who that last number belongs to?"

"Um. Hmm. That's strange. I'm getting that it's a nonworking. Maybe it's some sort of glitch. Can't really explain it, you know?"

"Oh, okay. Well, thanks anyway. Bye."

"Bye. And thank you for choosing TransMarket."

Mar got up, used the restroom, reset her alarm clock, and then went back to bed. "Place a hedge of protection around us, Lord. Guard our house, hearts, and minds as we sleep. And protect Trish. Thank you, Father. In Jesus' name, I pray, amen."

Chapter 5

"What is that incessant tapping?" thought Mar as she slowly walked toward it. She felt displaced and anxious.

Finally, she came to a clearing where the sound had increased, and was echoing. She stood silently, watching the bird. She'd never seen a woodpecker before.

"Mar, come on!" shouted Mitch. It was at this moment she realized she was still in a dream. As she bullied herself awake, the tapping turned to loud fist raps upon her bedroom door. She tried to sit up but failed. Had she answered him? She didn't recall.

"Mitch? What time is it?" she finally stammered.

"It's almost noon. Our brunch reservation is in just a little less than an hour."

Mar sprung from the bed, making quick assessment statements through the door. She listened as Mitch walked away, chuckling.

After a brief shower, Mar clipped up her wet hair and got dressed. She then grabbed her purse and headed out to the kitchen. There she found Mitch enjoying some coffee, and joined him.

By Dianne J. Beale

"Are we meeting anyone else?" asked Mar. "Or are we eating together, alone, this year?"

Mitch stood and rinsed his cup, then opened the dishwasher and loaded it in. He appeared to be thinking. When he noticed Mar had finished as well, he removed her cup and did the same with it. "I made the reservation for only two this year. Everyone else sounded as if they couldn't make it. I hope that's okay, Sis... just you and me."

"It's okay with me if it's okay with you. It's your birthday, after all. Whose car shall we take?"

"That can be your gift then, Mar. You can be my chauffeur for a day."

Mar agreed and they headed out the door. Neither noticed the blinking answering machine; they hadn't heard it ring. The ringer had been silenced for Thursday night Bible study and they had forgotten to turn it back on. So off they went to face the day and to enjoy the birthday they were celebrating.

It was late when they finally returned home. Brunch had led to a movie, a movie to the nearby museum, and the museum to the zoo. Now they were finally back. Mar readied the birthday cake while Mitch showered. He had no idea that a small get-together had been planned so was surprised when he heard the doorbell. It was nearly ten, after all.

He dressed quickly and hurried to the door. It was Tessa and Christopher — members of their weekly "life group." Mitch played with this phrase in his mind; why couldn't they just call it what it was? What he and Mar had grown to know as "Bible study" seemed to take on a new name almost monthly: small group, home group, cell group, and now life group.

As he pondered the church's obsession with naming things, Mitch noticed the blinking light of the answering machine. He crossed the room and turned up the volume. When he pressed the play button, the doorbell again rang. More people entered and were seated. But Mitch stood frozen by the phone.

When the last guest had arrived, Mar ushered them all to the kitchen. She pulled her brother into the room, as well, and they all sang to him, cheering upon the song's finish as Mitch squelched every candle's flame. Mar passed out the coffee and cake and then joined her brother. He was obviously shaken. Returning to the phone, Mar, too, listened to the message.

"Mitch? Margie? Are you there? Guys? Please pick up. I guess you're not home. I'll try Margie's cell. Um, if you've not heard from me when you get this message, can you please call? I'll be at my parents, though. I'll explain later. Gotta go. Call me: 601-555-0119."

"Did you call her? I don't understand. Why would she be at her parents'? First Chris and Tessa say they've been tryin' to get us all day—something about a break-in at the church—and now this. Mitch? What's wrong?"

By Dianne J. Beale

"I'm not completely sure. Trish is in some kind of trouble. Since she said she can't talk about it on the phone, she most likely wants us to drive out to her parents' house. I've not called yet, though. I thought we'd wait 'til we have no company. But I've never heard her so shaken. Not ever. I'm worried for her."

Mar told him how she'd been awakened to pray, but then forgot about it. She went to her purse to get her cell. It was frozen, so she had to dump out the battery and then replace it before she could read any notes. When it finished booting, she appeared to have both text and voice messages. She read the text messages first, but each message, although from Trish, was blank. Puzzled, she called the voice mail. Trish sounded frantic and confused. "Where are you guys? I guess maybe something's wrong with your phones. He's found me again. Well, you don't know anything about that, though. I'll be at my parents'. Call me. 601-555-0119. Call me. Okay?"

Mitch and Mar called together the group of friends and thanked them for coming. Someone suggested they pray for the church and another for Mitch's new year. Mar asked to pray for an unspoken request. Once all prayers had been said, hugs were exchanged and "good nights" were thrown about.

Immediately after the house had cleared, Mitch dialed the phone. The person at the other end hung up. Mar waited a few seconds and then dialed instead from her cell. A man answered, but soon, she was talking to Trish.

"Are you okay? We're so sorry. We just now got your messages."

"No. Tonight's not a good night for that. Maybe you can call again tomorrow."

"Is he with you? Is that why you can't talk?" Whoever "he" is, thought Mar.

"Yes. That's a great idea. Will you bring the cake when you come? You could freeze some."

"Should I call the police? Are your parents okay?"

"I'm sure my parents would love to meet you, too. But they're not well tonight."

"Okay, Trish. Hang in there, okay?"

"Sure I can. Thanks for the call."

As Mar hung up the phone, she realized that Mitch had already searched the Internet for an address to match the number and was on the phone with the police. She had to wonder… what did her brother know?

By Dianne J. Beale

Chapter 6

It was now past midnight and too late to call for replacements for the junior church. Mar would just have to call before services began in the morning and hope for the best. She obviously couldn't go to work. She hadn't realized it, but she was pacing.

Mitch was like a silent statue. Mar didn't know what to say. She tried to sit down next to him, but soon she was pacing again. Mitch didn't seem to notice.

They both jumped when the phone rang. Mitch grabbed the receiver. Mar could hear only tiny parts of what was being said, and Mitch's short comments didn't help much. Finally, he hung up the phone.

"That was Trish's mom. Her dad is in a coma at Saint Mark's, and the police are still trying to locate Trish. I'm going to drive out to sit at the hospital with Shawnda. Someone should stay here, too, though. Will you be okay here alone?"

Mar was struggling to take it all in, but she insisted that he go. She didn't want him to go alone, though, and talked him into calling the hotline at the church. Soon Pastor Andres had arrived and said that an older couple from the church would show up, shortly, to stay with her. When Mar said that it wasn't necessary, Andres became insistent.

Andres explained how Trish was being stalked by an ex-boyfriend and that he was sure that the guy had no problem with using her friends to get to her. Once he and Mitch were assured that Mar would not open the door for anyone other than the older couple, she was able to coax them onward, insisting she'd be fine during the short wait.

As Mitch and the pastor headed for the pastor's car, Mar again experienced the jetting pain in her leg and back. Although she hadn't made a sound, Andres turned his head around to look back at her. It almost seemed as if he'd perceived her discomfort.

Was the pastor limping? He appeared to be favoring his left leg. Mar had a flashing recollection of the backyard cat… the same limp had it favoring the left paw. And those eyes…

But she was being silly. How ridiculous a thought. She shook herself and waved as they drove off. Quickly sealing and locking the door, she went into the kitchen to pour herself some coffee.

At the sound of scraping blinds, she speedily reached under the blinds' edge and pushed shut the window, securing it with the locking bar. She then went into the adjoining room and flicked on both sets of outdoor lights. Peering out from this smaller window, she found herself a bundle of nerves. Just as she suspected, there was no cat. She scolded herself and returned to the kitchen for her coffee.

By Dianne J. Beale

The phone cut into the silence as if thunder inviting lightning. The Caller ID flashed a familiar name, and Mar answered, breathing a sigh of relief. But her steadied nerves were to be short-lived.

"Marge," said the voice, "we're not going to make it. Will you be okay by yourself? Our battery died and it's leaking fluid. We're sorry, Dear."

Mar responded as calmly as she could; she insisted that the couple need not worry but petitioned them for their prayers. As they hung up, Mar shivered. Her eyes scanned the room and her heart quickened with every shadow. Just as she was about to move, a key turned in the lock.

Mar jerkily erased the messages and caller ID numbers from the phone and then flipped off the ringer and the answering service.

Grabbing a nearby flashlight, she scrambled to the stairway's nearby crawlspace and dove into its darkness just in time. It took all her strength to maintain composure: Trish and Mitch were the only others who had the house-key. And she was sure that Mitch would not have returned without first giving her a call.

Chapter 7

Sitting in the dark, Mar was glad she had cleaned out the closet's spiders and cobwebs the past weekend. She also was relieved that her cell phone appeared to be in silent mode.

Her heart waned as she listened to Trish's voice plead with the man who had earlier answered Trish's phone. They appeared to be in the kitchen. Quietly, Mar dialed 911.

She didn't know what else to do. She felt helpless hiding in the small compartment, yet had no idea just how large the man who accompanied Trish was. She bit her lip as she heard what sounded like a slap to the face. The man seemed enraged as he threw out questions that were barely understood.

"911, can I help you?"

"Yes. A woman is being assaulted in my home."

"Can you speak up, dear? It is difficult to hear you."

"No. He doesn't know I'm here. I can't let him hear me. We're at 2143 Locket Avenue in Mayhaw."

"2143 Locket Avenue? Is that correct?"

By Dianne J. Beale

"Yes, Ma'am. He's hurting her. I don't know how bad she is. I think he put her dad into a coma earlier today, though."

"Just try to stay on the line, okay? Try to stay calm. You're doing fine. No matter what, stay where you are. Do not come out of hiding."

"No, Ma'am. I'll stay hidden. My phone battery is low, though. I'm not sure how long it will work."

"Okay, miss. Stay still and quiet, even if your phone does go off. Help is on its way."

"Yes. Thank you. I will."

The room had grown increasingly silent. Mar wondered if Trish had been knocked unconscious or if he'd killed her. Then she feared that she'd been heard and it was only a matter of time before she'd be dragged out. What was he waiting for? Was he maybe like a cat that plays with its mouse? It seemed he would be. Trish must have been with him for hours.

But soon, she heard voices again. Mar wondered if Trish knew she was there… just when she had needed to say the most, Trish had insisted on leaving the room to use the restroom. Now they were back nearby.

What seemed like an endless span of time had passed. Mar grew uneasy as she ignored text and voice messages from her brother. She feared he might return, but dared not use her phone; she couldn't risk losing the connection. The woman on the other end was giving occasional updates. Mar finally risked being heard as her desire to protect Mitch increased.

"Can you get a message to my brother? He's at Saint Mark's. He also has a cell phone. He's been trying to contact me, and I don't want him to come back to the house."

"We can try, Doll. What's the number?"

"Well, his cell is 601-555-0132. I don't know for Saint Mark's. He's with a Shawnda Everett. At least I think… I don't know the patient's name… but he should be Everett, too."

"Got it. Now try to stay quiet. The police should arrive in about five minutes. Don't let them know you are there."

"Okay. Thanks."

Mar's legs were cramping, and her back had a burning sensation. She tried to think of other things, all the while praying silently to God. Then she heard wood splintering and glass breaking. There were gunshots, Trish screaming, and now someone was running up the stairs with another in hot pursuit. Then came the pounding of each step as something moved downward… scuffing. A very calm and firm voice began reading out rights.

Next, light poured into the cubbyhole, and she and Trish were being transported to the hospital. Mar's last recollections were of yet another gunshot and the dull thump of her cell phone as it hit the floor.

By Dianne J. Beale

Chapter 8

There was that tapping again. She arrived at the clearing more quickly this time. As she fixed her eyes on the woodpecker, her vision began to blur. Then, hot tears were dripping off her nose. She raised her sleeve to her face, wiping at them. Just as her vision began to clear, she awoke.

The sunshine was bright against the pristine, white walls. A faint sound of shuffling reached into her from the hall. She believed that one voice belonged to Mitch but didn't recognize the others. She decided to sit up so she could maybe see the activity.

Mitch came toward her with what appeared to be a doctor and a nurse. He looked tired and harried. She hoped the smile she was visualizing had made it to her face. It was difficult to know for sure since Mitch's face was filled with concern.

"How ya holdin' up, Sis? Do you hurt anywhere? Are you doin' okay?"

Mar's voice was low and scratchy when she spoke. Mitch poured her some ice water, and she tried again. "How's Trish? Is Trish okay? Did they catch him?"

"Calm down, Mar. It's all okay. Trish should be fine. She'll be sore for a while, but she's a fighter, and she's doing well. Now, how are you?"

Mar had to analyze and think before she could answer the question. She finally decided the only apparent injury was the one she had given herself in the church parking lot. Her leg and back still seemed to be out of whack, but otherwise, she felt rather well.

Everyone was glad to hear her say so. She'd been unconscious for more than twelve hours now and had caused much concern. The doctor decided she'd need to undergo one last set of tests and then, if all was as it should be, she could go. The tests were set for the next morning before he left to continue his rounds.

Mitch stayed for the next half hour and answered with what little knowledge he had. He then asked if she minded his leaving her to visit Trish and to check in on Trish's dad. Mar agreed, of course, that he should go. She made him promise he'd also find time to get some rest. He hugged her, assuring her he'd be back, and then left.

A short time later, another visitor wandered into the room. He was rather thin, almost lanky in appearance. His eyes, nicely placed below a blonde tuft of hair, were a warm chocolate—the color of freshly baked brownies. Confused, she asked, "Can I help you, Sir?"

The man met her gaze and told her he hadn't meant to intrude but had wanted to check in on her progress. He

By Dianne J. Beale

explained that he had been part of the police force that entered her house and just wanted to see that she was okay. He then reached into his pocket: "I believe this belongs to you," he said with a smile.

Mar recognized her cell phone immediately and thanked him when he handed it to her. He nodded a "you're welcome" and then excused himself as if to go.

"Sir," Mar stopped him, "What is your name? If you don't mind sayin' that is."

"Luke, Ma'am," he answered.

"Well, I'm Mar. I just wondered... can you tell me what happened? I don't remember much and couldn't see from behind the door."

"I reckon I'd be needin' your doctor's okay on that, Ma'am." He reached into his shirt pocket, producing a business card. "You can call me when your doc says you can talk about it. For now, I think I best be goin'."

"Oh. Okay. I didn't, I... "

"I realize that, Ma'am. Don't trouble yerself over it any. It's all understandable, for sure." Luke smiled and then dismissed himself a second time. He had soon disappeared around the corner.

Mar studied the business card: "*Luke Smelding, detective.*" The design, although basic, appeared to belong to the local police station. Mar sighed and picked up her phone; it needed charging. She set both objects into the drawer next to her and turned on the television. Soon she had drifted off to sleep.

By Dianne J. Beale

Chapter 9

The morning was a bustle of x-rays and lab tests. Mar was growing impatient. Mitch had yet to return, but she was happy in the belief that he had taken her advice and gotten some rest. She just wanted it all to be over.

When she returned to her room, it was to a cold, tasteless lunch. She ate the crackers and drank some water but left the rest untouched. Grease spots had solidified along the soup's surface, and the milk was warm and unsettling. She decided to call Mitch in hopes of catching him on his way in. She could have him pick her up a snack. The home phone appeared to still have the answering machine set to off with the ringer silenced, and Mitch's cell went directly to his voice mail. She left a quick message and then succumbed to watching television.

Mar grew more and more restless, and every second seemed like an agonizingly endless space of time. She was about to push the nurse button when Mitch walked in.

"Sorry, Sis," he admitted sheepishly, "fell asleep on the chair by Trish and didn't get home until almost six this morning. But I'm here now, right?"

"How is Trish? How's her dad? Do you know yet how everything went down? And when are you gonna bust me outta here?"

"Sounds like someone's doin' a lot better. Um, Trish seems good; she was sitting up today. Her dad hasn't shown any promising improvement, though. I'm not sure how much Trish knows–she might not know about her dad. I haven't had a chance to talk to the police yet, but I've an appointment scheduled for tonight. As to you? Still waiting to hear the verdict. Sorry."

"I'm just glad you're here. I'm so bored! Will you still be here if I quickly duck into the ladies' room? You won't go anywhere, right?"

Mitch laughed. "Of course I'll still be here. I promise."

Mar entered the small restroom adjoined to her hospital room, and Mitch began to surf through channels on the TV. He was listening intently when Mar rejoined him.

We are here at Shepherd's Orchard on twenty-second street in the city of Mayhaw. This is the second break-in this week. The pastor, although justifiably shaken, says it appears that no more is missing than a box of Bibles. He adds that he is sure the perpetrators need them more than he does and urges them to read, rather than sell, them. Although nothing seems amiss on first glance, the police will be returning to investigate throughout the week.

This just in. Two other staff members have also faced tragedy this weekend. Patricia Everett, the church's daycare lady, is in the

By Dianne J. Beale

hospital, along with another staff member, Margaret Zeiler. One wonders if the events might somehow be related. No further information is available at this time. This is news' anchor, Ophelia Orlander, reporting, live. News at noon.

"Wow, it really does pour when it rains. I thought the police said they were gonna keep this all under wraps. I wonder who leaked your names to the press. If there was evidence, it'll probably be nowhere to be found, now. I'm so sorry, Sis."

"Well, at least they didn't mention Trish's dad. It'd be awful for her to find out that way. Maybe you should go find her Mom. Y'all might want to fill her in before she hears it from another. Oh, Mitch, you were right. Things are always more complex than they seem. Did you know about Trish?"

"I knew only bits 'n' pieces. I didn't know she was still in danger, though. She'd mentioned an old boyfriend she had lived with from before her salvation and how he had threatened her in the past, but she made it sound as if it was no longer an issue. I knew she was pushing me away, hesitant-like. I guess we'll see what comes of it once she's well again. Before this, she was insisting I should date others. But I'm not ready to do that. She isn't ready to hear this yet, but I think she'll be the one." Mitch sighed deeply.

"Well, for now, go to her with her mom. I'll be okay. I can text you if — WHEN — they decide to let me go."

Mitch passed a tall, boyish cop on his way out, but thought nothing of it. It was Luke Smelding.

By Dianne J. Beale

Chapter 10

A light tap on the door caused Mar to lift her gaze. She smiled at Luke, and he asked her if it was okay to visit. She invited him into the room, and they sat down in chairs that faced one another.

Luke explained that the police were hoping to step things up now, since the news had leaked the story. He asked if she could share what she remembered of the night in question.

Mar told him how her cell phone had flipped out, and how they hadn't gotten the phone message at home until well after ten that night. She explained how her call to Trish had resulted in cryptic messages that had led to their calling the police. Then, when she heard a key turn in the lock, she had the clarity to turn off the answering machine, silence the ringer, and hide.

After that, it was difficult to say. She'd been able to tell that a man was with Trish and that he was looking for Mitch. It had seemed he might be hitting her, interrogating her. He was enraged and insistent: *if he couldn't have Trish, then no one would*. Then she remembered hearing the sound of broken glass, cracking wood, running footsteps, and the reading of rights.

Luke filled her in on the rest of the events, and she breathed a sigh of relief when she heard that the man had taken his own life. Surprised that she had felt this way, guilt welled up inside of her as a result. She silently criticized her response; he most likely had not known the Savior.

Luke reminded her of the business card he had given her and told her not to hesitate if she remembered anything more or came across something she thought might be related. Mar thanked him, and once again, watched as he went out the door.

She got up to use the restroom and then situated herself on the bed. She turned the channel to music and tried to make sense of the chaos of events.

Just as she was dozing off, the doctor arrived. He took her pulse and blood pressure, and then listened to her heart. After many questions and answers, the doctor said he'd be sending a nurse with the paperwork for her release. Mar thanked him and then waited while he left to give the checkout orders. She decided not to call Mitch until she was actually ready to go.

By Dianne J. Beale

Chapter 11

Mitch was on a return trip to see Mar when he felt his phone vibrate. He pulled it from his pocket and saw that she'd been discharged and was ready to leave. He smiled as he thought of the wisdom of God's timing.

On the drive home, Mitch told Mar of how Trish's dad had come out of the coma directly before she would have had to bear the bad news. Instead, he and her mother had been able to offer hope and a good prognosis. Then, the doctor in charge of Trish also had good news—her rib was healing nicely and there would be no need for surgery. After much joy and sighs of relief, Mitch had said his "see you later" and had headed back to her.

Mar filled Mitch in concerning the attack. He was so happy to hear that Trish no longer would need to run. He thanked God out loud for this unexpected blessing. Mar's guilt began to fade in the shadows of Mitch's happiness. She smiled weakly and then closed her eyes and laid back her head. He popped in a CD and let his sister rest.

Once home, Mar awoke at the sudden silencing of CD and engine. She wiggled a stretch and then exited the car. She couldn't believe that tomorrow she'd be returning to work and soon it would seem as if none of this had ever happened. Was it really only Monday? She was almost afraid to ask about what had happened on Sunday.

Mitch popped a frozen pizza into the oven and then served some salad. He smiled across the table as he recalled the phone message he'd received about warm milk and cold soup. He had instantly put it out of his mind since he'd received it at the same time he'd picked up the text message about her having been freed for departure.

Mar interrupted his thoughts. "Have you heard anything about the church? Has other stuff been taken as well?"

Mitch teased that life moved onward despite her unplanned absence, but then admitted he hadn't heard a thing. He looked thoughtful, "Maybe they wanted us to concentrate on our own problems, so they didn't trouble us," he suggested.

Mar nodded her agreement and dug into her salad. Soon, they were feasting on pizza, as well. After they cleaned up, Mitch decided to return to the hospital. Mar asked him to give Trish her love and to tell her she'd try to visit her tomorrow. After checking to see if she was sure she'd be okay, he didn't ask twice for reassurance; he just grabbed his keys and headed out the door.

Mar unpacked her hospital bag and plugged in her cell phone. Then she decided to take a nice, long, hot shower. She had planned to soak in the tub but opted for the shower

By Dianne J. Beale

now that she was alone. She plugged her CD player into the safety outlet on the counter by the sink and then popped in some Bach. Then she cranked the volume and stepped into the streaming water.

A short time later, refreshed and relaxed, she recalled the state of the home phone when she had left and decided to check on it. Mitch had already corrected the settings, after all. She decided not to listen to the blinking message and instead set her alarm clock, reloaded the CD player, and climbed into bed. She began to read the Psalms aloud and soon found the pages were swimming before her. Closing her Bible, she dimmed the light and snuggled down into the thick comforter. She was asleep almost instantly.

Chapter 12

Was Mitch nailing something? It didn't exactly sound like a hammer. Mar slowly took in her surroundings. She walked forward, puzzling over why she knew where she was going. Soon, directly in front of her, there were what appeared to be three rough trees. Raising her eyes, she saw a woodpecker beating at the tree in the center. It appeared to be spelling something.

Mar laughed at her ridiculous notions and said aloud, "Birds can't spell." She tore her eyes away and looked to the tree on her left. It wasn't a tree at all; the tree had been altered by man—it was an empty cross. Suddenly, there was a rush of wind as the woodpecker grew and flew away—oh, an angel. Now she became aware of another cross on her right and forced herself to look on the cross in the middle. Just three words: FORSAKEN, FORGIVEN, and FREEDOM. Sap flowed downward from these fresh wounds, darkening the wood. Mar reached out her hand to touch the sap, but just then, everything disappeared.

She fell into confusion. The dream changed into chaos. A huge hole was opening around her. Pastor Andres appeared. He looked down on her with the same

By Dianne J. Beale

condescending expression he had used in the church parking lot. She was falling, and he was taking no interest in rescuing her. How could he just stand there and let her fall? Mar screamed and woke up.

She was sweating and felt as if she could not move. Had she screamed only in the dream? She must have since she didn't hear Mitch. It felt as if someone were holding her down. Although in a panic, her body remained stiff and unresponsive. She couldn't move. Was she still dreaming? She bit her tongue to prove she was awake. "Jesus," she whispered, "You were forsaken so I would never be. You gave forgiveness where I deserved death. Jesus, help me; free me." As she reached the word *free*, she was immediately able to sit up. She realized she was shaking, so she got up to find an extra blanket. The dream had seemed so real. She took some Tylenol and drank some tea, as well. When she returned to her room, she suddenly sensed she was alone in the house. She set down the blanket and went back out into the hall, edging her way slowly toward her brother's room. The door was open and the bed was neatly made up. The clock on the wall read two o'clock.

Walking back out into the family room, she turned on the television. The menu channel played familiar elevator music. She saw that Mitch's clock was correct. It was now a little past two a.m. She decided to leave the TV on as she went to the blinking message across the room and hit play. She didn't recognize the voice and assumed, at first, it was a wrong number. But the message was for Mitch, whoever it was. The woman's voice was that of a smoker. It was all rather mysterious—no number or name given—just "Hey Mitch" and a short message telling him to call. When the message finished, Mar left a short message after it, so the machine would continue to blink for Mitch when he finally returned home.

She went back to her room, feeling uneasy. Her phone was fully charged now, so she turned it on. There were no messages of any kind. She set the phone's alarm now, as well, just in case, and then climbed back into bed.

Again, she read aloud from the Psalms. Restless, she decided to try copying the verses onto paper. When this failed to comfort her, she crossed the room and began to go through her CD collection. She put the chosen CD into the player and then crawled back into her bed. Snuggling down into her comforter, she closed her eyes and began to pray. Finally, she was able to sleep.

By Dianne J. Beale

Chapter 13

The alarm was relentless and undesired when it went off at six. Mar stumbled across the room and shut it off. She figured the cell phone's alarm would wake her in an hour, so she crawled back into bed.

It seemed she had only just laid down her head when the cell's alarm also went off. She was about to hit snooze when she remembered her brother's empty room. She shut down the alarm and dragged herself out of the bed.

Mitch's door was closed. She couldn't remember if she had done that, or if this meant he was home. She hated to risk waking him but gently tapped the door. There was no response, so she gingerly cracked it. Either he had come and left already, or that bed had never been slept in.

She tried to rationalize by saying he'd most likely stayed at the hospital. After all, he'd fallen asleep in the chair by Trish just the other night. But when she finally headed out toward the kitchen, the answering machine was no longer blinking. She pushed play twice to make it play without its notification, but the message had been erased.

Mar was feeling more than a little uneasy when she got into her car to drive to the church, so she chose to skip breakfast. Mitch was not answering his phone, either. She didn't know what to think.

At the church, she opened the outside door with her key and then waited for it to shut. She noticed that the security cameras were all off but then remembered that this was often the case. When she came to her office, she was startled to see an open door. And where was the customary scent of brewed tea that she had come to expect?

Papers were everywhere! She went in cautiously and then breathed a sigh of relief when she was sure she was alone. Ignoring the mess, she reached toward the computer to switch it on, but she stopped in midair. It was on already. She grabbed a tissue from a nearby box and used it to quickly start the monitor. The church directory was open on the screen, and Trish's name was highlighted. Next to the phone number that Mar recognized as Trish's home number was a newly formed column that contained another number. She pulled out her address book and wrote the number down—somehow it seemed familiar: 601-555-0197.

Mar then called Luke. He was, after all, the detective assigned to her case. Besides, no one was due in the office for another hour, and she was spooked. Luke took down the number and said he'd be over as soon as he had run it. He then told her not to touch anything, and hung up.

Mar decided to distract herself by playing some games on her phone. She noticed she had received a message so opened it first. All it said was "call me." She located the

By Dianne J. Beale

time, date, and number for the call and gasped. The number was registering as having called twice, and both were text messages. She located the second message, but it was completely blank. It was the message she had never received—the one that TransMarket had mentioned on the night she'd prayed for Trish. Chills began to climb her spine. She realized she was shaking. The number on her phone was the same number she had just given to Luke. She set her phone on the desk as if it were poison.

When Luke finally buzzed, Mar was a wreck. He was surprised that she sounded so frantic and pulled out his gun in case she wasn't alone. When he arrived, she was standing in front of her office, looking in on the chaos.

Luke set the safety on his gun and sheathed it. Walking toward her, he spoke quietly, hoping she'd calm. She grabbed his arm when he came near, so he covered her hands with his own. He convinced her to let go and then moved her chair into the hall so she could sit, watching.

First, he quickly gathered fingerprints from the computer. Then he scanned the floor of papers. One particular paper stood out, capturing his gaze, so he picked it up with gloves and put it into a plastic bag. Then, he pocketed it. He first took photos; then, after printing a screen capture of the open document on the screen, he pulled out a disk to save the computer's documents to it. Then he turned to Mar, "Are you okay? Did you see anything?"

Mar gathered her wits and explained how the number was on her phone and the strange circumstances surrounding it. She also asked if he'd found out any information about it. He told her how he had considered it to be a dead end, but not now, since it appeared on both her computer screen and phone. He wrote up a report and then checked to be sure that there was no one else in the building. As he was getting ready to leave, Pastor Andres arrived.

"Garnet," he sulked, "you know the policies."

When she refused to show any shame, he continued. "Why wasn't I called?" he bullied. "I suppose you've already signed release papers, too."

Since it was more of a statement than a question, Mar chose not to answer. Instead, she simply picked up her belongings and followed Luke.

The pastor was left standing in the hallway as Mar and Luke made their ways out of the building. She knew he'd be angry and was sure that payday would come. But she was appalled at his lack of concern. Could she maybe still be trapped inside her early morning dream?

By Dianne J. Beale

Chapter 14

When they reached the parking lot, Luke offered to follow her home. She declined his offer and apologized for her lack of professional conduct. He gave her another business card and reminded her that this was his job. Then they both got into their cars, but he deliberately waited until she had safely left before he, himself, drove away.

Mar arrived home to the smell of Mitch's amazing spaghetti. When he saw her, he immediately crossed the room.

"Pastor Andres called. He says I need to go clean your office out as your services are no longer needed. Mar, what happened? Can he just fire you like that? Shouldn't there be a vote or something? He seemed furious."

"Did you tell him we want that in writing? I'm not going to just stop showing up for work because of a phone call. He didn't even have the courtesy to talk with me? I am *so* not happy right now."

Mitch moved back into the kitchen to stir the sauce. He knew there was no reasoning with his sister until she calmed down. He waited for her to continue, but she didn't. The room fell silent as she left to put away her stuff, leaving Mitch to wonder if they were done talking.

While Mar was in her room, the phone rang. She ignored it, knowing Mitch could grab it. Pulling off her office clothes, she carelessly threw them onto her bed. She then kicked off her shoes and did not even care when one knocked over her desk lamp. Her stockings ran, then tore, so she tossed them into the trash on the way to her closet. Here she yanked her most comfortable sweats from the shelf and pulled them on with an unaccustomed roughness that caused her to trip and then fall forward onto the floor. Without rising, she jerked her foot through the offending pant leg and then forced on the matching shirt. Then she marched herself back out to the kitchen.

She could hear that Mitch was still on the phone, but she wasn't sure with whom. When Mitch saw she'd returned, he said he needed to go but would call back later. This reminded her that she had wanted to find out where he was last night.

"When did you get home last night?" she asked. "Did you fall asleep at the hospital again?"

"Yeah. I got in sometime after three this morning. Then I woke up when your alarm went off at six and couldn't get back to sleep. So, I got up so I could visit Joe before getting back to Trish."

"Joe?"

By Dianne J. Beale

"Trish's dad… Joe Everett. Joe and Shawnda Everett. Trisha Everett. That kinda rolls off the tongue, don't you think? Maybe I should take her name, instead," he joked.

Mar missed her brother's implication completely. She was too deep in thought to have caught the subtle hint that he had just dropped. She shook her head, hoping to clear her mind.

But then she was falling. Mitch caught her just in time; she had fainted. Neither noticed the shadowed shape as it jumped the fence and tore off down the road.

Chapter 15

When Mar came to, she was disoriented. She was sure she had checked out of the hospital, but here she was again. She pushed the nurse's button in hopes of getting some answers.

A male nurse entered, asking her what she needed. She felt silly but asked anyway, "Can you tell me why I am here? Is my brother here, too?"

The nurse said he'd just signed on and he'd have to check the files since she was a new patient on the floor. He apologized for not knowing more and then left the room.

Mar closed her eyes against the bright lights. She had such a headache, as if she'd hit her head. She didn't remember anything. She felt confused and lonely.

Just then, Luke came into the room. She opened her eyes when she heard footsteps. He seemed awkward. Deciding he needed help, she spoke up, "Hey, Stranger, long time no see."

Luke relaxed a little. Mar was glad to see him smile. He asked how she was doing, and she told him that she honestly had no idea. He laughed a hearty laugh at her veracity.

By Dianne J. Beale

Mitch came in next. He was relieved to see Luke. He filled him in on all that had happened. Luke told them that the doctors had found traces of poison on Mar's fingers. They had wanted to put her under psychological supervision, but Luke had assured them that she was not suicidal. He had taken the paper that he had removed from the crime scene for analysis, and there was not only type O blood, in the shape of a thumb, but there were traces of arsenic, as well. The hospital had verified that this was the same poison they had found on the patient.

Mar suddenly felt sick. There appeared to be more to this church than met the eye, definitely more than she wanted to believe. Faces and names, long since gone, began to come to mind. She asked for some paper, and a pencil, so she could write some of them down. She also wrote down names of other files she had archived. She even remembered a conversation she had overheard not too long ago. Pastor Andres and the new staff counselor had been talking to Trish. At the time, she hadn't thought anything of it. Now, she began to relate her suspicions to Luke and Mitch.

"You know, last month Trish was supposed to have a meeting with our church staff, but when she arrived, they told her the meeting had been postponed. They told her that the pastor in charge of the church's business had been called away and that no financial decisions could be made without him." Mar paused, taking a sip of her nearby water.

"But after Trish left," she continued, "we still had our weekly meeting. Basically, we were told that Trish wanted a raise and that it had already been decided she'd have to give up her benefits for the raise to go through. Then we were told that the church could not afford the increase she was asking, even with the sacrifice of benefits. It was decided she'd be given half of what she was asking, but only if she agreed to forego her benefits. There was no discussion. The decision had already been made. The meeting with Trish was only postponed so that we would all be in agreement when we actually met with her."

Mar began to experience other, similar meetings that she'd been a party to, as well. They were marching across her mind as clearly as a slide show. Willing herself to resume, she imagined shutting off a projector with its switch.

"It just occurred to me that we finally met with Trish directly before all this trouble started. She handed in her resignation, stating that she could make more and do less if she worked for *Wal-Mart*. The meeting ended abruptly with them accusing her of betraying God and the church. Later that day, I showed Pastor Andres an online report that showed she was asking for less than what was considered fair and he just dismissed it by saying we shouldn't compare what we do for God with those who serve in the secular world. He took my research, put it through the shredder, and said, 'You are either for God or against Him, Garnet. We

By Dianne J. Beale

don't have room for God's enemies.' He told me to stop wasting the church's money by using my time for trivial matters and to do the job I was hired to do. I was being paid to work, not to think."

"Wow. That's pretty harsh, Sis. Why didn't you or Trish mention this?"

"It's just he has a way of making you feel like you're the one in the wrong. Not one person on the entire staff dares to disagree with him. He fired me, not to my face but instead by calling you. And you can bet when you do go to get my stuff, the paperwork will be ready. Trish didn't even bother returning for her last two week's pay!"

Luke was disgusted. "And they don't keep minutes of the meetings, either, right? Why do you go to this church?"

"Well, I did keep minutes," Mar quietly admitted, "but it seemed that I could never get anything right, so I stopped. I had it in writing–dated–but I was told again and again that things didn't happen the way I'd written them or that I had misunderstood what had actually been decided. I was even accused of changing the notes to suit my own agenda. I began to question my own sanity because of it so just stopped taking the notes."

Luke grunted. Mitch ignored the note-taking as he was still stuck on Mar's previous statements. Convinced that Mar was wrong about any paperwork having been readied, he countered, "No. Andres will calm down and apologize. They can't find anyone else who will accept the low pay you accept and yet do all the things that you do."

Luke smiled, "I hope you're right. We could use that to our advantage—if Mar was willin'." He winked at her.

Mar said that she'd have to think about it. Mitch was right to say that she was underpaid. But she still felt it was somehow justifiable since she was doing it all for God. She didn't consider that all the men made more than her yet were responsible for far less. Some didn't even have the appropriate education for the posts they held. But she'd accepted Christ at this church. Somehow she just wasn't quite ready to give up on it. She wanted to believe that she could still make a difference and was not ready to admit that it was not—and might never become—the church of her aspired perception.

By Dianne J. Beale

Chapter 16

A week later, Mar still woke to an IV in her arm and with the sun streaming into the room. A nurse walked in with a warm smile. I think you're goin' home today," she said.

"I hope so," quipped Mar. "It feels like I've been here an eternity."

After taking a pulse, checking blood pressure, and analyzing the IV, the nurse continued her rounds. Mar suddenly recalled that Trish was still in the hospital as well, so picked up the phone.

"Hello?"

"Hi Trish. How're you doin'? No one has told me anything."

"Margie! It is so good to hear your voice. Mitch told me what's been happening. Are you okay?"

"Yeah, I'm okay. But you?"

"Well, well. Yes, good. Did Mitch tell you?"

"Tell me what?"

"We're engaged! I've never been happier. Oh, but I think he wanted to tell you himself… "

Trish's voice trailed off. Mar wasn't sure what to say. "Um, I think I kinda recall him tryin' to tell me, but I'm not sure. Everything is sorta a blur since I fainted."

"Oh," answered Trish, "I'm sorry."

"Why are you sorry? You didn't plan for any of this to happen. I'm just glad you're okay."

"Margie, I gotta go. The nurse is here now with the doctor. Hope I get to see you soon. Bye."

She hung up before Mar could answer. It was just as well, though. As she hung up the phone, Pastor Andres walked in with the praise minister.

"Garnet! We came as soon as we heard! What a fluke, huh?"

Mar pushed out a smile. "A fluke? What do you mean?"

"Oh," said Pastor Andres, "we just assumed you'd been told. The church counselor got a call concerning your health and we just thought you'd be aware of it."

"Who called?" asked Mar.

"The hospital, of course. Who'd you think?"

"I didn't know what to think. Why would they call the church?"

Pastor Andres gave her his most pleasant, consoling smile. "They wanted to know if we knew how you'd gotten arsenic poisoning. We didn't, but we think we figured it out. You know where we store all the paper?" He waited for Mar to either nod or shake her head. She did neither, but he

By Dianne J. Beale

continued as if she had. "Oh, well... we keep it in the furnace room. It seems that our heating oil has been leaking out, and it got onto some of the boxes. The arsenic is in our heating oil. A fluke, right?"

Mar was annoyed at all the beating around the bush but kept her pleasant demeanor. "Wow. Really? Who woulda thought," she answered. "Has Mitch been by to get my things?"

Pastor Andres looked wounded and puzzled. "Your things? Why would he get your things? Is there something we don't know?" He exaggerated a glance toward the praise minister who accommodated him by returning raised eyebrows and a shrug.

"You fired me, remember? I wasn't supposed to call the police on my own? You should have been notified first? Ring a bell?"

Pastor Andres was looking at her as if she were changing colors or something. The praise minister also wore an expression of genuine surprise. Pastor Andres chuckled. "Now, Garnet, why would I fire you? We're family, right? Brother and sister in Christ. We at the office love you. Who told you that you'd been fired?"

"Why are you doing this? You know you called Mitch and... "

"I should have guessed. Of course it was Mitch. He's been after you to change jobs forever. Hmm. Let me think. Yes, ever since the day I told him that Trish was not God's choice for him. Sure, he still comes to church, but maybe not so often now he's decided to follow his own path rather than God's." The praise minister just hung his head, shaking it sadly. Andres went on, "I hope we'll see you back in your office where you belong. Oh, and Garnet? Don't follow your brother's example. We're your family now." He looked at her as if he were a parent who had just scolded his child for repeating an offense that had resulted in punishment at least once before—disappointed and hurt.

Mar was seething, but she also was confused and irritated. She wanted them to go. She wanted to talk with Mitch. She forced a calm response. "Maybe it was all just a misunderstanding," she conceded, despite knowing that Andres was the one who liked to rewrite history, not Mitch. "My brother would not lie to me. You must not have been clear with your message," she stated. Even as she said it, she knew that he had been more than clear in what he said to Mitch and that he was lying to her.

But Pastor Andres was quick to reassure her: "No, I didn't mean that he'd lie to you, not intentionally anyway. I just meant that he heard what he wanted to hear. I did talk with him, but I had called to talk with you. I mentioned that we had had a few words and that I was concerned because you'd left work early and were obviously angry, and you were driving. I told him I didn't want you to think your job was in jeopardy and that I understood your mistake after all you'd been through. Come on Garnet. The kids adore you!

By Dianne J. Beale

We can work this all out, right? For the kids? Just get better, okay? We can work this out later, when you're well."

    Mar did not appreciate the intonation he used as it implied much more than physical healing was what was needed. But she was glad to see that once he'd finished his speech, he was ready to go. He motioned to the praise minister and they left. Each was shaking his head as if deeply sorrowed and feeling pity for her. But Mar had to wait before she could talk with Mitch. The doctor had arrived with another nurse.

Chapter 17

"Your church counselor called today. He wanted to reaffirm that the police had come by and analyzed the paper and that the arsenic was accidental, not suicidal. It must be nice to have so many people in your life who know you so well and care so much." The doctor paused as he read over Mar's chart. "We planned to send you home today, but we're just a tad concerned about your pulse and blood pressure. We're going to keep you overnight for observation, just to be sure."

Mar thanked the doctor and watched as he and the nurse left. She wanted to tell the doctor if he were really concerned for her, he'd keep people from her church away. Instead, she picked up the phone and dialed her brother. When he didn't answer, she remembered that he was probably at work. She left a message on both the home phone and the cell, but kept it simple. "Hi Mitch. They're keeping me here again, overnight. I had visitors today. Call me when you get a chance. I really need to see you, to talk. This is Mar."

She ate her lunch and then took out the provided notepad from the drawer. She had planned to write down all she could remember since she was beginning to question everything. But the pencil was missing. So were her earlier notes. Had she given them to Mitch? Just as she was about to ring the nurse, Luke walked in.

"What's wrong? Should I come back at another time?"

Mar looked up into his face and the concern she saw resulted in tears slowly moving down her cheeks. She reached out her hand so he'd see that she didn't want him to leave.

Luke knew it was never a good idea to get involved with those connected to a case, but he felt that if he were to refuse her hand, she'd burn and crash. He sat down on the chair next to her and took it in his. Then he waited.

After about ten minutes, Mar was finally able to talk. "Can I ask you something?" she stammered.

"You can ask. I, however, can't guarantee an answer. What's up?"

"Can paper that has no noticeable stains have residue of arsenic on it if that arsenic resulted from a furnace oil leak? I mean, wouldn't the paper be stained?"

"I would think there'd be stains, yes. Why?"

Mar looked wary, but still confided, "Well, two of the pastors came by from the church today. They said the arsenic was because we store our paper in the furnace room and that the oil is leaking. They also claimed that Mitch lied to me about being fired. They accused him of altering the message so I'd quit. Then, when I insisted that my brother doesn't lie, they said maybe he just heard what he wanted to hear since it was no secret he wanted me to change jobs. I'm supposed to believe I was never fired. There was no apology because it never happened."

"Sounds odd to me. Is Pastor Andres denying what happened? I was there, remember?"

"No. He says it was understandable that I reacted the way I did since I had to have been charged emotionally after all that had happened to me. He even admits he talked to Mitch. But he claims he called to talk with me but then, since Mitch answered, told him that my job would never be in jeopardy. He insists that he did not, in fact, fire me."

"Do you believe him?"

"No, I don't. Mitch has never lied to me, and he says that the pastor called to fire me. And Andres, I know he rewrites the past if it suits him to do so. I've watched him do it. He does it so well I think he even convinces himself. He seems so convicted and sure… " Mar's voice trailed off, doubtful.

Luke continued to talk with Mar and he decided her idea to write things down was an important step. He took a pen from his pocket and they began to list events as Mar remembered them. Mar talked, and Luke did the writing:

1. Overheard church counselor and Andres tell Trish her meeting had been rescheduled.

2. Discussed Trish at meeting anyway; the contracts had already been drawn up.

By Dianne J. Beale

3. Trish resigned at the new meeting.

4. Mitch and Mar received strange messages from Trish.

5. Mitch called Trish at parents' house.

6. Whoever answered and hung up.

7. Mar called Trish at same number from her cell.

8. Strange man answered. Spoke to Trish. Cryptic messages.

9. Called police to send to parents' house.

10. Mitch and Andres leave together in Andres' car to go to the hospital to sit with Shawnda, Trish's mom.

11. Older couple from church can't make it to stay with Mar. Car won't start.

12. Key turns in lock. Mar grabs cell and turns off home phone's machine and ringer.

13. Mar calls 911 from hiding place.

14. Mar and Trish are rescued.

15. Discover man with Trish killed himself.

16. Mar returns to work; ransacked office, so calls Luke.

17. Number on cell and computer screen is invalid.

18. Luke gets prints off computer. Also arsenic and Type O blood thumb print on paper.

19. Andres livid because Mar called police.

20. Andres calls Zeiler home; tells Mitch Mar is fired.

21. Mitch takes Mar to hospital after she faints.

22. Pastor Andres, with praise minister, says arsenic is from heating oil and that Mitch is wrong about Mar being fired.

23. Left message for Mitch as he was at work.

24. Luke helped make this list – heating oil is an odd explanation.

When Mar had finished talking, Luke set down the pen and handed her the list. He jokingly told her that she'd need glasses after reading his writing. But Mar didn't even smile. She looked tired. He told her she should get some rest and then decided to make a copy of the list, just in case. When he returned from making the copy, Mar had fallen asleep.

Luke placed the notepad on her night stand and then quietly walked away. He stopped at the nurse's station to get a prognosis on his way out. Apparently, the doctors weren't in agreement that the arsenic was the cause for Mar's fainting. He had questioned that as well.

By Dianne J. Beale

Chapter 18

Mitch entered the room quietly, but Mar was awake anyhow. She'd had the dream again, but this time she was not afraid at all. This time she'd been ready when the ground gave way around her. She had wrapped her arms around the cross and was safe. She ignored Pastor Andres when he had arrived and just kept clinging to the cross. She had conquered the dream.

Mar smiled at Mitch and asked how Trish was. He said she'd seemed fine when he had called but that he hadn't gone to see her yet. He had wanted to see Mar and find out who the visitors were.

Mitch waited as Mar looked for something. She was looking through a drawer. She took out a Bible, a pen, and some tissues, but then the drawer was empty. She then replaced everything, after shaking out the Bible. She had not found what she was looking for.

"It's gone," she announced. "I guess I'll have to rely on my memory after all." She sighed. "Where do I start?"

"What's gone? Is that notepad yours? Is that what you want?" Mitch picked it up and handed it to her.

Mar took the notepad, but the writing was gone. Had she just dreamed it all? Had Luke ever really visited? She thanked Mitch and put everything into the drawer.

"Well," offered Mitch, "I've not seen you since last night, if that helps. Why is the doctor keeping you overnight?"

Just then, Mar's dinner arrived. She thanked the nurse and watched her leave.

Finally, it was time to relate all that had happened. Mar seemed nervous and on edge, but Mitch waited for her to start.

"Well, first, I called Trish. Congratulations, by the way. I'm so happy for you! She couldn't talk long though. The doctor arrived, so she hung up. Then Pastor Andres came with the praise minister. They were super friendly and said they'd come as soon as they'd heard. Can you believe that? As soon as they'd heard? An entire week's gone by for Pete's sake! Anyway, they said the hospital had called the church, but the doctor said it was the other way around. But I'm getting ahead of myself. Um, they said the arsenic was from storing the paper in the furnace room — something about leaking oil. But Luke and I think that's odd: the paper had no stains. Anyhow, he — Pastor Andres — implied you'd either misunderstood or lied about me being fired. He claims he said my job would never be in jeopardy and that it was you who wanted me to quit. He claims you're still angry 'cause he told you it would be a mistake to marry Trish. Did he

By Dianne J. Beale

really say that to you?" Mar waited to see her brother's response. He merely nodded a yes, so Mar went on, "Then, shortly after they left, Luke came to see me. Oh but first the doctor came by, and I called you and left messages. Then, I ate lunch. Then came Luke." Mitch remained calm and waited to hear if there were more. Then he quietly asked how her visit with Luke had gone.

"Oh, it went great. He listened and wrote down stuff as I tried to organize everything. Pastor Andres has a way of making me feel inadequate and stupid. I start questioning myself, my memory. I've been feeling lost and alone ever since you changed employers. I don't trust myself anymore. I have so many doubts. So we decided to write it all down so I would have the truth in writing and wouldn't feel so inclined to doubt myself. But he went out to make a copy for himself and now I don't have a copy. But Mitch, I get so confused!"

"Mar, you know I would never lie to you. I might not like you working at that church, but I wouldn't deceive you to get my way. Besides, I wouldn't ask you to quit unless you already had another job, not unless I thought you weren't safe somehow. Mar, you *know* me. It's like what the professor said in The Lion, the Witch, and the Wardrobe. You remember, right? Something about how logic should compel you to trust what you know to be true, even when everything else seems to contradict it?"

"I told them you would never lie to me. Then they tried to say I misunderstood them and that all they had really said was that you had misunderstood, not lied. Then they left, and Luke came."

Just then, there was a tap at the door and the doctor entered. He asked Mar a few questions and then told her he needed to have a nurse come in and take a few more blood samples. Mar expressed frustration about not knowing what was going on, and the doctor apologized. He assumed someone had explained already. "Your blood pressure is slightly low, and your pulse has been normal to high. The traces of arsenic have cleared, but these other symptoms have continued. Your blood's been slightly off balance and we've not been able to determine the reason. Some tests pointed to vein dilation but others seemed to show vein compression. This is probably the reason you fainted. It is quite likely that this has been going on for some time, weakening your immune system and causing you stress. We also suspect you may have a form of anemia, but we need to be sure. There are different treatments for different types. Do you drink a lot of coffee or tea?"

"I have only one cup of coffee before work, but I drink tea almost all day. But it's not caffeinated. I only drink herbal. I do know I should drink more water, but the tea is brewed in the morning, and I keep the pot in my office. I would need to go to the church kitchen if I wanted to drink water."

By Dianne J. Beale

"What kind of herbal tea is it?"

"I drink mostly a mood tea. The office staff got it for me. They think I'm kinda emotional. It tastes good, though. So I ignored their reasoning and drank it anyway."

"Does it have St. John's Wort? This can be an effective herbal antidepressant, but drinking or taking it for prolonged lengths of time can deplete iron."

"I believe it does, along with maybe six or seven other herbs. I'm not one hundred percent sure, though."

"Well, we should check those ingredients out. But we'll see what the tests say first, okay? The nurse will be in shortly."

Mitch saw that Mar looked worried and decided not to mention the office attitude. He watched as the nurse took more blood. As she then left the room, he mentioned how tired Mar seemed, and told her he would move on to visit Trish and then go home.

Mar nodded and excused him even though she really wanted him to stay. Then she rolled over onto her pillow. Changing the television to music, she closed her eyes. She didn't even have the strength to pray. But she knew that God was with her and that He understood. Soon she had fallen asleep.

Chapter 19

The next day came early. The doctor was scheduled for vacation and introduced her to the doctor he often teamed with. He also wanted her to hear the results from himself.

Mar did appear to have anemia, but thankfully, it was the easiest to treat. He told her she would need to lower her tea intake, even herbal, and avoid too much caffeine. He also prescribed a liquid iron and gave her an initial diet. He then instructed her to schedule an appointment with the nutritionist, as well. There was a short discussion between the two doctors and then they added a daily vitamin. They told her that if she were a vegetarian, she'd need to change her lifestyle by adding either chicken or fish. They also emphasized the need to drink plenty of water and not to skip meals. She was then handed all of the paperwork, asked if she had any questions, and told to sign her discharge orders. Once she had signed, she was told that she could go.

She packed up her things, checked the closets and the drawers, and then picked up the phone. She was about to dial Mitch at work when Luke entered the room. She put the receiver back on its base and told him she was about to leave. He invited her to lunch with him, and she accepted.

They had decided to drive to a *Denny's* but then chose a nearby café instead. They sat across from each other and waited for the server to return with the drinks they had ordered. The greeter had gone back to her post by the door, but they had seen her pass their order along.

A short time later, their drinks arrived. Mar had forgotten how much she enjoyed strawberry lemonade. Today, it tasted like absolute perfection. She watched as Luke sipped his *Coke*.

Silence normally would have caused Mar to babble; she occasionally did this whenever her nerves kicked in. But she was tired and felt that it was too late to impress Luke now. He'd seen her at her very worst. She would never have believed it if she could hear Luke's thoughts. He was actually rather surprised at how strong she seemed.

When their food finally came, Mar was suddenly reminded of the missing notepad that had contained his notes. She thought about how to bring it up but then just risked sounding crazy. "Luke, didn't we make notes the other day when you visited me at the hospital? You were going to make a copy for yourself and leave the original with me, right?" she queried.

Luke paused to finish his chewing before he spoke. "Yeah. Why?"

"They're missing," she explained. "All I have is an empty notepad of paper."

"Is that all that was missing?"

"I think so. Well, no. My other notes that I had scribbled in pencil were gone as well. I told Mitch I was beginning to think I was losing my mind. He doesn't plan on going back to that church. I told him about how they tried to convince me that he was lying about my being fired and that Pastor Andres then claimed that he hadn't called him a liar but had only said that he had obviously misunderstood. But Mitch has been planning to leave for some time now. I knew that changing employers had been only a first step. He says the church is a disgrace to our parents' names." Luke didn't seem surprised, but she pressed on anyhow. "Do you still have the notes we wrote?" she asked. He just nodded his head; he was chewing again. Mar was embarrassed at her poor sense of timing and fell silent.

When they had finished, Luke suggested that she rent *Gaslight*. He told her it was a movie in which she could easily play the main character. He suggested she not watch it alone, though. She immediately thought of Trish and Mitch. Maybe they would enjoy it, as well. It never occurred to her that Luke might want to be the one she shared it with.

Mar thanked him for the suggestion and was about to dig through her bag when he said that the lunch was on him. He seemed preoccupied and in a hurry, so she didn't argue. He did, however, take the time to drive her home.

Once inside, Mar called Mitch's cell to let him know she was no longer at the hospital. Then she listened to the messages, but none were pressing enough for her to return a

By Dianne J. Beale

call. She decided she'd just go to bed, even if it was still early. In the comfort of her own room, she soon was sleeping soundly.

Chapter 20

It seemed as if only minutes had passed when Mar awoke to the repeated sound of the doorbell. At first, she thought she'd only dreamt it, but then pounding knocks joined the chime. The urgency expressed by the caller caused a huge knot to form in her stomach. She crawled out of bed and was thankful she had not changed into her pajamas. She cautiously and quietly went to the door. Squinting out through the peek hole revealed a very wet Mitch. Someone was with him, but she couldn't tell who. She unlocked and opened the door.

A relieved Mitch entered the house, followed by a woman that Mar did not recognize. Yet somehow, she seemed familiar. She was a petite woman, with a delicate, shapely figure. Her dark eyes were almost black in color, making it difficult to distinguish her irises from her pupils. But her expression was warm against her worn, vanilla-toffee skin.

Mitch closed the door behind them, locking it quickly. Mar was about to ask why he'd not used the garage, but he shushed her. He was making a phone call, so Mar decided her questions could wait. The woman stood awkwardly, shifting her weight from foot to foot. Remembering her manners, Mar directed the woman to the kitchen. Mitch, realizing he was only adding to the tension, sat down at the table as well. Mar put water into the tea kettle and set it on the stove to heat. She then quietly explained she was going to get some towels and would be back shortly.

While she was in the restroom getting towels, she recalled a bag of clothes she had planned to drop off at the Salvation Army. She grabbed those, as well, and then headed back to the kitchen. Mitch appeared to be on hold, but he took the towel and began to dry off. The woman seemed surprised, but grateful. She entered the nearby half-bath with the towel and bag of clothes. There were even a few unopened bags of underclothes in the mixture. Mar often purchased such articles on sale so she could provide these as new when she gave to the poor.

When the front door's bell rang again, Mar knew it would be difficult to feign absence, since Mitch had not parked in the garage. She was about to check who it was when Mitch stopped her with an extension of his arm. He went to the door, instead. He returned to the kitchen with Luke at his side. The woman came out from the restroom. Luke appeared to recognize her. They shook hands but didn't talk since Mitch was on the phone.

The kettle whistled, and Mar set up four cups for warm drinks. She put the water-filled cups on the table, along with choices of teas, instant coffee, hot chocolate, and instant cider. She also set out creamer, sugar, and spoons. Then, she sat down at the table and waited quietly with the others. All three jumped when Mitch closed his cell and swore. "On hold for what seemed an eternity," he explained, "and then I'm transferred to a message that gives office hours and hangs up! I thought they told you that was the 24-hour emergency number." He was apparently talking to the woman.

The woman began to shake again. Mar was just now realizing that this had not been entirely from the cold. Mar thought that it might have been her brother's agitation that awakened the new trembling. She turned to Mitch and questioned, "Whose emergency number?"

The woman seemed to gain a little strength at the sound of Mar's voice. "That's the number they gave me. But I've had it for almost a year and have never used it. Maybe it's changed," she offered.

Mitch, although he was not happy with the answer, accepted it. Then he seemed to get a better idea. He turned to Luke. "What am I thinking? You're a cop. Why don't we just get instructions from you?"

Luke eyed Mitch with caution, "What kind of instructions? I might not know any more than you do. We do have different departments, you know. What information do you need?"

By Dianne J. Beale

The woman was suddenly frantic and agitated. She obviously did not like that Luke was a cop. She began to plead with Mitch to just let it go.

Mitch knew enough to know he could do nothing without the woman's testimony, so he agreed to drop it. Mar could tell he was not happy about it, though. She watched as his right eye began to twitch. This often happened when her brother saw injustice that was beyond his control.

Luke had also hoped the woman would talk. He'd seen her before. She only wanted to be free, but without testifying. Why couldn't she understand that her testimony was the only way to gain her freedom?

Mar realized she was the only one left in the dark and didn't like it. But she knew only the woman could change that, and she wasn't talking. Mar did manage to place the voice, though. This was the mysterious woman who had been leaving messages for her brother. Since Mar was hungry, she decided ordering a pizza would lighten the mood.

Chapter 21

After her uncanny ability to change the topic, the kitchen became a buzz of activity. They all pooled their cash and realized they had close to forty dollars. It was amazing that they all could agree on the toppings to order, as well. Mitch called in the order.

"Thirty-four, ninety-two," Mitch related, "perfect. I think he'll earn the five-dollar tip in this downpour."

The table became a place of laughter and joking, and the time passed quickly. The pizza arrived, and soon they were all eating, instead.

When they had finished, Mar cleared the dishes to the sink and began to rinse them. Luke apologized for having to eat and run, but he had to work a double shift the next day. "I need to get my rest while I can."

The mysterious woman still had no name. Luke offered to take her home. She took the bag of clothes with her as they went. Mitch saw them to the door.

Mar suddenly felt cold and alone. She realized the window was open and shut it. As she reached to pull the blinds, she felt her heartbeat quicken. The rain had long since stopped, and staring at her from the fence was a dark

By Dianne J. Beale

shadow with piercing yellow-green eyes. She let down the blinds so quickly that they clanked against the window ledge below. But she still felt as if she were being watched, so she loosed the curtains, as well. Foolishly, she believed that it had spoken to her. But cats can't talk. It had to be her imagination.

She finished cleaning up just as Mitch rejoined her. He saw her agitation but assumed it was with him because of the secrecy. He apologized but told her that the woman's story was not his story to tell. He did give her a name, however.

"She's Trish's half-sister," he explained. "Her name is Amelia. That's all I'm at liberty to discuss. Sorry, Sis."

Mar was used to her brother's secrecy. As a counselor, he often was not "at liberty to discuss." This was the main reason he had left the church. The other staff members felt it was their business to know Mitch's clients, and their stories. They often would say that for the leadership to be unified, they must all be equally informed. She had even heard Andres once say that *confidentiality was overrated*. But Mitch would not divulge either name or reason. He also kept his files here at the house and had been furious when his office Rolodex had obviously been given the once over. He had served as counselor and youth minister. But when he felt that confidentiality had the potential to become compromised, he had accepted a fellow counselor's invitation to join his practice and had left the church. He had graciously continued to attend church with Mar, however. But there would be no more of that. Not now. Not without Trish there, as well.

Without Mitch at the staff meetings, there also were no more disagreements—everyone seemed to cater to Pastor Andres Loukatos. If Andres wanted it, he got it. If he didn't, then it didn't happen. Mar was uneasy with these thoughts and was not looking forward to returning to work.

Mar realized that Mitch was still standing nearby, waiting for her to respond. She assured him that she understood, and they hugged each other. Then each went off to their rooms. They'd forgotten about the car in the driveway and Mitch's lack of a key.

By Dianne J. Beale

Chapter 22

"Garnet… Garnet… why must you be so stubborn? Don't you see? Mitch has left the narrow path and put your life in danger. He's thinking only of himself. You should move away from him. God need not punish you, too. Leave Mitch to face God's wrath alone."

Mar was standing in her backyard, talking to the cat. But cats can't talk, she reasoned, so turned to go inside.

Suddenly, Pastor Andres stood in front of her, blocking her path. Mar protested, asking him to move. He gently kissed her forehead, instead. "Garnet," he reasoned, "I'm your pastor. I want only what's best for you. Let me lead you."

Mar knew she had to be dreaming again and tried desperately to wake herself up. But the pastor continued. He put his hands on her shoulders and looked her in the eyes. "Such sad eyes," he sympathized. "They used to smile. You were to be my prize, but not now. A pastor's wife must believe in him and be willing to forsake all others. But you serve your brother. You've put him before even your God. Our children would have been so beautiful… beyond beautiful. But you've chosen to ignore God and follow a path of your own."

Mar began to panic. She turned away from the door and instead headed for the gate. As she turned, she noticed that the cat had left the fence. She opened the gate, went into the side yard, and let the gate slam shut behind her, hoping if Andres followed, he'd be slowed down. Moving to the house's front, she began to scream at herself: "Wake up! Why don't you just open your eyes and wake up?"

A rusted, rundown car loomed before her. It had been stripped completely; only the basic frame remained, along with a steering wheel. She gasped as she realized the car belonged to Mitch–the very car he had earlier left in the driveway. The steering wheel remained intact, protected by the personalized cover that Trish had given him.

The church counselor seemed to appear from nowhere. He stood in her path, wielding more accusations and lies. "He's followed his own way, Garnet. He has chosen to be the driver; he's not even allowed God to remain in the back seat. It has led to death… look at the car; it has wasted away. He traded God for Trish. Run from them; choose us instead. Our road leads to life, his to death. You were meant for the pastor, but he's chosen another. You already have second best. You turned away and God took away your planned blessings. Don't choose Mitch over God–he is selfish and unkind. You know it is the truth. You've seen how he's changed. Why won't you grab onto the truth?"

By Dianne J. Beale

Mar backed away from the raving counselor, but recalling Andres, the shady feline, and the gate, she slowly edged sideways to alter her course. She began to pray. "Jesus," she managed, "Please help me. Where are You? Where is the cross that set me free? Oh, Jesus, my Lord."

Suddenly the car was rising into the air. The cross she had seized in the woodpecker dream was growing upward from under the car. It rose above the counselor, lifting the car as it climbed. As it soared onward, the car began to change. Rust fell away to be replaced by strong, beautiful metal. The tires, the missing shell, and the doors all returned. Witnessing the car's renewal at the appearance of the cross, Mar dove forward. Throwing herself against it, she secured her hold, grasping it tightly. She, too, was lifted to safety. She pulled herself upward and entered the car. Stretching herself out on the back seat, she felt peacefully cradled by the cross below. She was safe. "Thank You, Jesus," she breathed, "Thank You."

Chapter 23

When Mar didn't make it to breakfast, Mitch grew concerned. Realizing that if he didn't walk out the door right at that moment, he'd be late, he called his secretary and told her he wouldn't be in for the day. Then he phoned the church where Mar was expected. Not surprisingly, he got the machine, so left a brief, nondescript message saying that Mar would be out until Monday.

He then went to her bedroom door and quietly knocked. When she didn't answer, he knocked a little louder. As a final resort, he opened the door and went in.

Covers were scattered all over the floor and she was still dressed in her clothes from the night before. He walked over to the closest bedding and picked it up to place over her. When he drew nearer, he noticed she had beads of sweat on her face and arms. Touching his wrist to her forehead, he discovered she was burning with fever. Gently, he woke her.

Mar opened her eyes. Seeing Mitch, she smiled. But when she tried to talk, she winced in pain. Mitch walked to the sink and filled a cup with water. She drank it quickly, as if parched, so he returned for more. When she had finished with this second cup, she again tried to talk: "You, car?"

Not understanding what she meant, he decided she was confused due to the fever. At least she seemed peaceful. He explained he was going to go out to the kitchen to get her some medicine, and then he would return. When she didn't answer, he turned and left.

She was asleep again when he came back, so he set the medicine on the night stand, allowing her to rest. He retrieved the remainder of the bedding from the floor and laid it over her. He'd return later to check on her. She could take the medicine then. As he left the room, his mind transported him into the past.

"Mitch, why does my throat still hurt?" asked a much younger Mar. "I feel as if my skin is stretched, pinching me almost, and it's hard to breathe."

"The doctor said it would take time for the antibiotics to work, remember? I don't like how swollen your glands look, though. I'll call the after-hours nursing staff and see what they say. Okay?"

Mar had just looked up at him with pained eyes that were pleading. He left to make the call and had been told that she had tested positive for mono.

"I'm sorry, Sis," he told her. "The only solution they offered was for me to try ice." He laid a baggie of ice onto her hot skin, causing her to wince in shock. She had begged him to remove it, but he told her they needed to get the swelling under control. He never mentioned how frightened he'd been; the nurses had also said to call 911 if she quit breathing. He had watched her that night as if one of many vultures, circling above their dying prey. He had never before sought God so fervently.

The ringing phone jarred him back to reality. Recognizing the church's number, he did not pick up. Instead he waited for the machine to answer, hoping they'd leave a message.

"Hello?" an unfamiliar voice said. "Ah, this is Jasmine. Um, right, you probably don't know me. I'm the new receptionist at Shepherd's Orchard. I just started my job today."

She sounded unsure of herself. It was almost painful to let the machine record on. "Someone called earlier–to call in sick–and I just want you to know that I'm the only one here. The entire staff is out with strep. You might want to get tested. Ah, okay, hope this helps. Bye."

Mitch knew it was risky, but he saw this as an opportunity to get Mar's personal property out of their grasp. When he had worked there, he had emptied his office of personal touches a little at a time until nothing even resembling him had remained.

He remembered Mar's teasing and jokes, but wanting to protect her, he just took it all in stride. She was never aware of the things he had seen and heard.

By Dianne J. Beale

Now he wished he hadn't sheltered her so thoroughly. He was convinced that if she'd seen staff members fired and dragged out of the church, or his counseling clients being questioned and badgered, she'd have had an entirely different view. One of his former colleagues was instructed to fire his own wife, and when he refused, they both were escorted out to the sidewalk. Mitch had later gathered their things and returned them to them, but he did this against church orders.

Mitch called Trish's mom to stay with Mar while he stepped out. She was honored that he trusted her enough to ask for such a favor, and arrived quickly. He explained that he needed to run an errand and asked if she could also call Mar's doctor to set an appointment since most of the church staff had been diagnosed with strep. She took down the name and number and assured him that everything was going to be okay. She had mistaken his nervousness for hesitancy in leaving while Mar was sick, so motherly shooed him out the door.

Jasmine was more than happy to let Mitch in. She was climbing the walls with boredom. Besides, she hadn't packed a lunch and wondered if he'd man the fort long enough for her to run across the street for a sandwich. She hadn't even asked who he was; this was just far too easy.

As soon as she was out of sight, Mitch set the church's system back to automatic answering and then raced up to Mar's office. The mess of the other day had been cleared, so his job became even easier. He pulled the wadded bag from his pocket and began loading it with his sister's personal stuff: tea bags and boxes, pictures, stuffed animals, stationery, post cards, greeting cards, a sweater, her empty tea pot with matching plates and cups, a mug with her name on it, and the Bible he had purchased for her to keep at the office so she wouldn't need to cart one back and forth. He scanned the room, checked drawers and cupboards, and finally was content that he'd gathered it all. He tied the bag shut, and was about to leave, when he noticed the computer was on.

He quickly moved the mouse to pull the monitor out of standby. The browser was opened to a popular, free email service–one he had used in the past. A program was also running. He analyzed the program closer and found that it seemed to be systematically creating and trying passwords at the open site. But the user name it was using belonged to him! Were they trying to crack his password and get into his private email? He had read about such programs but had never actually seen one.

He quickly took out his camera phone and snapped a few pictures of the screen, and then the computer's surroundings. He then set the computer to return to standby and went back down to the main office. Jasmine had not yet returned. He was able to leave the church, put his sister's stuff into the trunk of his car, and slip his cell phone safely

By Dianne J. Beale

inside, as well. He closed and locked the trunk, set his car's alarm, and then went back into the church.

Jasmine was back behind the desk, eating her sandwich. She was surprised to see him coming in from outside, but he explained how he had set the automated system to answer any incoming calls and then gone to his car to wait for her in case someone really did stop by. He went on to say how he hadn't wanted to get her into any trouble and thought that people were more likely to excuse a quick restroom break than they would her complete absence. This seemed to satisfy her and, after explaining the automated system, he was able to leave without further incidence.

Chapter 24

Once home, he found he could breathe again. He parked in the garage and went directly into the house. Trish's mom was in the kitchen. She had made homemade chicken soup. He thanked her and then asked about Mar's appointment. She apologetically informed him that the doctor had not been able to fit her in, despite the possibility of strep, and that he was to take her to the hospital emergency room if things got worse before her eight o'clock appointment the next morning. He thanked Shawnda again, asked her how things had gone, and walked her out to the car. After returning to the house and securing all the locks, he practically ran back out to his car to retrieve his phone and Mar's stuff. He immediately went to his business laptop, ignoring their home computer.

First he surfed to the site where he could sign in to his old email address-the one he believed to be the target of the possible hijack. He hadn't used it in a while, but it was still possible it stored private and confidential matters. He changed his password to a fourteen character phrase that was spelled out using numbers, symbols, and both capital and lowercase letters. He then wrote out the password for future reference and switched to a search engine where he could hunt for another site that offered free email. He wanted a site that he had never heard of. Once he found one he liked, he signed up for a new email account and created a different, but equally difficult password.

Next he uploaded his camera photos into the computer. He saved them with the numerals they had been given as identity by the program rather than labeling them, so they would seem generic and unimportant. He signed into his business account, changed its password, just in case, and then composed a letter with the pictures as attachments. He sent this letter to the new account that he had created just moments before.

Then he signed out of his business account and back into the one that he had witnessed being attacked. He began to sort the mail and tediously forward any that might prove important, or was considered confidential. He deleted these, one by one, knowing they would sit safely in the trash, so he'd remember what had been viewed and already forwarded.

Remaining signed in to this account, he quickly checked the new account to verify receipt of the pictures and forwards. Once verified, he signed out of his new account and went back to the old account once more. He deleted all of the remaining sent messages that would reveal his new account, and then emptied the trash. He scanned the account, and once satisfied, signed off. Finally, he went to check on his sister.

Mar was sleeping peacefully, undisturbed, just as Shawnda had said. He left her to sleep and went to the kitchen to look in on the soup. He decided to whip up a batch of dumplings to drop in on the top. Once accomplished, he turned the soup down to a simmer and covered it. If Mar was not awake within the next half hour then he would wake her to give her medicine and something to eat. As he walked past the refrigerator, Luke's business card caught his eye. He determined he should call him and get his take on things.

Surprisingly, it was Luke who answered. His voice cheered a bit when he heard a familiar voice. He listened silently as Mitch discussed the possibility of sending him the pictures he had taken. Luke processed what he'd been told and concluded that Mitch, for some reason, wasn't willing to discuss the contents of the pictures over the phone. Yet it also seemed he was suggesting he'd like Luke to get them as soon as possible. Luke thought this over and told Mitch the safest and best bet was for him to email them to his email account at work. The address was on the business card he had given to Mar.

Just as Mitch was about to hang up, Luke changed his mind and asked Mitch to hold while he checked to see if he was free to leave the office. Mitch agreed to hold but then realized he could forward the pictures to Luke's cell phone.

By Dianne J. Beale

This seemed to be the easiest and quickest option. So, as he waited, he pulled out his cell phone and forwarded the pictures he had taken. He then saved each picture, using a password to lock them, and returned the phone to his pocket.

Growing impatient, Mitch switched to the nearby portable and began to busy himself preparing iced tea to go with the soup. When he opened the soup pot, the soup had evolved into more of a stew, so he removed it from the burner. He went to the pantry and got out some crackers, setting them down on the table.

Finally, Luke's voice came over the phone. He had been waiting for his boss's approval when the pictures had arrived to his cell. They had recognized the cracking program at once. It was one they'd been tracking for months. His boss okayed his departure and he would be heading over just as soon as he and Mitch hung up. Mitch breathed a sigh of relief.

Serving the stew into bowls, he then went to check on Mar to see how she was doing. Finding her door closed, he knocked. She had managed to walk herself to the restroom and was on her way back to the bed when she heard him. She went to the door and opened it. Although she still seemed slightly weak, she sounded much better. Mitch told her of the soup that Shawnda had made and asked her if she had taken any of the medicine he had left at her bedside. She told him she wanted to try to eat something and that she hadn't taken any medicine but definitely would now that she was awake. He told her to get back into bed and he would bring her a tray. She thanked him and went to the night stand to take her medicine before lying back down.

On his way to the kitchen, the doorbell rang. He went to the door, and seeing it was Luke, he opened the door and motioned him inside. After securing the locks, he gestured that Luke should follow him to the kitchen.

Mitch explained that Mar was sick as he prepared a tray to take to her room. He put two bottles of water on the tray deciding that caffeine would not be a good idea, especially while she was sick. He filled a bowl with crackers and then set it on the tray, along with one of the bowls of soup. He told Luke to help himself and explained he would return shortly.

Mar's color had returned and she was sitting up, propped against pillows, when he came in. He set the tray up around her and then explained he needed to get back because Luke had stopped by and was waiting in the kitchen. She asked him to say hello for her and also wondered if he'd mind calling a pharmacist for her. Her tongue was slightly swollen and she wondered if there was anything she could take that would help. Mitch insisted on looking it over and then agreed that he'd call the pharmacist since it wasn't too swollen and she was seeing the doctor in the morning anyhow.

By Dianne J. Beale

Luke smiled as Mitch apologized and told him he'd be right with him. He spoke with the pharmacist and they concluded that Benadryl would be the best option. Upon hanging up, he dug through their kitchen shelves and found a bottle of liquid Benadryl that was still good. He excused himself one last time and then returned, joining Luke at the table. He finally was able to eat the soup he had smelled for most of the day. And it was good.

Chapter 25

Luke's phone rang, and he realized he needed to take the call. He went into the other room to talk while Mitch continued enjoying his supper. Shortly, Luke hung up and returned. He smiled mischievously. "It must madden your sister now that she has two men in her life who must withhold information," he said.

Mitch laughed. "I guess now I know what it's like for her. Maybe it's my fault she no longer asks questions."

Luke then moved right on to business. "Those pictures were taken at the church, right? Wasn't that Mar's office?" he asked.

Mitch nodded. "She's been sick all day and the receptionist called to say she'd need to see a doctor. The entire staff has strep. Anyhow, I took this opportunity to go by and grab all her personal stuff, just to be safe. Besides, the doctor had wanted the ingredients to the teas she drinks."

Luke stored that thought as a follow-up question and directed the conversation back to the church. "So, you must have noticed her computer was on?" Mitch nodded, so Luke continued. "It was on the day she tried to return to work, as well. Is it normal for it to remain on like that?"

By Dianne J. Beale

Mitch told Luke that he believed it was encouraged for the staff to shut them down when they left for the day. "But," he added, "It seems the rules tend to change almost weekly. They did, at least, while I worked there."

"Oh," replied Luke, "I hadn't realized. But I guess that would make sense. Wasn't it once your parents' church?"

"Yeah," Mitch faltered, "but it wasn't an Orchard church back then. It was called the Shepherd's Fold. We had more ministries then. And counseling was left to the professionals, not to those who just claim to have a gifting."

Luke sensed some anger, maybe even bitterness. "Your parents didn't approve of counseling?" he asked.

"Oh, no," quipped Mitch, "they just knew that counseling was rather important and that sometimes the basics weren't enough. They believed in God's power to heal, but they also thought it was dangerous to assume He would. My dad was famous for saying that even Luke—from the Bible, you know—was a doctor and that knowledge is sometimes the only thread between true healing and surface healing. Mom always said that it takes God's wisdom and discernment to be *shrewd as serpents and innocent as doves* and that we are responsible for learning as much as we can about His world."

Luke had figured they had to be practical to have raised a son like Mitch, but he prided himself on being thorough. "Sounds like you had yourself some good parents there. What happened?"

The Uninvited

Mitch sighed at the memory, and Luke was just about to take back the question when Mitch answered. "A drunk driver ran a red light and totaled the van from the side. They died instantly, it's believed. The only comfort Mar and I had was that they were in heaven praising God that the youth group had already been dropped off."

Luke told Mitch he was sorry and tried to change the subject. Mitch, sensing Luke's discomfort, suddenly realized that maybe Luke had meant the question differently. Maybe he'd been trying to lighten the mood by joking about how Mitch and Mar had turned out.

After a few seconds of discomfort, Luke continued, "Did you get everything that belongs to Mar?"

"I believe so. I even checked her drawers and cupboards. Why?"

"You mentioned the doctor had hoped to get the ingredients to her tea. Do you have her stuff where we can get to it without disturbing her?"

Mitch and Luke moved to the family room to poke over the contents of the bag. Luke had him throw down a white sheet on the floor. Then the viewing began.

By Dianne J. Beale

Chapter 26

After having poured the contents of the bag onto the sheet, Mitch quickly gathered up the Bible. It had landed in a heap, pages folding and crimping. He smoothed out the Bible, watching as a slip of paper fell from within. He felt bad about going through Mar's things, as if he was now the one doing the spying. But he knew it was more of a matter of being concerned for her health. He set the Bible gingerly to the side and picked up the paper.

My darling Maggie, I've so enjoyed our times together. I know we both believed that our love would last forever, but I've come to see that it is not our love that matters. Ours is a greater mission–the increase of the Kingdom. We lack a combined charisma–a charisma I will need if I am to bring people to side with our cause. I never meant to hurt you. Keep the ring. I had it resized and told them that it will be you who pick it up. You will need your license to show that you are the right person. It's paid for in full, just as our lives are in Christ. I release you to Him who owns your heart. Anthony.

"What a crock of you-know-what! I wondered what had happened to him. I didn't know he'd proposed! Why would Mar keep this a secret from me?"

Luke was quiet. He was reading the back side of the note: *I will store you here. Psalm 41:9.* He asked Mitch to look up the verse.

Mitch read aloud, "Even my close friend, whom I trusted, he who shared my bread, has lifted up his heel against me." Next to the verse in the Bible was written, *Mitch must never know.* Mitch slid the letter between the two pages and laid the Bible back on the floor. He and Luke chose not to discuss it. Instead, they continued their search.

Opening a box of unlabeled tea, they discovered a small, plastic bag instead of tea bags. It had a smudged tag that was used as a closure. Fortunately, it was still legible: *An Enchantress's Entanglement.* On the back was a disclaimer: *All herbal teas, especially custom made, should be cleared with your health provider.*

Luke unclipped his cell phone and called his office. Soon, he was asking if he could be patched through. It must have been possible since it appeared he was now talking to someone new. "Yes, I was interested in possibly getting a personalized blend of tea? Yes, I can hold."

He explained to Mitch that he was being transferred to the herbalist employed at *An Enchantress's Entanglement.* He then began talking again on the phone. "Um, yes I recently shared some tea at a friend's and was wondering if it is possible to order my own custom blend. Um, yes. Oh, I see. Well, okay, I'll try to make the time to come in then. No, it's okay. I understand perfectly. Okay. Thanks."

By Dianne J. Beale

Luke hung up the phone and quickly jotted down a few notes. Then he related everything to Mitch. "Well, it appears that the majority of their teas are completely safe prefabs," he explained. "But if the tea isn't bagged, and comes in an unlabeled box, then it is one of their custom blends. Usually they choose what herbs go into each of their teas, but occasionally they do allow requests. In this case, I would need to come to the store with my friend since the tea is custom, and they can't be sure of the ingredients without knowing who ordered it. My friend would need to okay the disclosure, as well. They value privacy rights rather highly. Certain herbs even require a doctor's written permission before they'll use them."

Mitch thought this over. He wondered aloud, "Do you think the doctor from the hospital would be willing to analyze this mix? I think it's reasonable to assume that since the teapot has a filled tea ball in it, I'd say that this is most likely what Mar's been drinking the most. The other teas all were of the conventional type–tea bags with brand names attached."

Luke seemed to agree with this assessment. He said it wouldn't hurt to offer it to them and then added that he'd take some to the police lab, as well.

Mitch then offered to call the tea shop himself to be sure that Mar hadn't been the one to order it. Since Luke had been transferred, he didn't have the number. Looking it up in the phone book, Mitch then dialed the phone.

"An *Enchantress's Entanglement,* can I help you?"

"Hi. I hope so," he answered. "My sister recently finished off a box of tea that I especially enjoyed, and she mentioned she planned to order some more. I wondered if she'd been in to place the order. It's a custom tea, I think, so I really cannot order it myself."

"Can I have her name, please?"

"Yes. It's Margaret Zeiler."

"With a Z sir?"

"Yes, that's correct."

"We don't have any customers in our files that match that name. Are you sure that it was a custom tea?" she asked.

"I thought that was what she said. It was in the form of leaves rather than bags, if that helps."

"Well, it does, but could it be maybe she buys it with another friend? If her friend buys from us, and the blend doesn't require a doctor's approval, we'd let her purchase it, as well–if her friend were with her, of course."

"Oh, I didn't realize. Sorry. I'll just remind her that we're out, then. Thank you for your help."

"No problem. Thank you for your interest in our teas."

Mitch turned to Luke. "She's not on their customer list. She did say the church staff had purchased her a mood tea. Do you think maybe this is it?"

Luke looked over the contents on the sheet once more. "Well, none of those others claim to be for moods. They all

By Dianne J. Beale

look rather basic, like department store tea. I'd say this must be the tea she received as a gift."

Mitch had Luke pour some of the tea into a baggie so he could bring it to the lab and then did the same so he'd have a sample for the doctor. He tied the rest back up in the plastic bag it had come in and stuffed it back into the plain box. He walked Luke to the door and they agreed not to discuss it with Mar unless something came of the analysis. Once Luke left, Mitch retrieved the tray and dishes from his sister's room and then left her to continue sleeping. He'd forgotten to tell Luke that she had said to say "hi."

Chapter 27

Mitch took Mar to her appointment the next morning. She didn't have strep as they suspected, but she did appear to be having an allergic reaction. The doctor also suspected she may have had the twenty-four-hour flu. He prescribed a couple of allergy medications and insisted on the importance of pushing liquids and getting lots of rest. He also told her she should not return to work until Wednesday, at the earliest.

After dropping Mar at the house, Mitch went back out for the prescriptions. He was relieved to have this time alone so he could also stop by the hospital. The doctor was intrigued with the tea and looked forward to the analysis. He showed little interest in the ingredients Mitch had copied off the other tea boxes: Echinacea, chamomile, licorice, St. John's Wort, and peppermint.

Mitch gave the doctor his cell phone's number as the one to call with any news and then went by the pharmacy to pick up the prescriptions. He also purchased bottled water so Mar would have no excuse to not drink water once she had returned to work. Besides, these would be easier to monitor for tampering.

On the way home, he stopped at a favorite sub shop and picked up some dinner. With his free hand, he called Trish. He was surprised at how reasonable and understanding she was being, even before he explained Mar's illness. He promised to stop by later once Mar was settled in for the night.

He arrived home to an open front door. He stopped in the drive and hopped out of the car. Once inside, he saw Mar was sitting on the couch, unharmed. Luke was standing between her and the door. He quickly moved around Luke to cross to his sister, analyzing her as he went. "What happened? Why's the door open," he asked.

Luke explained it had been his fault. He had come to talk with Mitch, but Mar had answered the door. Then she had swayed a little, mentioning she felt a little tipsy, so he had helped her to the couch. He was just returning to get the door when Mitch had come in.

Relief flooded Mitch's body. He saw Mar was nodding in agreement, so excused himself to move the car to the garage and retrieve the purchases.

He and Mar each shared a third of their subs with Luke, despite his protests, and then she took her medicine and obediently headed off to bed. When they were sure she was out of earshot, they began to talk.

Neither had much to share, but each had received good initial responses. They were both wrapped in anticipation.

The Uninvited

They couldn't wait to have results so they could compare and discuss them.

By Dianne J. Beale

Chapter 28

The weekend passed without church and Mar was able to call in sick, on her own, once Monday had come. She began to bemoan the day she'd return, but she felt she needed to do it.

Wednesday was her first day back since the day she had rushed home to hear she'd been fired. Yet she walked into the church as if she'd never been gone, heading directly for her office. As she entered the room, she was shocked to find it devoid of all personality. Mitch had forgotten to mention his ransacking.

She went to the main office to question if anyone had noticed, and they all acted as if she had never had any personal items. They each insisted that personal items hadn't been allowed for the last few months and that she must have just forgotten that she'd taken them home.

In reality, they had noticed. They had discussed just that at the meeting the day before and had all taken their personal items home that night. It was decided then that if asked, the response would be one of disinterested surprise that implied she was the problem–didn't she remember the change in policy? They watched her carry it to her car, etc. If

Mar didn't bring it up, they'd assume she had somehow managed to remove her stuff herself and then question her loyalty because of it. Problem solved.

Due to this meeting, Mar never even knew Jasmine had served as secretary. They had fired her on the spot. They threatened to reveal secrets she had confided while attending their healing ministries if she attempted to report them or complain. Insisting that her peppered past implicated her, they shamed her by saying that they regretted giving her a second chance. Knowing they had no evidence, they only pretended that they planned to involve the police. She was so hurt and angry that she decided not to mention the man who had come and gone on her first day at work. Their treatment made her all the more determined to keep it a secret. So Jasmine had come and gone and Mar was none the wiser.

After only a few hours of the office staff joking at her expense, she began to doubt herself. Had she taken the items home? She was sure that she had not, but an entire staff of people couldn't be wrong, could they? She consoled herself by commending herself on the amount of work she had been able to accomplish. It seemed no one else had done anything. And she had returned to stacks of papers, some which were not even her responsibility, but which she often gave in and did.

Mitch's call broke into her thoughts. She agreed to meet him for lunch. Taking her bag of water, snacks, and

By Dianne J. Beale

medicine with her, she unaccustomedly locked her office and headed out.

When Mar related the morning events of her day to Mitch, he felt terrible. He told her that he had gone in on a day when there was a new receptionist–maybe secretary, he wasn't sure–and picked up her things because her firing/unfiring had unsettled him. He apologized but said they would have probably found another way to accost her if she hadn't mentioned it.

Mar was puzzled. "Did you say a new secretary?" The same old staff member that made a habit of complaining that her job was really better described as being for two, had just been complaining that morning. She had gone on more than usual about how they had said they'd find her an assistant and yet she still didn't have one.

"Yeah, I take it she wasn't there this morning. Her name began with a J. I think it was a flower… Jasmine… yes, her name was Jasmine."

Mar was suddenly furious. "Can you believe them? They hire a new assistant while I'm gone and then act as if I'm crazy when I mention my stuff is missing. I'll bet they thought she took my stuff, or at least blamed her for it, and fired her. Then, as usual, they cover it all up with lies. Let's make up a pleasant alternate reality and tell that story instead. How dare these people patronize, label, and judge me! I'll bet our Jasmine attended their so-called healing classes, too. What's it called? Oh yeah: Wild Springs. They act as if everyone needs to attend and if you choose not to, you're just in denial. 'Everyone's broken somehow, Garnet. You'd understand if you'd just attend.' I've seen them talk behind people's backs, gossip over others' pasts by sharing prayer requests and pretending it's all out of concern, even boast about how they've succeeded so well in healing the terminal. Oh, please! As if! You'd think they were God Himself! My refusal to attend was how they convinced Anthony that he couldn't marry me... 'Look at her, Anthony, if she's not willing to trust the anointed of God, if she refuses to submit even to Him... well, you can imagine, right? You do understand why she's just not right for you.' Oh, but you never knew he'd proposed. I'm sorry, Mitch." Having just revealed a long-held secret, she deflated in defeat.

"It's okay, Mar." Secretly he was glad he had already run across her secret. "I'm sure you had your reasons. I've not always shared everything with you. Don't worry about it. Sometimes secrets are healthy. You can't hide anything from God and not everyone finds healing through others. Sometimes it can only take place in the secrecy of your room–a private affair between Him and you. Remember Eustace from <u>The Chronicles of Narnia</u> when he was the dragon? He faced Aslan alone before he was freed."

Mar knew exactly what her brother meant. She hated that she had to return to work and finish out her day. She told Mitch she intended to leave them all in the dark.

By Dianne J. Beale

As she gathered her stuff to head back to the church, she thought of the miserable people she called her co-workers. They talked of freedom but knew only captivity and they spoke of light while they walked in darkness. They wore their wounds and iniquities like badges and spoke of the Kingdom, but rarely the King. Dethroning the King, they had redefined the Kingdom. And their reign, while speaking of mercy, dealt instead, swift injustice.

Chapter 29

Just as Mitch arrived home, his cell phone rang. He decided to take the call as he drove around the block.

"Hello?" he answered.

"Dr. Wiltenger here. I'm calling about Margaret Zeiler and the tea sample her brother dropped off."

"Yes. This is Mitch Zeiler. Margaret's not available now, but I can take down the results." Mitch pulled into the parking lot of the nearby park and pulled paper and pen from his pack. He then began to write as the doctor spoke.

"Lime was the main component found in the tea," he began, "Basically harmless, possibly even beneficial. But the other ingredients are of great concern: yohimbe, skullcap, and betel nut. Betel nut, in large doses, can result in sedation. Smaller doses might increase energy or cause euphoria. Skullcap, if used incorrectly, can cause confusion. Large doses can also induce shaking, or even a stupor-like state. But yohimbe causes me to have an even greater concern: if used in excess, it can increase heart rate, change blood pressure, cause nausea or cramping, and has been known to possibly increase body temperature. If Margaret was taking large enough doses, she might not have anemia

By Dianne J. Beale

at all. She needs to call so we can get a better idea of how much of this tea she may have drunk."

Mitch thanked the doctor, wrote down the number he gave, and promised he'd have Mar call. He then hung up the phone, praying for wisdom when he'd have to face his sister. Next, before going home, he called Luke.

Since Luke wasn't at work, and Mitch didn't know his home number, he decided that Luke would have to wait. Besides, he needed to talk with his sister, anyway. He started his engine and drove the short way back home.

Parking his car next to Mar's in the garage, he got out, grabbed his pack, and went into the house. The smell of lasagna filled the air, and he knew that Mar was feeling better than she had in quite some time. He went to his room, washed up, and then tore off the notes he had taken while talking to the doctor. He put them into his pocket and headed back out to the kitchen.

He opened the fridge and grabbed a soda, then sat down. Just then, Mar came into the room. She announced that they were going to have company for dinner. Mitch said that it would be a nice change and then asked when dinner would be ready. She laughed and said, "When the doorbell rings."

Mitch decided he'd have to wait for the company to leave before he could talk to her. He half-expected their guest might be Luke, but then decided it was unlikely. If he didn't have Luke's home number, then Mar didn't either.

Besides, she was never the one to make the first move. He didn't have to wonder long: Trish, Joe, Shawnda, and Trish's half-sister, Amelia, were soon at the door. Mitch was pleasantly surprised. He offered drinks while Mar set the table. Then they all sat down together, and began the meal.

After dinner, Mar asked if everyone wanted to watch a movie she'd been recommended. They all agreed, since it was still early. The movie, *Gaslight*, proved intriguing. Mitch seemed to enjoy it the most. But since they all had to work the next morning, they decided any discussion would need to be postponed. Mitch walked them to the door as Mar cleaned up. Tomorrow would be an interesting day.

By Dianne J. Beale

Chapter 30

Mitch woke early. He had set his alarm to be sure he would see Mar before she left the house. As he prepared the coffee and toasted the bread, he prayed. He wanted the conversation with Mar to go smoothly.

When Mar finally appeared, she seemed relaxed and happy. Mitch almost hated to share the news he had. But he knew she needed to hear what the doctor had discovered.

Mitch began cautiously. "Remember how the doctor from the hospital requested your herbal tea ingredients?" He waited for a response, but Mar seemed to be waiting for him to continue, so he did. "Well, I dropped off samples on the day I retrieved your personal stuff; you know, on the way home." Mar still didn't say anything. Mitch was growing nervous. "Um, he called yesterday with the results."

Mar finally spoke. "Yes, I know he called. It was on the machine," she stated. Mitch didn't think this was possible, but waited for her to continue.

When she didn't, he felt obliged to speak. "Oh? What did he say?" he asked.

"He wants me back at the hospital for more testing. He didn't say why. It was just a message requesting that I set up an appointment."

Mitch realized that it was probably the hospital's follow-up call and that Mar hadn't really known about the tea after all. He decided to try again. "Well, he called my cell, as well. The herbal tea contained three potentially dangerous herbs. He said too high a dose could have caused some of the same symptoms of anemia, so he wanted to test you again, now that the teas have been out of your system. I wrote down the herbs and stuff if you want to read it. I didn't want to forget."

Mar didn't seem upset at all and seemed even less surprised. "It was Pastor Andres' idea for the staff to get me that tea for a gift. I recognized the vender. I remember setting it aside and hadn't planned on using it. But the tea was steeped before I got to work most days, so I felt obligated to drink it."

Mitch was puzzled. "Why didn't you just bring it home and say we were enjoying it together? Why would you leave it at the office if you thought it might be bad?"

Mar became agitated. "Oh, please, Mitch! You worked in that environment. I really didn't think it was dangerous, I just assumed it was another way for him to control. The whole office thinks I'm an emotional wreck because Andres made sure they knew about Anthony. Once I tasted it, I

By Dianne J. Beale

decided that lime seemed safe enough so didn't want to risk making waves."

Mitch realized he had made her feel badly when there was nothing she could do to change what was done, and he felt terrible. "I'm sorry, Mar. You know I forget to think sometimes. I'm just so angry that he'd risk harming you. I hope we can prove that harm was his intention."

Mar hated arguing with her brother. She knew he didn't mean to make her feel dumb. She also knew that she hadn't been hypersensitive until Andres had come to work for the church. She had accepted a cut in pay when she had left her public school position because she had expected her stress levels to go down. At first, it appeared she had made the right decision. But since Andres, her pay decreased again, her bills had increased, and her self-worth had plummeted. She also had more to do, not less. Mar walked over to her brother and hugged him. "I know, Mitch. And I want you to know that I am looking for work again. But no one else can know that. Okay?"

Mitch returned her hug and said he was glad, reassuring her that he wouldn't tell anyone. Then they both sat down and had their toast and coffee. After breakfast, Mar called the hospital and set up the appointments she needed. Then they went out to the garage to their separate cars and jobs.

Despite her calm exterior, Mar was angry and hurt. She had stopped liking Pastor Andres some time ago, but she hadn't thought badly of him. Her dreams began to flood her mind, and she laughed. It was right there in front of her the entire time.

By Dianne J. Beale

Chapter 31

When Mar arrived at the church, she decided she should change her predictable routine. Instead of parking farthest away, as if she didn't matter, she parked in one of the closest spaces. She then locked her car, armed the alarm, and went into the church. No one else had yet arrived. As usual, she was the first. This struck her as odd for once. How could the tea have been brewed prior to her arrival if she was always the first one in the building? She began to analyze that assumption and realized that there was one other person in the building by the time she arrived–the janitor. She decided to go find him, but needed a ruse, just in case. She chose to use the need for new copier or printer paper due to the arsenic. Then her search began.

She found Paco in the children's building. He was building a new storage area that she had requested some time ago. Determined, she walked right up to him. "Paco," she said quietly. He jumped at her voice, nearly hitting his head, but recovered quickly.

"Yes, Ma'am," he answered. "Is there something you need? I couldn't brew your tea for you. Someone took all your stuff. I thought maybe you was gone."

"No, Paco. I'm still here. I wasn't worried about the tea. I was just hoping to get new paper since mine's been contaminated with arsenic."

"Arsenic, Ma'am?" He seemed genuinely confused. "Why would your paper have arsenic?"

"Oh, maybe I misunderstood. Pastor Andres said something about a heating oil leak that had contaminated the paper."

"No, Ma'am. No leak. I'd had noticed a leak. I'm the only one goes in there. Besides, there's no room in the furnace room for more than the furnace. A person can barely slide in. The paper's kept here–in your air conditioner's room. I can get you some now if you need it."

"No. It's no hurry. Bring it whenever you're goin' to be over our way. I don't need any special trips."

"You sure, Ma'am? Pastor Andres, he made it quite clear that things should be ready for you when you arrive. He said not to upset you by gettin' in your way, that you preferred to be alone. He was the one who suggested I even get your tea ready for you. He'd be mad if you don't get your paper when you need it. But no one told me 'bout the arsenic problem. I didn't know."

"Oh, Paco, I'm sorry to have been so much trouble. I had no idea you'd been given special orders. Don't worry about me. In fact, I'll just take one ream of paper with me now. That's more than enough. I don't need a whole box."

By Dianne J. Beale

"Okay Ma'am. Can I get back to work or do you need somethin' else?"

"Oh, sorry. Don't let me keep you; I wouldn't want you to get into trouble on my account. Thanks for your help." Inside her head rang seven additional words: *you've helped me more than you know.*

Mar grabbed one pack of paper from the room Paco had mentioned and then went back to her office. She began her usual day but soon became aware of distant voices. She was the only one who worked in the office who was aware of the intercom system. It hadn't been used since her parents had died. She began to play with the switches, searching for the room with people. When she came to the youth room, she stopped. She didn't know why, but she also hit record on her cell.

"You always were the theatrical one." She recognized Luke's voice immediately. "I got rid of the tea he gave me and the pictures he took, as well. You worry too much. They trust me."

Andres spoke next. "I know. I know. I've had a lot on my mind lately. I'll try to leave being a cop to you. Go now. We'll talk later."

Mar was in shock. How could Luke? But she came to her senses quickly. She shut down the intercom, slid it back into the hidden drawer, and locked it. Then she sent the recorded message to her email and to her brother's phone.

She had just password protected it and cleared the screen when she heard someone approaching.

"Hasn't anyone else arrived yet?" Andres asked nonchalantly.

"I haven't seen anyone. Why? What time is it?"

"Oh. I guess you're right. They won't get here for at least another ten minutes. Are you better now?"

"I think so, Sir. So long as I bring my bottled water, I should be fine."

"No more tea?" he asked.

"No. Not even herbal. I guess it was sapping my iron. But at least my anemia is the type that's controllable."

"Yes, may God be praised for that. Well, don't let me keep you."

"Have a good day, Sir. I'm sure the others will get here soon."

Mar couldn't believe she made it through the rest of the day. She was dying to talk with Mitch. Pictures? What pictures? And what did he think of the conversation she'd taped? But she did make it through the day like the professional she was. She had also almost caught up all that had been allowed to pile up like clutter and was surprised to find herself singing on her way out to the car. She couldn't wait to get home!

By Dianne J. Beale

Chapter 32

Mar couldn't even park in her own drive when she arrived home. She pulled up next to the mailbox, pulled out the mail, and then parked along the front edge of their yard.

Once inside, she realized that everyone who'd watched the movie was there. Not only these, but the small group members were there, as well. Everyone cheered when she'd shut the door.

Mitch pulled her aside and said they'd talk about the interesting message she'd sent later. He also pointedly made her aware that the subject of that message was also here. "He just popped over after work. Said they'd found nothing unusual about the tea. I didn't see any way to suggest he leave without giving away what we know."

Mar smiled and quietly answered while waving back at Luke from across the room. "Don't worry. I've been acting all day. I've gotten quite good at it, actually."

The rest of the night was more of a party than a small group meeting. The members said they were celebrating her recovery. Mar thanked them repeatedly.

Finally, the whirl of pizza, people, and soda stopped. It was well past ten, and all but one of the guests had left.

Trish's half-sister remained. She said she'd wanted to talk privately. Mar was about to leave when she insisted it was her desire to talk to both of them.

They sat down around the table and Trish's half-sister began to talk. "Trish insists I can trust you two, so I've gotta take a chance. I don't like that Luke character, but that's a whole other story. Can I trust you like Trish says? What's said here will go no further?"

Mar was suddenly aware of watching eyes. She went to the kitchen sink, closed the window, and pulled the blinds. Her brother seemed thrown. "Mar, did you hear the question?"

Mar smiled weakly. She was exhausted. "Yes, I did. That's why I didn't like the idea of an open window. I know this is going to sound silly, but I don't trust that cat. I've had other real-life encounters with a cat that looks just like it. I've also had dreams where that same cat was bad news. I just wanted to be sure our conversation does actually stay safe."

Mitch shook his head, but the woman at the table looked completely serious when she said, "You, too? I thought I was being crazy. I've tripped over what could have been the same cat on more than one occasion. And I've had terrifying dreams–it grows to the size of a panther and then attacks!"

Mar sighed, relieved. She, too, had believed her feelings to be crazy. Now she remembered the same limp–the cat and Andres. She decided not to share this and offered input,

By Dianne J. Beale

instead. "Not crazy. I tripped over what I believe was possibly this cat, as well. I'm just realizing we all need to be way more careful. Spiritual warfare, you know? Not flesh and blood."

The woman nodded, "Amen to that." Then she continued, "Up 'til now you've known me as either Amelia, or Trish's half-sister. We've been careful not to say my full name. But tonight I'm sharing with you that my name is Amelia Loukatos. I was once married to Andres. Be careful who you trust; Luke was Andres' best man. I don't know him, and never saw or heard of him before or after the wedding, at least not until he showed up the other night and here, again, now. But this is a past that Andres no longer owns. No one knows he was ever married–only me, Trish, and our parents. And, of course, Luke."

She continued, "I was shocked when Andres moved back to this town. He has a restraining order to stay away from me. I had hoped it would keep him away from here, as well. My mom signed for him to marry me when I was just sixteen. I was so much in love that I relentlessly begged her to. But a year later, she was fighting to get me out of the local psychiatric ward."

She paused, trying to slow down her tumbling speech. "Andres had beaten me, drugged me, shared me with his buddies, and even tortured me. Then, when he grew tired of it all, he slipped me hallucinogenic herbs until I was mad–

crazy mad. He put me into a nut house, paid them for me to have an accident, and then left me for dead."

She tried to smile. "But God spared me. Years later, he has now returned as a minister. It suits him; he thrives on control. And all his yes-men? They have shady pasts too. But no one knows. Well, I do, and my family, and now you. And now he runs a church. I know it's a cover for something; I'm just not sure what."

When she stopped, Mar and Mitch were wordlessly numb. Finally, Mitch cleared his throat. "Can we pray together?" he queried.

When Amelia nodded, and Mar had agreed as well, they began. They prayed for the church, the church members, those who'd been harmed, and for each other. They prayed for strength and courage and asked for discernment, direction, and wisdom. And then Amelia finished the prayer. "Destroy the evil one, Oh God. Destroy the stronghold he has at Shepherd's Orchard. Destroy those who serve him. Divide their tongues and cause confusion. They have broken covenants and taken the form of flatterers. Bring them down. Reveal the truth. Rescue us as we cast our burdens on You. We trust You. We will not be moved. Amen."

Mitch and Mar added, in unison, "If it is Your Will, Father, so be it." Then they group-hugged and Mitch went with Amelia out to her car while Mar got her keys. They checked the cars and then climbed in. Mar drove into the garage, and Amelia drove away. As the garage door closed, Mitch watched a black shadow slink inside. He went into the house, locking the doors. Then, he joined Mar in the garage. They chased a familiar, black cat back outside and shut the door. Then, they went inside, checking all the locks and windows one last time.

Chapter 33

Despite her exhaustion, Mar found she couldn't sleep. The fact that a woman named Jasmine had both come and gone while she'd been out was eating away at her. And now that she knew of a connection between Luke and Andres, the gnawing had increased exponentially. She knew Mitch was telling the truth, so who was this woman?

Mar chose to pray. "Dear Father, Shepherd's Orchard is Your church. You see all and know all. I'm asking You, Father, to publicly expose the leaders for who they are. I don't need to have all the answers, or to know all the details. It may be better if I don't. But harm is coming to Your sheep. Many, when they found You, came to this church believing that healing could come only through You. So they joined Wild Springs and devoured the literature–the program that would set them free. Yet the leaders involved, although they use the literature, do not believe. And those who wrote the literature have grown accustomed to the lifestyle it has provided for them; they do not correct those who exploit others through its use. Wearing their wounds and iniquities as badges, pride applies deceiving bandages to hide their pain–to conceal the truth. They claim to offer healing but instead breed dependency and instill fear. Oh, Father, where do Mitch and I fit into this? Where do we go from here? What is Your purpose in revealing such evil to us? Show us what to do. Help us. We are nothing without You. Thank You, Lord. May Your will be done. In Your Son's Holy Name, Jesus, I pray. Through the precious blood He shed, I ask this. Protect us. Give us strength. Amen."

Switching on her reading lamp, she was about to reach for her Bible when she remembered her folder of directories and mailing lists. She got out of bed and quietly went to their combination library and office. Opening the filing cabinet, she took out the church directory and then, changing her mind, she put it back and booted up the computer instead. The search would go much faster on the computer.

She activated the search feature and typed "Jasmine" into the correct box. One by one, documents began to fill the search window. Once it had finished, she began to open the documents one at a time. Finally she came across what she'd been looking for. In a prayer email that had been sent only to staff members, the name Jasmine appeared. Next to it was written "pray for Paco's wife–Paco is the janitor–both are attending Wild Springs session–wife does not attend church with husband." Mar printed out the email, highlighted the information, and then shut down the computer. Then she returned to her room, set the paper down on her desk, and climbed back into the bed.

The Uninvited

As she turned to shut off her lamp, she knocked her Bible to the floor. When she picked it up, she realized papers had fallen from it, so began to gather these, as well. One particular paper caught her eye: it was a bookmark that highlighted a sermon her dad had once given. She read it out loud. "Second Timothy 3: 1-5. This know also, that in the last days perilous times shall come. For men shall be lovers of their own selves, covetous, boasters, proud, blasphemers, disobedient to parents, unthankful, unholy, without natural affection, truce breakers, false accusers, incontinent, fierce, despisers of those that are good, traitors, heady, high-minded, lovers of pleasure more than lovers of God; having a form of godliness, but denying the power thereof: from such turn away."

Mar placed the papers and bookmark back into her Bible, set it all back on the desk, and shut off the light. Snuggling into her bedding, she prayed, "Thank You for that reminder, God." Then she sighed with satisfaction, remembering the depth of His care, and decided to get some sleep.

She awoke the next morning, feeling refreshed, as if she'd finally caught up on her lack of rest. She popped in a CD and readied herself for the day.

Just as she sat down to breakfast, Mitch appeared. After the initial greetings, they each fell silent. The phone rang and they let the machine get it. "Yes, I'm trying to reach a… Margaret Zeiler? I'm holding her resume and job application

By Dianne J. Beale

in my hand, and would appreciate if she could call me. We'd like to set up an interview, if she's still interested. I can be reached at 601-555-0166. My name is Todd Ferguson; our school is known as *Making Sense*. I should be in until eight tonight. Looking forward to your call. Thanks."

"Making Sense?" laughed Mitch. "That's a school? Where'd you find that job?"

Mar answered simply, "I didn't." Although puzzled, they had to ignore this new development. It was time to leave for work.

Chapter 34

Although arriving early, as usual, nothing else even resembled normal activity. Why were there so many cars? As she meandered the parking lot, she found no place to park; so, she pulled back out onto the road. She turned down a side street and then stopped a little further down after taking a left.

She exited her car, grabbed her things from the back, and then armed the alarm. As she made her way back toward the church, she miscalculated while avoiding a dip in the sidewalk, breaking the heel off her left shoe. Relieved that she'd not fallen, she continued onward despite the discomfort.

The door was unlocked, held slightly ajar with a slab of wood. Mar began to sense a long, laborious, unpleasant day was ahead. As she pulled open the door and edged her way inside, her purse strap slipped from her shoulder, falling to the floor and spewing its contents. She dropped her backpack, setting her keys atop it, and bent to gather her things. Hastily she threw all that was salvageable into her purse. As she reached for the bottle of perfume, the upper portion of the bottle, just beneath the top, broke off. Cutting

By Dianne J. Beale

her finger, she dropped it once again, the cut searing from contact with the alcohol. She pulled some tissues from her purse and began to gather the bits of glass.

A shadow cast itself over the area. Before he even spoke, she knew it was Andres. "You've cut yourself, Garnet," he purred. He knelt down beside her, bringing her finger to his lips. She kept her eyes lowered as if concentrating on her task. Andres continued. "Go care for yourself," he insisted. "I'll have Paco finish up here." Sensing her hesitancy, he dropped her hand and added, "Look. I'll begin the work myself."

She thanked him and rose to her feet. But forgetting the broken heel, she lost her balance. Andres swore as her remaining heel came down, hard, on his hand. She then fell, her knee crushing the other. "There's no mysterious animal to blame this time," he pointedly noted, as he rose swiftly to his feet.

Mar blushed. "I'm sorry, Sir," she stammered. "I've always struggled with this door; it's just so heavy. Maybe I need to join a gym."

Andres, disgusted, acted as if he didn't believe her. "Maybe you should," he grunted, disdain etching his normally calm, handsome features. He turned on his heels, tossed the tissue he was holding down at her, and left.

Mar realized she had practically been holding her breath, so let out a long, tired sigh. She finished drying up the floor, checked it for any remaining glass, and then headed to the restroom. After washing up, she set out for her office. When she arrived, her nameplate was gone and her key no longer worked in the lock. Backtracking to the main desk, she asked about it.

The entire staff, minus Andres, appeared to be discussing something. She interrupted, "What happened to my office?" she demanded.

Bewilderment crossed the faces as if a rippling wave at a football game. Finally, the receptionist spoke up. "Your office?" she inquired. "We assumed you were making copies. Your office is in the opposite direction, you know."

At the confused, frustrated look Mar gave her, the youth pastor interjected. "It's where it's always been." He gestured with his hand, implying a direction. He looked genuinely puzzled.

Just then, Andres popped in. "Is there a problem?" he questioned. He looked at the faces around the room, stopping on Mar's. She could have sworn that she saw a moment of smug satisfaction cross his face. Before she could answer, the praise pastor chimed in.

"Mar seems to be somewhat disoriented," he said. "I suppose she has been out quite a lot lately." He turned toward her, "Are you feeling okay, Sweetie?"

Mar didn't know how she should feel. She decided to just forget it and play along. She apologized, saying she'd just gotten off to a bad start. This caused Andres to zero in on her. His eyes met hers; they were filled with pity.

By Dianne J. Beale

She thanked them for their help and then proceeded down the hall that they had indicated. Once out of their view, she removed her shoes and continued on in her stocking feet. Next to the janitor's closet, on a door that had once led to storage, emerged her name plate. She took out her key and fit it easily into the lock.

"Okay," she pondered, "so, not only are there way more cars than it appears there are people, but I'm also supposed to be delusional, or something. Interesting." She turned the key and entered the room, switching on the light as she did.

Everything looked to be normal, so she set down her backpack, put her keys into her purse, and sat down. Turning on the computer, she was surprised to see that her computer's picture had changed. She clicked on the folder of documents. It was empty. She thanked God that she had a CD at home on which she had recently copied everything; she'd definitely not be bringing that CD into this church anytime soon.

As she studied her computer's programs and other folders, she realized that it looked as if it had returned to its original factory settings. Had someone used the recovery disk to return the computer to the initial defaults? She began to count the number of times that this had happened and sought to recall the reasoning behind it. Suddenly she felt vulnerable, suspecting that maybe there was more to these inconvenient, scheduled resets than met the eye. And she was right.

By Dianne J. Beale

Chapter 35

When noon arrived, Mar made her way to the front office once again. Since they had not yet hired an assistant for the regular receptionist, it was Mar's job to man the fort while everyone else ate during this time. She would screen calls, sign for packages, manage files, and work on bulletin inserts.

Today only continued to challenge her sanity. "Can I help you with something?" queried a young girl, maybe early twenties at most. She was sitting behind the desk.

"I was about to ask you the same question," Mar replied. "I assume you now work here?"

The girl visibly bristled. Although her eyes were shooting daggers, her demeanor was calm and professional. "Yes, I work here. For almost a week now. You?"

Mar decided she didn't need an enemy when those she had considered friends were behaving so hostile. She changed her manner. "I'm sorry. I have been out some lately so guess I wasn't told. I'm Garnet." She held out her hand.

Ignoring this sign of courtesy, the girl did manage to at least introduce herself. "Jodi. My dad's the pastor at the sister church across town."

Mar brushed her hand off on her side. "Oh, I've met him once. You've got his nose."

Still defensive, and maybe slightly agitated, Jodi responded impatiently. "Yeah, I do. Lucky, I guess. My dad's nose is rather, well, perfect. But mom's is slightly crooked. I think this is why some people think she's snobby; it's almost as if she's looking down her nose at people. But she's actually more sociable than dad." Jodi seemed uneasy, ready to return to her work.

"I've not met your mom," Mar commented. Jodi just shrugged. When the phone rang, she waved Mar away, as if to dismiss her, and answered it.

Mar went down the stairs and on over to the café. She got herself some water and sat down with her lunch. As she said her prayer, she felt someone approaching, so finished quickly and then looked up. It was a man in a janitor's uniform, but it wasn't Paco. Mar, despite the day's belligerence, decided to chance a dialogue. "Sir," she began, "did they finally hire someone to help out Paco? Do you work here?"

The stranger stopped working to turn and look at her. "Paco?" he questioned. "I'm sorry. Who is Paco?"

She was beginning to feel as if she was trapped in another of her ridiculous dreams, as if this day might never end. "Paco's been the janitor here for as long as I remember," she answered.

By Dianne J. Beale

"Well, I wouldn't know anything about that. I was hired just today. Lucky break, I guess. Name's Jeb." He held out his hand for her to shake, so she took it.

Mar could have sworn that Andres had mentioned Paco that morning. Hadn't he suggested that she let Paco clean up the perfume? She was sure of it. Had Paco quit because of her clumsiness? Had Andres just been unreasonable due to her? Had he fired Paco because of her reluctance to bother the janitor to clean up her mess?

She was suddenly aware that Jeb was still standing near her, facing her, probably waiting to be sure he'd been dismissed. "Forgive me if I seem preoccupied," she obliged. "I'm Margaret; I work with the children. Everyone here calls me Garnet, though." She paused, taking a drink.

"Oh, so you're Garnet," he stated, knowingly.

Mar decided to ignore the condescending edge she thought she detected in his voice. Already she was *so* not liking this man. Without Paco, she felt afloat in a sea of unforgiving sharks. "It's nice to meet you, Jeb," she said resignedly.

"Ma'am," he returned, and then went back to his chores.

She finished her lunch, excused herself, and returned to her broom closet of an office. She had been the last to take her break, but the first to return. "Well," she thought, "Nothing unusual there."

She sat at her desk, moved the mouse, and readied her fingers to type in her password. But the computer was already signed in and seemed to have a mind of its own. The mouse was buzzing around the screen and occasionally folders would open then close. When a game of solitaire opened, she reached over and manually shut the computer down. It was a computer, possessed.

Unplugging it, she then closed her office door. Not wanting to be interrupted, she reopened the door, hung out her "do not disturb" sign, and then locked the door as it once again fell shut. Then she lowered herself to the floor, using her chair as more of a table, and prayed, "Oh, Lord. My Dear and Precious Father. I'm tired. I'm confused. I'm angry. Reveal Your presence to me at this moment. I can't do this alone. I am nothing without You. Show me what to do. And please, Lord, help me to finish out this never-ending day."

Leaving her door shut, she unlocked it and then plugged her computer back in. This time she was asked to log in, so did. To her surprise, it appeared her computer had been restored to the personalized settings she had set from before this day began. The picture on the desktop had changed back to the one she had chosen, and the verse for the day was just what she needed to read: *Wait for the LORD; Be strong, and let your heart take courage; Yes, wait for the LORD–Psalm 27:14*. She remembered this Psalm. She knew it

By Dianne J. Beale

began, in the first verse, with *whom shall I fear? Whom shall I dread?*

Opening her folder of documents, she found it full once more. She slipped in an empty CD and copied all the files as a backup to the CD she already had. Then she found the document she needed to alter. Just as she sent the updated document to the printer, the computer restarted itself and the printer merely hummed before shutting off. Exasperated, but comforted, she turned the computer off and on once more. The screen reverted back to the factory presets once more and the documents were again, gone. She laughed to herself as she uploaded the document from her disk, altered it once more, and again sent it to the printer.

Once she had the hard copy in her hand, she removed the disk from the computer, pocketed it, and shut everything down. It was time to head home.

Grabbing her personal items, she left, locking the door behind her. She stopped off at the copy center, copied the document in her hand, slipped the extra copies into her backpack, and then left a copy in the in-basket on the secretary's desk. She was surprised to realize she was humming a hymn as she made her way to the exit that would lead to the freedom of outdoors. She couldn't remember the last time she had sung a hymn and was thankful that she could silently still recall the words.

Chapter 36

With no window in her new location, Mar hadn't realized that it was pouring. Now, as she opened the door, she recollected hearing the familiar spatter above her head. She enjoyed the rain and the sound of it beating against the roof was soothing to her. But she had tossed her broken shoes that morning, forgetting that Mitch had cleared her office of all personal things. So, she had no shoes and had parked far from the building. She was about to walk out the door and soak herself when Jeb came up beside her.

"Hi Garnet," he said. "You're still here? I thought everyone had gone. I was about to lock up."

She didn't even have the energy to force a smile. "Yeah, I'm often the last to leave. I guess that's why I got so used to Paco. He kind of looked out for me. He still remembers our father–mine and Mitch's that is. We went to youth group together. Never met his family, though. I was away at college then. I, um, was just about to brave the weather."

Jeb perceived that she was apologizing but decided to ignore it. She also seemed nervous. "Where are you parked?" he insisted.

"Oh. On a side street. I meant to move the car during lunch when the parking lot was maybe less crowded, but forgot. I didn't remember to call Mitch, either. I had planned to ask him to bring me shoes." She looked down at her feet, embarrassed.

Jeb realized he was parked right down the road from her. "Look, I've got an umbrella and have to walk that way myself," he started. "If you'll just wait here while I shut down, turn off, and lock up, you can walk with me."

Mar wanted to refuse, but she knew it would seem ungracious and probably would further knit the perception the rest of the staff had implanted in him. "That's very nice of you," she managed, instead.

Jeb left to complete his day and Mar sat down on a nearby bench to wait. She pulled out her cell phone to check messages but then remembered that she rarely had a signal in this place. She closed her eyes and laid back her head against the wood.

"Ready?" Jeb had returned much quicker than she'd expected. She hadn't even heard him approach and wondered how long he'd been standing there. "I brought you a couple bags you can rubber band around your feet, if you're interested," he said.

She explained what had happened to her shoes as she slid her feet into the plastic bags he had brought. "Thank you," she said quietly, feeling like a helpless, clueless, shy little girl. She felt her cheeks flush.

Jeb just smiled down at her. "Well, you said it's the janitor's job to watch out for you, after all." He opened the umbrella and they walked closely together toward her car. Once she was buckled in, with the engine running, he gave her a quick nod and left.

Inside her dry, warm garage, Mar was relieved Mitch wasn't back yet. She'd had enough to deal with for the day and didn't think she could handle his teasing. He would have been sure to notice her make-shift footwear. She gathered her stuff, got out of the car, and unlocked the door that led into the house. Then she closed the garage door, waited for it to touch bottom, and went in.

She might not have felt so safe without her brother had she seen the pewter gray Mitsubishi that had followed her home. It quietly drove on by without so much of a pause.

Mar first went to her room to change from her office apparel. Then she turned on the heat and went into their family room. Noticing the blinking answering machine, she pushed play. The message was nothing more than a loud hang up.

Walking into the kitchen, she grabbed the tea kettle and filled it with water. Placing it on the stove, she then went to the cupboards and hunted down some crackers. Setting them on the table, she got out cheese spread from the fridge and grabbed a knife from a nearby drawer.

As she sat snacking, she felt she was being watched. She couldn't bring herself to look toward the window, so

By Dianne J. Beale

pulled out her cell, instead. Turning it on, she was relieved to see the signal bar at full capacity. Immediately message notifications began coming in. She decided to ignore the text messages for the moment and called her voice mail.

"You have two new voice messages. To listen to your messages, please…" Mar interrupted the programmed voice by pushing the number one. The first message was blank and had registered as an unknown name, unknown number. She instinctively hit delete and moved on to the next message. It was Mitch: "Mar? Is everything okay? I'm hoping this is your message center 'cause it's your number I dialed. What happened to your greeting? I expected you'd be out of work by now, but maybe you've stayed late again. Can you give me a call when you get this? It looked as if you had quite the meeting or congregation at your church this morning. I just wondered if you know what's up. Call me, okay? It's Mitch. Bye."

Mar still had the creepy feeling that she was being watched. Why hadn't her water heated? She rose from the table, careful to avoid looking out the window, and moved to the stove. She'd forgotten to turn on the burner so switched it to high and then went into the family room to make a call. Forgetting she hadn't wanted to see the window, she looked up while waiting for the phone to connect. The blinds were down, but there was a distinctive human shadow cast upon them. She turned as if she hadn't noticed, casually walking off in a different direction. The voice on the phone startled her.

"Can I help you?" the voice said. "Hello? Can I help you?" Mar was pulled back to the phone and remembered she had been trying to reach her brother. She had planned to call his cell but had dialed his work number by mistake.

"Um, yes. Is Mitch Zeiler in?" she asked, knowing that he wasn't. She was unexpectedly cold again. She felt chilled and shivered.

"No, Ma'am. May I ask who's calling? He's gone for the day. Can I maybe take a message?"

"Oh, no, thank you. I'm sorry I bothered you. I had believed I was calling his cell."

"Never a bother, Miss. We're here to serve. Have a good evening."

"Thanks. You, too. Bye." Mar hung up the phone and switched to calling her brother's cell. When he didn't answer, she hung up. The tea kettle began to whistle, so she returned to the kitchen. The shadow was gone.

Turning off the burner, she filled her cup with hot water and then added a spot of cold water to the kettle so she could return it to the heated burner without it whistling. Her mother had often done this very thing and one day Mar had asked her why. She was told that it was dangerous to leave a heated burner uncovered, especially with kids, but that without the spot of cold water, it would continue to whistle. Mar remembered laughing and joking with her

By Dianne J. Beale

mom about how she and Mitch weren't really kids anymore. Her mom had said it was never a good thing to underestimate the possibility that someone might be distracted and get burned anyhow.

Slicing a lemon, she added a slice to her tea and then sweetened it with honey. Just as she sat back at the table, she heard the garage. With a sigh of relief, she picked up the knife and returned to spreading cheese on the crackers.

Chapter 37

Mitch came into the kitchen, completely soaked through. He seemed as relieved to see her as she was to see him. After greeting one another, he went to his room and changed, just as she had done. Once back in the kitchen, Mitch began to spread and then eat crackers, as well. After a short silence, he asked, "Did you get my messages?"

Mar told him how she had just listened to the voice message but had forgotten that she had text messages as well. She took out her phone to check these now, but the notification had been cleared. Checking the text messages anyhow, she found only one new message and it was blank. The number was the same she had received that night in her room; the one that seemed to have erased her phone's memory. Believing that Luke could no longer be trusted, she related the entire number story so far. Both Luke and the phone company had said the number was a nonworking number. Yet somehow it was showing up just fine on her phone. It was also the number that she had found next to Trish's name.

Mitch took her phone, blocked his cell number, and then called the number on her screen. He got a message center: "The number you have called is not accepting messages at this time. Please try again, at a later time."

Although disappointed, it did seem that the number, in fact, did belong to someone. Mitch suspected it might be one of those *pay-as-you-go* phones since a client of his had such a phone. He told how, if the person lets the minutes slide, then the person calling gets a message center that explains the person is not available. It doesn't allow the person to leave a message, though.

They each sat drinking tea and eating crackers for a bit, but then Mitch voiced his concern. "Maybe we should change our cell numbers, Sis, and not give them out to anyone–well, not anyone we're not sure we can trust, anyway. You can allow the church to believe that we don't have cell phones at this time. It just seems that whenever you get anything from this number, your phone goes crazy. I can call and change our numbers in the morning and I'll tell them we don't want a forwarding message, as well."

Mar agreed. "I think that's a good idea. I'll keep my phone off at the church and hide it in my pack. It doesn't work half the time, anyway, when I'm there."

Once they were in agreement, Mitch asked if she'd called back the job lead from that morning. She admitted that she hadn't. She explained she'd had a very rough day but that she didn't want to talk about it at the moment. Respecting this, he suggested that maybe she should call back about the potential position even if she hadn't applied for it.

So Mar dialed the phone and waited for someone to pick up. "Boo, doo, doo, boo, doo, doo. The number you have dialed, 9, 2, 8, 5, 5, 5, 0, 1, 6, 6 is not a working number. Please check the number, hang up, and dial again."

Mar hung up the phone. Checking the number, she was certain it had been dialed correctly. Just to be sure, she had Mitch call as well. "Boo, doo, doo, boo..." He hung up the phone.

The Caller ID had registered no information, so Mitch called information. There was no listing for either a Todd Ferguson or *Making Sense*. Mitch thanked the operator and then had an idea. He quickly used the Call Back feature and Mar wrote down the numbers as they appeared across the phone. Before the call could connect, Mitch hung up. But then Mar remembered the hang up call from earlier and told Mitch that this would be the number for whoever hung up, not for the man who had left the message. Mitch decided to call back information and get a report on this number, as well. But the operator apologized, saying the number was an unpublished, private number for which she could give no information.

So, Mar blocked their number and called the number, instead. She got a machine. An automated, mechanical voice answered: "Hello. No one is available to take your call. Please leave a message after the tone." She hung up.

By Dianne J. Beale

Things seemed to be getting stranger and stranger. Mitch suggested they should go out for a bit and Mar readily agreed. Each had faced days of mystery that had led to much frustration. They agreed they'd discuss it all at their favorite place to relax–a place where they had never run into fellow church members.

Taking Mitch's car, they drove to their favorite café. Once inside, they ran into Trish and Amelia. Saying hello to their fellow outsiders, they were asked to join their table. They, too, had come to relate strange events of their days. Amelia jokingly suggested they'd been sucked into an alternate reality–another plane of existence. They all laughed and ordered their drinks.

Mar was asked to get the ball rolling. First she told how Paco had been replaced and then related how a new office girl, who had to be new just today, had claimed to have been there for at least a week.

Next she mentioned how her office location had changed and how the entire staff insisted that it had always been that way. She told how she had broken her shoe and then had crushed Andres' hands.

But most curious of all, she never determined why there were so many cars. She hadn't noticed any extra people at either the church or the school across from it, all day. But the cars eventually left–they were gone when she'd gone to sit in the café for lunch. It was all rather curious.

She didn't mention the shadow on the blinds once she was home; she had begun to think maybe she'd imagined it. She also forgot about the computer problems.

Mitch picked up from there. He told how Mar had received only one of his three messages and how there was a mysterious number that kept wiping out her phone's memory. Then he mentioned the strange job opportunity that Mar had never applied for. He went on to relate the mysteries throughout his day.

A stone had come through his office window, breaking it, and although the street was crowded, no one saw a thing. Later, when he went out to his car, it wasn't where he had parked it. This seemed impossible, since he had an alarm, but he was sure he had parked it where he always does. Yet when he left work for the day, it was in a different location.

After checking it over, he had shrugged, climbed into it anyway, and started toward home. Once on the highway, although he had filled the tank just that morning on the way to work, he noticed the gas gauge was nearly empty. So, pulling up to a station, he drove over glass. Once he filled the tank, he was about to change the tire when he was asked to move from the pumps to keep them open.

Not another car was in sight, but he honored the gas attendant's request and pulled out from the provided cover to the side of the lot. He changed his tire in the downpour, jumped back into his car as soon as he'd finished, and was never gladder to be home.

By Dianne J. Beale

Trish shared her day next. She had arrived at work only to be met with an intense cold front. It took her more than half the day to discover why. Her boss had received a call from a so-called prospective employer who was checking on her credentials and references. The man who called had known all about her. It was extremely difficult to convince her boss that she'd made a commitment and had not applied elsewhere. She had, after all, gotten this job only through the recommendation of a friend and she wouldn't betray that trust so easily. She finally had to sign a statement that she would not leave her present job without giving at least a full two weeks' written notice. This seemed to satisfy them and the office thawed a little.

But Amelia's day topped them all. She had been trying to legally change her name from her married name back to her maiden name for years; she had been so relieved to be granted the divorce that she hadn't seen the clause that insisted she keep Andres' surname.

Well, she had finally overturned the original ruling and was free once again to use her maiden name. But when she tried to change her social security card, it was discovered that another already shared her number and was using it with this name. The same happened when she tried to change over her license.

So, for now, she was stuck with Andres' surname since the FBI had been tracking this other woman. They made her go home and make copies of her birth certificate, her marriage certificate, and her divorce papers, along with creating a list of all the places she had ever lived or worked over the years. They even took finger prints to insure they matched the birth certificate.

Although they had suspected this other woman was not who she said she was for some time, they had lacked the proof. So now Amelia had been instructed to live and breathe with her married name until this could all be straightened out. She was also given a case number and an important document to carry with her until the time came when she could take back her stolen identity.

It all seemed incredible. They finished their food and drinks about the same time they had finished their stories. The meeting had not been planned, but they all felt better because of it. They decided to travel over to Mitch and Mar's house for coffee and ice cream. Finally, as the night came to an end, they prayed together. Trish and Amelia said their good-byes, and Mitch and Mar waved them off. They then returned to the house, locked up, cleaned the kitchen, and headed off to bed.

By Dianne J. Beale

Chapter 38

Mar was still uneasy as she readied herself for the night. She wanted badly to find a new job and leave her present atmosphere behind. Just as she climbed into her bed, the cell phone rang. Who would be calling her at such a late hour? She didn't recognize the number so waited for the voice message she hoped the caller would leave. No voice message alert came through, but the family land line began to ring. She felt compelled to answer so ran out into the family room to grab the receiver.

"Hello?" she answered.

"Miss Garnet?" Paco's voice sounded urgent when it came over the phone.

"Yes, Paco, this is Garnet," she said in a rush. "Are you okay? I've had a bad feeling all day, since meeting your replacement."

"No, we're not okay. Me and my wife, we're scared. I wouldn't've called so late but we don't know who else to trust. Your dad–he was good man. But I can't protect his church no more. His church–it gone. Been gone a while. They threatened us; said they'd deport us. But we're here legally, Miss Garnet. You dad, he made sure. All I wanted was for them to pay her for her day's work. I wanted them to pay too for her arm he broke. They say we have no story to tell and no one will believe us if we do. They fired me when I asked about Jasmine's arm–I thought it, um, misunderstanding, but my wife right. They bad people."

"Who broke her arm, Paco? Pastor Andres?"

"No. No. The new guy. The counselor man. The church said she took your stuff so they not pay her. She told them no, she didn't do it. They say she need to leave. But my Jasmine stood her ground, demanded her money. The counselor man manhandled her, pushed her out on the street. When I ask about it they say she was lying. But that night her arm was all swollen, even with no bruises. So I took her to doctor but kept working at the church 'cause they said they help. Then I go in today and they give me only half my pay and fire me. We can't pay the bill, not now they don't pay us."

Mar felt hot tears pouring down her face. She told Paco she needed to get Mitch since he knew more about these things. Paco promised to wait and Mar ran to her brother's room. He was still awake and fully dressed. When he saw Mar, concern filled his face. She quickly relayed all she'd been told and then handed Mitch the phone.

"Paco?" Mitch asked. "Oh, good. I do know you're legal. Dad kept the records here at the house as well as at the church. I know an immigration lawyer, too. I volunteer at my new church and sometimes give members a small discount. They have a fund for emergencies like this. Ah. Uh, good idea. We'll meet you there in about thirty minutes then. Okay. No. We're glad to help. Okay. No problem. Bye."

Mar waited for Mitch to talk. Instead he immediately made another call. This person seemed to be meeting with them, as well. Then he made one last call. The person said he could stop over and he told them he'd be there in a little more than five. Finally, Mitch included Mar and they each rushed to get ready. They locked up the house, Mitch handed Mar a folder of papers that he said they'd need to copy, and they got into his car. It was nearing midnight when they left the house.

The first stop was the parsonage of Mitch's new church. The pastor's wife was standing ready with a check from the church. She explained that they had a limit of $500.00 for the month as other emergencies had taken place, as well. But if they needed more they might be able to help again the following month. She just needed the left line, usually used for remembering the check's purpose, to be stamped by the hospital and then signed by Paco so they had it on record as proof of charitable use. Mitch thanked her and got back into the car. He handed the check to Mar, who carefully put it into her purse as it was a blank check of $500.00 for the moment.

They finally arrived where they were meeting Paco. Another car–the lawyer's–pulled in next to them. They all got out and went into the twenty-four-hour copy shop. As the lawyer read through the papers, he assured them all was in order and agreed to go with them to get their legal Social Security numbers. They had been using the assigned Employee Identification Numbers, not realizing they were already approved citizens who could now be assigned Social Security numbers. It turned out that this is also why they'd waited to start a family. They had feared their children might someday be separated from them.

Mitch made triple copies of all the papers: Mar kept the originals, Mitch had a folder of copies, and then Paco and the lawyer had the others. The lawyer set up a time when the three of them would meet in the morning, handed Paco his business card, and then left.

Mar and Mitch went with Jasmine and Paco to the hospital's emergency room. They were able to help them fill out forms requesting financial aid, and they also got the hospital to reduce the bill since Mitch told them the church planned to pay the first $500.00. Mar pulled the check from her purse, copied the name of the hospital onto the appropriate line, and then handed it to Mitch. Mitch explained the need for the hospital to stamp the remembrance line and then Paco signed next to the stamp. He gave the check to the hospital and they gave Paco a receipt, showing that the first $500.00 had been paid toward the bill. The hospital handed Mitch a copy of the receipt, as well.

By Dianne J. Beale

Paco and Jasmine thanked them for all of their help and explained that the phone he had used was a pay phone near their old address. They had just moved and were glad that the church would not have their address or any of their numbers. He apologized for not trusting them at first, but he couldn't take any more chances with his family. Mar and Mitch assured them that they understood and explained that Mar was planning to leave the church as soon as she could find a new job. Once Paco and Jasmine were sure that they hadn't offended them, they all went off in their respective directions. Mar and Mitch returned home, thankful that today would begin their weekend.

Chapter 39

Back in her room, Mar was too tired to go back through the routine of readying herself for bed. She grabbed an afghan off her nearby chair and threw herself down on top of the covers. Her prayer was short and to the point and her light went out in record time. Sleep engulfed her.

Mar was surprised at the strength of her voice; she sounded firm and authoritative. Her prayer seemed to echo around her: *break the strongholds that hold Your church captive, Lord; awaken those who have been deceived; free the sheep.* These three phrases had a life of their own–an unending echo.

Opening her eyes, she found she was standing among the church offices. The words continued to blend in an increasingly loud, yet amazingly clear hum that all seemed to come at once from within her. It was as if the three phrases were being spoken together, layered as separate, clear thoughts.

A sudden splintering of wood, followed by rushing water, caused her to turn. The wall at the far left was crumbling away as a huge termite emerged. What Mar had believed to be water was blood. It was pouring out from the hole that now sat above the counselor's office. The door burst open and locusts began to swarm.

Above the ongoing hum, Mar begins to quote Scripture: "for they have shed the blood of Your saints and prophets, and You have given them blood to drink as they deserve." Again she hears splintering. Turning, she witnesses further destruction.

Another termite has emerged. Above the worship minister's door is a subsequent tear with blood flowing downward as if a waterfall. As this door, too, bursts, more locusts swarm the hall. Almost immediately it's as if a mirror image has erupted across the hall. Blood continues to fill the hall and the air is now dark with locusts. Three huge termites sit above the three doors. Andres sits behind this newest door. He seems oblivious to the truth of what is happening. He continues to quietly contemplate the sermon he will give.

Mar was astounded that she was not only continuing to speak the Scripture, but the hum of the other three phrases endured as well. She watched Andres as he ignored his surroundings. Almost in anticipation, she found herself turning again, looking back down the hall at the door across from the counselor's. A fourth wall section gives way. The flow of blood increases and the door bursts forth with even more locusts. Smaller termites emerge with the final giant termite. They move to cover the walls. The locusts have turned the air around her black. Yet she finds she is uncannily calm. The youth room streams in an endless flow of blood, termites, and locusts. A final Scripture now joins her hum: "God will raise up a shepherd that will eat the choice sheep and will tear off their hooves." Her eyes meet Andres as he comes into the hall. Sadness fills her and waves of tears are added to the chaos.

Mar woke up. She was calm—neither frantic, nor sweating. But she remembered the dream. She first went into the restroom and then quietly went out to the kitchen. After brewing herself a small cup of green tea, she rinsed the cup, put it into the dishwasher, and headed back to her room.

But throughout the night the dream repeated itself with little or no variation. As soon as her eyes would shut, it would begin again. Finally, she turned on her lamp, took out her notebook, and wrote the dream down. "God, I'll remember now. Please let me rest. I'll find the Scripture and do my best to spread Your message. Let me sleep now. Thank you, God. Amen."

The next thing Mar remembered was the sound of a mower outside her window. She got up, noted it was a little after eight, used the restroom, and then returned to bed.

It was nearly two when she finally rose to face the day. She got freshly dressed and padded off toward the kitchen. Finding no coffee, she set about making some. Once it was brewing, she went to find Mitch. She knocked on his door and got a muffled "Yeah," in reply. She decided to leave him be; if he chose to join her for coffee, then she'd be glad for

By Dianne J. Beale

the company. But she knew her brother well enough to know that if he chose sleep, he needed it.

Drinking her coffee, she poured herself a bowl of cereal. She'd forgotten that she had noticed that there was no milk when she had opened the fridge and added half and half to her coffee. Returning the cereal to its box, she instead took out six eggs and some cheese.

She was moving the omelettes to plates when Mitch appeared. He took out some summer sausage and sliced it. They each ate in silence, drinking their coffee. Mitch finished first, rinsed his dishes, thanked her, and then was gone.

Mar sat alone, pondering the dream she'd had. Suddenly the move of her office, despite the lack of a window, was a blessing. She'd been in the center of it all.

Remembering what Paco had said about the tea and the paper, Mar decided she'd be smart to check the mysterious number for herself. She rinsed and loaded her dishes and then headed for their computer. The security suite found and removed a virus at startup and then rebooted before she could do anything. She decided to gather her notes, her phone, and any other materials she might have. Then she returned to the computer in hopes of beginning her research.

As she sat down, she noticed there were programs that were updating themselves. She chuckled at the thought of each program having an addiction to the Internet connection, desperate to receive the data that it could provide.

She placed the disk from the church into the drive and waited for it to load. Instead, a strange whirring sound emerged. Then the computer again restarted. But once Windows began to load, the computer froze. Mar forced a manual shutdown and then started the computer once more, removing the disk she had left in the drive. ScanDisk ensued, due to the improper shutdown.

Finally Mar gave in and went to ask if she could use Mitch's laptop, instead. Although frustrated, she didn't want to risk causing problems on her brother's laptop so decided to only check and answer her email.

By Dianne J. Beale

Chapter 40

The next morning went smoothly. All the volunteers showed up, and the lessons completed without a hitch. Mar was collecting trash, checking rooms, and locking up when Betsy showed up.

"Marge?" she queried. "Is there anything I can do to help?" Betsy had been an extra pair of hands for the past two years. Her daughter was also always quick to offer assistance.

"No, I'm just about finished here," Mar said as she straightened from refitting a new bag to the can next to her. "Thanks, though."

Betsy turned to go, but then moved back toward Mar. "We're celebrating Liza's birthday today. We'd love if you could join us for lunch."

Mar looked as if she would refuse but then thought better of it. "Sounds like fun," she offered. "I'll just need to stop by the house to drop off a few things that Mitch needs, and then I can meet you. Where y'all planning to go?"

Betsy's face brightened with a smile. "How is Mitch?" She asked. "Is he enjoying his new job?"

Mar breathed out a long, sustained sigh. She had been ordered not to talk about Mitch. "He's well. It would seem he's enjoying himself. We've not had much time to converse since his engagement, though." Mar shrugged, hoping the subject would change before anyone else showed up.

"Oh, I heard!" Betsy beamed. "We're all so happy for them! Trish and he make such a great team! I'm sure that the staff regrets losing them, but there's no point in fighting God. It must have been a difficult decision."

Mar finished what needed to be done, tucked away the rogue hair that kept obstructing her vision, and then picked up a stack of books and a bag. She nodded her head toward the door and then began to walk forward.

Betsy, realizing she was blocking the way, stepped aside, apologizing. She then followed Mar to the door. She held it open as Mar exited, grabbing the keys to lock it. Returning the keys, she then walked with Mar to her car.

Liza and Karl came up behind them just as Mar was about to set the stack of books onto the top of the car. Karl's hands encircled the books, and Liza's reached for the bag. "Oh," she blurted, "Thank you." She hastily opened the car and motioned for the stuff to be set onto the back seat. Karl and Liza complied.

"So, can you come, Miss Margaret?" Liza asked. "We weren't sure we could go until Friday. Sorry I didn't ask sooner."

By Dianne J. Beale

Liza was no longer a part of the children's department, except when she helped as a volunteer. She had moved up into the youth just a little over four months before. Mar was about to answer when Betsy spoke up, "She's gonna meet us there."

Karl quickly jotted down directions to the restaurant and handed them to Mar. Then he thought better of it, retrieved the paper, and added their three cell phone numbers at the bottom. Mar thanked him, and they all parted company. "Well, a person's gotta eat," Mar reasoned to herself. She swerved to the right, avoiding a familiar cat that had seemed to come from nowhere. Gathering her wits, she turned out from the parking lot and onto the busy road.

Once home, she pulled into the garage, leaving the door open to save time. She shut off the engine, got out, retrieved the bag and books, and went into the house. She jotted down a note for Mitch and placed it onto the pile of books, laying her pen across the top to help it stay in place.

Crossing the room to return to the garage, she checked her pockets for the directions. When her search came up empty, she moved back to the table and began shaking out each individual book. Once convinced the directions weren't there, she replaced the note and pen and took the bag into the other room. She dumped it out and then quickly sorted the contents, placing them back into the bag. Still no paper with directions. She put the bag back onto the table with the books and traced her steps back out to the car. The paper was nowhere to be found.

"What was the name of that restaurant?" she badgered herself. "Leave it to me to lose directions I was given only moments before." She rattled her brain for answers and then remembered that the Carringtons had been carrying their cell phones. She took out her cell, switched it on, and then looked through the phone book. It again had no numbers–all had been erased. Remembering the printed document from Friday, she went to the computer room and pulled it out from among the clutter. She breathed a sigh of relief and called Betsy's cell.

Although it hadn't rung, Mar could hear "Hello? Hello? Marge?"

Mar answered quickly, "Betsy? I've been trying to call."

"You're still coming, aren't you? We've saved you a spot."

Mar explained what had happened and next heard Karl's voice. She wrote new instructions as he spoke them over the phone. Then she left the house, backed out of the garage, signaled the door to close, and almost hit her brother as he drove into the driveway; he barely avoided the collision. But Mar didn't seem to notice. She just mechanically drove away, leaving Trish and Mitch in a state of shock.

By Dianne J. Beale

Chapter 41

Mar returned to the house a little after four. Betsy was in the car with her. She had agreed to look at Mar's home computer.

Mitch wasn't home, but Mar decided not to call him. She had hoped to leave him a message so he wouldn't be surprised by Betsy's visit. But Betsy went straight to work.

First, she explained she would put the computer into safe mode. When this didn't work, she manually shut it down to try again. This time, it worked. She took out a disk she had in her purse and tried to run it. But the program wouldn't work in safe mode, so she removed it again.

Then she double-clicked the security suite, found the anti-virus program, and told it to run. Mar was quietly listening, taking notes. She asked how long the scan would take and decided they should make some tea and find something to do while they waited.

Spotting Mitch's laptop, Betsy asked, "Do you think I could get onto the Internet?" Mar merely nodded an okay. So, as Mar prepared the tea, Betsy busied herself with downloading a few small, but useful programs. She then saved them to an empty disk she was carrying and went to check on the other computer's progress. It claimed to have fifteen minutes left to run, so she joined Mar in the kitchen.

Mar had finished the tea and was sitting behind a cup at the table. The books and bag from earlier had been pushed to the very end to make room. Betsy sat down behind the other cup and began to sip the warm, flavorful liquid. Mar had served Betsy many times over the last two years and hadn't needed to ask how she took it. This was the third time that Betsy had come to salvage their computer. Mar hadn't planned to burden her this time, but Betsy always seemed to know; she was ready to lend a hand.

After the tea, they returned to the computer room. The scan reported the removal of three viruses and one Trojan, and it strongly suggested restarting to remove any traces that could not be successfully taken care of without it. Betsy moved the mouse to click on the command to reboot and the computer responded. Upon restart, Betsy loaded the newly prepared CD and installed the three new programs, explaining each as she did: one was a user-friendly firewall; one was for actively detecting and blocking threats before they could download; and the last was for cleaning off unnecessarily stored clutter. She carefully explained how the security suite would soon expire and would need to be renewed, but that it would continue to run, conflict-free, with these three programs.

Although Mar did not really understand, and was only half listening, she shook her head as if she were taking it all

By Dianne J. Beale

in. After the three programs had run, Betsy again showed Mar how to Defragment the hard drive. They allowed it to run while they worked on ideas for next week's lesson. When finished, Betsy restarted the computer, allowing it to run in normal mode once again.

"Praise God!" Mar shouted. "I thought I'd lost everything! I know you told me to back things up, but I was about two weeks behind on saving my stuff to disks," she explained.

Betsy used her cell phone to call Karl and let him know she was ready whenever he was. Then she backed up all the documents and pictures onto yet another blank CD. Just as the copy finished, Betsy's cell rung. She hugged Mar, apologizing for the unfixed printer; it needed a new driver and she hadn't found any that were compatible. Betsy, knowing it was unlikely that Mar had understood, left a note for Mitch. It wasn't necessary, but Mar didn't know this. Mitch's plan was to just buy a new printer, despite his sister's protests.

Chapter 42

Mitch came through the door. "Was that Karl and Betsy? Was Liza with them?" he asked.

Mar nodded and sleepily said, "Yes. Betsy fixed our computer again. I'm not sure where Karl and Liza went. It's Liza's birthday and we ate lunch together."

Mitch didn't answer. He had merely been surprised and was sorry he'd missed them. He enjoyed the Carringtons. Liza was a very bright and talented youth, and he doubted she'd enjoy the new youth leader's classes. Most of the church-grown youth were older in Christ than the new teacher, and Mitch expected they'd be left unchallenged. But he kept this to himself and changed the subject. "Have you heard from Luke lately?" he asked.

Mar seemed to find a sudden burst of energy, "No. You?" She appeared to be analyzing her memory just as she would a case of files. "Not since the party, right?"

Mitch couldn't recall. "I'm not sure," he answered. "Been awhile, though."

This led them to wonder if he knew that they had overheard his conversation with Andres. Mar looked at the

By Dianne J. Beale

clock. How could she be so tired when it was not yet nine? She decided they should call him.

"Hello?" The voice was soft and silky, almost sensual. Mar nearly lost her nerve, but forced herself to plow forward, instead.

"Is Officer Luke Smelding available?" she managed. "This is Margaret Zeiler. I believe he's in charge of the case I'm involved with."

"One second, Ma'am. I'll get him," the voice purred. Mar heard the receiver click against a hard surface and could barely make out what was being said. She did recognize the words "Luke" and "phone," however.

"Luke here," a deep sigh followed. "How can I be of service?"

"Hi Luke. It's Margaret... Margaret Zeiler? I was just wondering if you're still working on our case. Is it still open, or did the death finalize it?"

"Oh. Hi, Mar. Um, I'm not sure. I've been out of the office for the last few days. I can check on it for you tomorrow if you'd like."

Mar could hear jazz music and what sounded like kisses in the background. She found herself bristling despite herself. She forced a nonchalant calmness into her voice. "Oh, Okay. I guess we weren't informed. Is there someone else I should call instead?"

Luke seemed impatient. "No. That's okay. I'll call you with the details tomorrow. Or has something happened that made you want to report it now?"

"Oh, no, nothing like that. I'm sorry I bothered you. It didn't occur to me to just wait 'til morning. I apologize for interrupting your evening."

"Yeah. Okay then. I'll get back to you tomorrow. Or maybe I'll just have whoever's in charge give you a ring. Sorry I couldn't help."

"It's okay. I wasn't thinking, obviously. Have a good night."

"Bye then. You, too." And Luke hung up before anything else could be said.

"Mar?" Mitch queried. "Why so agitated?"

"You can tell I'm agitated? You don't think he could tell, do you? I suppose he did, though. Why am I being so ridiculous?"

Mitch assured her that the only way Luke could have picked up her agitation would be if he could see her. Her voice did not match her body language. Then he tried again, "Well? What's going on?"

Mar explained how she'd been caught off guard when a woman answered. Then, she passed along the mysterious details as they'd been related to her. They decided to read their Bibles together, pray, and then head off to bed.

By Dianne J. Beale

Chapter 43

The following week went by quickly, and without incident. Mar was beginning to hope that things would once again go back to normal, settling into a routine. Having Jeb at work was almost akin to working with Mitch once more at her side. As she pondered the past few days, still not having heard back from either Luke or the police station, she prayed, read her Bible, and then got into bed. Tomorrow was again another Sunday, and she needed her rest. After tossing and turning for about an hour, she finally yielded her body to sleep.

Mar could hear voices, but they seemed to echo and were not distinct. Believing she recognized them, she headed toward where they seemed to be coming from. Her feet seemed to drag heavier the closer she came to the place where they should be.

Suddenly, all noise stopped. Complete silence met her as she continued forward. She opened the door to the meeting room to find it was empty. A notebook lay in the center of the table next to a box of nearly empty breakfast burritos and one small jelly doughnut. She picked up the doughnut, aimlessly nibbling as she read: it was a list of names. Her name hovered nearby with a question mark next to it. All others had left the church.

Next, she found herself in the office hall once again. The walls were bleeding, and there were swarms of locusts and termites.

Just as suddenly, the hall fell empty again, and quiet. Tears streaked her face as she prayed. Her words faded in and out with a repeated phrase that was permeating her mind: "God will raise up a shepherd that will eat the choice sheep and tear off their hooves."

It began again. Wood splintered behind her. So she turned to watch as the expected termite broke out of the wall ahead on her left. Blood began to pour out, and the door swung open. Locusts swarmed from the office and filled the hall.

Continuing to pray, a feeling of familiarity overwhelmed her, causing her to turn back toward the other end of the hall. To her left another termite materialized, another hole splintered, and blood began water-falling. Again, the door opened and more locusts began to swarm.

About to turn away, she stopped. The wall on the right also splintered. Another termite appeared, and another door opened with more locusts, more blood.

Behind her, hearing running feet, she turned to address whoever might be approaching. But another wall–the youth wall–tears open, dragging her attention back. This time, the large termite begins to eat along the entire wall and smaller

By Dianne J. Beale

termites spread to all the walls. The force of the blood is so strong that all remaining doors open and locusts now congest the hall, making it difficult to see.

She tries again to address whoever had approached. But when she tries to speak, wanting to explain to those who've come into view, they're staring blankly. They cannot hear her; she can hear only them: "I told him she was a problem." "Right. And we're supposed to believe she had nothing to do with this?" "Why didn't Pastor Andres fire her when he had the chance?" Everything seemed to run together into a mumble, yet she managed to hear and understand it all.

Then, finding her voice, she at last speaks. But the words aren't at all what she had planned. She's eerily calm, and as if pondering. "For they have shed the blood of Your saints and prophets. You have given them blood to drink as they deserve."

Wading toward the bystanders, she realizes they've continued to deny and to blame. "They have ears, but they do not hear." Yet she had no fear. She was God's messenger; for her, all would end in Him. Mar woke up.

How long the alarm had been ringing, she couldn't be sure. She pulled herself out of bed and shut it off. Now that she was closer, she could see it was only a little after six a.m. She had another hour before she would need to get ready. Why had she set the alarm for so early?

The Uninvited

She took out the notebook that contained the last dream she'd had, and opened to a blank page where she could write. Soon she had mapped out the office hall at the church. She had to talk to Mitch. The first office belonged to the church counselor, the second was the office of the Worship Director, and the third was Andres'. The final room was a combination youth area–office, classroom, event room, etc.

Mar decided to read her devotions, pray, and then wake up Mitch so they could efficiently eat and chat at the same time. She wasn't surprised when the passage was again from Second Timothy three–the devotional talked of recognizing true godliness and a form of godliness that was in place solely for man's glory.

It struck her suddenly. They all talked about authenticity–being real–yet she knew little to nothing she'd consider "personal" about any of them. They easily shared only what they wanted to share; she knew nothing of their real lives. She shivered at this revelation.

She desperately needed to get a new job. "But you promised your Dad, Mag," a nagging voice prodded. "Are you now going to fail him? His greatness dies with his dream."

Mar shook herself and then threw on a robe. She knocked to awaken Mitch and then headed out to make breakfast. She was startled by what she came upon in the kitchen.

By Dianne J. Beale

Chapter 44

"Good morning, Mar," said Mitch. "I thought I'd let you sleep in." He was standing next to a seated Trish, and Luke was also sitting at the table. She hoped that they hadn't registered her surprise and was glad for her extra large, frumpy robe.

"Good morning," she returned as Mitch handed her some coffee. "And I thought I was going to surprise you," she added.

Mitch smiled. "Well sit down and have some doughnuts. Trish brought them. We had planned to work on Wedding stuff but then Luke stopped by. He had intended to just drop off a folder and leave but we discovered he hadn't eaten so invited him in."

Mar sat down, set her coffee on the table, pulled a napkin from the holder, and then grabbed a doughnut. As she set the doughnut down, she paused to study it. It closely resembled the doughnut that had commenced her dream, only larger. "Hi Luke, Trish," she managed. She turned to look at Luke. "Long time no see," she added.

"Yeah," Luke looked down at his coffee. "I took a bullet while investigating a crime on my beat. Then I guess I've been so busy moping that I hadn't realized how long it's been. I'm not allowed to work, so my mom and dad came to stay with me." Luke paused and raised his eyes to meet Mar's. He then added, with a smile, "And their little dog, Polly, too."

Mar smiled back. "Polly?" she laughed. "Were they maybe hoping for a parrot? And do I detect a hint of 'Oz' in your voice? You know…"

Luke interrupted. "Yeah. *I'll get you, my pretty, and your little dog, too.*" Luke laughed. "She's been a real pill. But seriously, though, they adopt rescue dogs. When one dies, they get another. And they never change the name that comes with them. Mom thinks it's wrong to further traumatize them after all they've been through. But that's not important, really. How have you been?"

Mar found his charm to be irresistible and mentally chided herself because of this. He did look genuinely concerned, however. "I'm doing okay," she reasoned. "They did move my office, though. I no longer have a window and am not even in the same hall. They put me next to the janitor's closet."

"Really? Wow. That really reeks. Why'd they do that?"

Mar shrugged. "I think it's all a game to them. They act as if it's always been this way. I'm sure it's to keep me out of the loop because Andres has his eyes set on a new prospect. Her name's Jodi and she's the new secretary. Pretty little thing. She's gotta be at least a good twenty years younger than he is."

Mitch finally decided to join them at the table and sat down. But it was Trish who spoke. "Well, I'm glad he's finally taken his hooks out of you... but really? Twenty years?"

"Definitely... maybe even more. She seems very young. Her parents pastor the sister church across town."

Mar reached for another doughnut just as Luke was retrieving one and their fingers touched. "I'm glad he's backed off, as well," he offered.

Blushing, Mar responded, "Yeah. Me too. And actually it's nice being away from them all... no one drops by extra work so they can spend the day either chatting or telephoning online. It is all actually worth not having a window." Mar took in some air and forced a sigh.

Sensing her discomfort, Mitch changed the subject. "So, are they closing our case? And do they know how Trish's ex-boyfriend found out where she was?" he asked.

Luke looked tired. "That's a good question. The guy they replaced me with is never available for conversation and when I went by the station they handed me this folder and told me to go back home. The file's incomplete, too. There is no mention of the hostage situation and, if it has been closed, it's missing the final report. Seems odd. It doesn't sit right with me, but that's all I know."

Trish looked rather culpable as she spoke up. "He found me because I was stupid enough to attend Wild Springs, the church's so-called *healing* class. I thought I mentioned it. Sorry. Andres was angry at me because I refused to break it off with Mitch, despite his attempt to blackmail me with the confidential information I had shared. So he leaked my whereabouts to the ex. I think he was hoping more to get rid of Mitch than he was me. He finds me to be a nuisance, but Mitch has stood in his way far too many times. He blames Mitch that Mar and he are not yet married."

Mar and Mitch both flinched visibly at the thought of Mar's union with Andres. Each insisted that it was understandable that Trish forgot to mention what she knew and told Luke that he shouldn't worry himself further, reminding him that no one had informed them of his injury. Trish then chimed in to say that if they didn't plan on being late, they all needed to head off to their churches. Rising from the table all at once, Luke went for the door, and Mitch and Trish followed. But Mar ran for her room in a panic; she wasn't even dressed and definitely wouldn't have time for a shower.

By Dianne J. Beale

Chapter 45

Mar stepped into the children's building with trepidation. She didn't want to be there today and feared the children might sense this. She said a quick prayer as she went about her preparations. She looked up when she heard the door, saw it was Jeb, nodded an acknowledgment, and returned to her work.

"Ma'am," offered Jeb. As he began to set up and repair a table, his tool belt dropped, hitting the floor. Mar realized she might have appeared as rude so went over to help him.

Jeb flushed. "The clip's broke," he stated. "Haven't had time to get it fixed."

Mar nodded, holding it up next to him so he'd have quicker access to the tools he needed. "What's this table for?" she ventured.

"Don't know, Ma'am," he stated. "I jus' do what I'm told, I'm sure. They said you needed it."

Mar searched her memory and landed on an unsettled portion of last week's staff meeting. Now she really didn't want to be there. She decided to just hold the tools and to keep her mouth shut.

When Jeb straightened, he bumped into Mar since she was preoccupied and hadn't noticed his movement. He put out his arm to steady her, apologizing for his clumsiness. She was suddenly acutely aware of his towering height and powerful body. Why hadn't she noticed how attractive he was? He had an earthy quality to him. His hair was a distinct dark, bronzy, brown and his skin was smooth and firm against her. She felt strangely safe, protected. When she raised her eyes, hazel eyes met hers for but a moment.

Flustered, she readily acknowledged that she'd been to blame and told him she was the one who should be apologizing. He just smiled down at her, shyly told her not to worry about it, and then took his tools and was gone.

Mar remained motionless as she pondered the expression she had seen in Jeb's eyes. Not only did she sense deep concern, but he also appeared older and more intelligent than he chose to portray. She touched her lips as she thought of his warm, full smile.

Realizing she hadn't moved, she scolded herself. "Always the wrong men, Mar. You got to stop reading between the lines. At this rate you'll be a ripe old maid, still working here for peanuts, and answering to Andres' children." She forced herself to return to her unfinished task and ignored Jodi when she entered to ready the table.

The feeling appeared to be mutual. Just as Jodi left, kids and parents began to pile in. Mar used this as an excuse to analyze the table's new contents.

By Dianne J. Beale

On the left were ridiculously gaudy buttons. They sported fluorescent colors that one might associate with the '70s and tastelessly stated, "Love Me, Love My God." A small puppy shape disrespectfully appeared behind the word "God."

The center of the table displayed expensive pamphlets that paraded similar colors on a high-gloss sheen (and she was lucky if given permission to use even the most basic of colored papers). They appeared to advertise an upcoming event. Not wishing to draw attention to the exhibit, Mar refused to give in to her curiosity, resisting the urge to pick up and leaf through one of them.

At the right end of the table there were Bible-based fortune cookies placed next to an enthusiastically scrawled "love me, love my god SIGN-UP SHEET." Decorated pens and pencils were also placed nearby in what appeared to be small, bright vases.

Mar moved away from the entryway and returned to the counter she had earlier left. The kids were playing in groups on the floor as they waited for others to arrive. So far she was the only adult. She pulled her notepad from her purse to check on who had volunteered for the day.

When Betsy arrived, she offered to stay. She often filled in when others did not honor their commitments. As Mar accepted her suggestion, she explained that this still left them short. State law required that at least two other adults serve for even the amount of kids who had already arrived, and another ten to twenty kids were the norm. Liza, who was with her mom, also agreed to stay.

Mar decided she should seek out the other volunteers that had not arrived even though experience had taught her not to expect to find any of them. Two that she thought might not show were a teen that relied on parental transportation and a single mom with multiple health challenges. The latter had two kids who had not yet arrived, so the outlook seemed even less promising. Rarely did volunteers call when they could not make it.

On her way out, Mar grabbed a pamphlet and stuffed it in her pocket. Betsy and Liza stayed to watch over the kids. Only a few minutes had passed when Jeb caught her eye and said he'd been sent to help. As they walked back toward the children's building, Mar tried to reason with him since Sundays were supposed to be his day off: just because he attended the church he worked for did not mean that he should be taken advantage of. She had to relent when they were joined by the out-of-breath single mom with her two trailing kids.

Betsy, in the meantime, had also sent a text-message to her husband, Karl. He agreed to join them once he had finished playing with the worship team. This would make five adults and one teenager to work with the children. Mar quickly tallied the number of children and determined that they could just slide by without Jeb, leaving four adults, since Liza also planned to stay.

By Dianne J. Beale

She was about to insist that Jeb should go when Karl walked through the door. Behind him were another six children. Resignedly, Mar thanked Jeb as she realized that his help would still be needed. She hadn't fully understood how much she had come to depend on Betsy and her family until today: only one of the original six volunteers had arrived.

The rest of the morning went by in a haze. Soon the kids had gone, and it was time to clean up. Mar said her thank yous and good byes and then turned toward the nearly empty table.

Betsy was holding one of the two last pamphlets and her eyebrows were raised. "Love me, love my God?" she quipped.

"I know. Not my idea. They set it up this morning while I was preparing for the lesson. Does it say who's in charge?"

"So once again our ideas weren't even considered. Whatever happened to the children's planned performance?"

"Apparently it was never planned. Oh, and hymns are for old folks, not a church service."

"Who said that?"

"Never mind. I shouldn't have said anything. I'm much too emotional, anyway. But I'm working on it." Mar feigned a smile that did not reach her eyes.

Betsy sensed she should change the subject. "Do you know this Jodi person? It seems the table was her idea."

"She's the new secretary. Any other names mentioned?"

"No. It just says to call for details. Didn't *sign-up sheets* used to imply commitment? Oh, sorry, did I just say the C-word?" Betsy saw that Mar wasn't laughing but knew it was more likely to be disappointment than anything aimed at her.

Mar finally took the time to read over the pamphlet:

Love Me, Love My God!
Build a bond that can't be broken!
Form a fence that can't be forced!
Raise missional kids that increase the Kingdom!
Relationship, Boundaries, and Community!
We've got it all–even the PIZZA!
Come one, come all–bring the entire family!

As she read, her face became pinched. "Is *missional* even a word?"

Betsy was shaking her head. "I guess it just may be now that churches are more concerned with impressing the lost than they are with keeping their members."

When Mar finally raised her eyes to look at her friend, it appeared as if Betsy was just about ready to vomit. But instead, in silent understanding, they went back to the cleaning so that they could leave.

By Dianne J. Beale

Exiting the building, neither saw Jeb as he stood across the road, watching. They walked steadily toward their cars and soon were driving off in opposite directions. Although no one seemed to notice, a pewter-gray Mitsubishi silently followed Mar as she drove off to her and Mitch's home.

Chapter 46

Mar parked in her garage, shutting the door almost as soon as she'd entered. Mitch's car already sat beside hers. She was looking forward to seeing him. She went inside and closed the door, locking it behind her. After changing and using the restroom, she ventured into the kitchen, surprised to not find Mitch. She checked all the rooms and then knocked on his door. When she still received no response, she peeked inside. The room had a feeling of emptiness, so she shut the door quickly.

She returned to the kitchen, put on water for tea, and then sat down. Turning on her phone, she answered the message icons by first calling her voice mail. The message, although from Mitch, was garbled. She hung up and moved on to the text messages instead.

"Don't go home. I'll explain later. Luke." "Oh, call me, okay? The number isn't mine. Use the one sending this text. Luke." "Trish and I are going to *Denny's*. Join us. Mitch. You know which one." "Mar, where are you? Call me. Mitch."

Mar shut off the tea kettle. As she turned back toward the table, she saw a man's shadow on the blinds. Maybe she hadn't imagined the shadow of the other day. She poured water into a cup, deposited a tea bag, and then casually left the kitchen. Grabbing her purse and keys, she went over to the garage, locked the house, got into her car, and opened the garage door with her remote. She pulled out, lowering the door as she drove away, and headed out toward *Denny's*.

The gray car appeared familiar as she shot past it. It was parked along the dead-end street that she and Mitch lived on. She recognized the man only after she'd made it safely to the through street. It was Jeb.

Why was he sitting in his car across from her home on a dead-end street? Well, he couldn't have made it to his car that quickly, so to whom did the shadow belong? But she was sure that she had seen Jeb… and now she felt vulnerable and weak.

Unfortunately, she didn't see her familiar animal friend because of her preoccupation with Jeb. But there it sat, sunning in her driveway. And its eyes were following her, long after the car had passed from its sight.

When Mitch and Trish spotted her entering, Trish decided to go over and greet her. She had just reached her side when the waitress arrived to seat her. Trish told the waitress that Mar was with her and guided a pale, shaking Mar to their table. Mitch eyed her carefully and then ordered her a drink.

Mar somehow managed to eventually speak. She told how Mitch's voice message had been useless but that she'd received two strange text messages from Luke, along with their own invitations to *Denny's*. Then she had looked up to see a man's shadow against the blinds of the kitchen window, and fearing the worst because of Luke's instructions, quickly went back out to her car and had driven here.

She then mentioned how Jeb had been parked out in his car in front of the house, across the street, and how she was sure the shadow on the blinds couldn't have been him because he was in the car, sitting peacefully. The shadow man didn't have the necessary time to make it to where she'd encountered Jeb.

When she finally winded down, Mitch took her phone and looked up the text messages from Luke. Both came from the same number, but it was not a number that he recognized as Luke's. He hit the option to call the number and waited.

"Mar," Luke said. "Is it you? Are you okay?"

"This is Mitch, Luke. Mar's here with me. Can you meet us at *Denny's*?"

"No. That's not a good idea. I don't think we should be seen together. Is Mar okay? Did she get my message? I knew that calls don't go through at that church but couldn't take the risk. Is she okay?"

Mitch decided to be somewhat guarded. He didn't like that he couldn't see Luke's face. "She's here. She's okay. She got your message." He heard a sigh of relief.

By Dianne J. Beale

"I'll call later, then. I don't want to interrupt your meal. Maybe we could meet later somehow, but not at the house. I'll be in touch. Tell Mar I'm glad she's okay, and that I'm sorry if I've alarmed her. I just… well, there was no other way. I had no choice. I'll call later."

The rest of the meal was eaten in calm silence. Even the waitress commented on the change in demeanor. She threw a look of concern at Mar and then gave her some free coffee. She explained that it appeared she needed it.

Trish had a meeting that she had to get to and they had lunched longer than they had planned. So Mitch took Mar's keys, they parted company with Trish, and he drove the car towards home. It was not long before they were exiting the car and entering their house.

The tea Mar had left by the stove was gone. Not even the cup remained. She tried to tell Mitch this, but he was too busy calling the police–two muddy footprints sat directly in front of the door that led to the back yard–the yard behind the kitchen window. The kitchen, itself, had paw prints all over. But the house remained locked, and there was no sign of a break-in; all valuables appeared to be untouched. But he and Mar decided to wait for the police before moving on to more of the house.

They tarried almost an hour before the doorbell rang. Luke appeared with three other police officers. He looked both wane and wan. He also seemed worried. They set about taking photos and samples of everything. Luke even opened the trash bin–there was the cup… empty of tea, but stained with what might have been blood. It was broken. Luke used gloves as he placed it into a sterile sample bag.

Once they were finished, the police insisted that Mitch and Mar pack their bags and leave with them. When they heard that Mitch had lost his house key months ago, Luke went out to buy new locks. Once these were changed, as well, Mitch was given the new keys. The original knobs and locks were placed into further sterile bags. It was this final gesture that sent Mar into jitters once again.

At the police forensics, Mar and Mitch were also given new cell phones. Their SIMs were analyzed and determined to be safe, but the phones were replaced. They sat in a friendly coffee break room while they waited for Luke. But it was Jeb who came through the door. Mar went from pale to colorless. Mitch warily followed him with his eyes. It was then that Luke joined them and Jeb finally spoke.

By Dianne J. Beale

Chapter 47

"Do you know a Jasmine and Paco?" Jeb questioned. Luke nodded at them, urging them to answer.

"He used to be the janitor at our church," Mar answered. "But we only met his wife once."

"No, Mar," Mitch corrected, "You only met his wife once. Jasmine was the receptionist or secretary the day I went to empty your office of your things. I've met her twice. But the first time I didn't know she was married to Paco."

"Right, I forgot," said Mar. "I met her once. Mitch met her twice. But we both knew Paco rather well… before he left the church."

"Do you know where they are now?" Jeb continued.

"No. They didn't want us to know. The church. Um. One of the pastor's, I think… I can't remember. The new counselor, maybe? Someone at the church threatened them. Mitch recommended a good lawyer, though. But we hadn't heard anything since. Are they okay?"

Luke placed his hand on Jeb's shoulder to stop his flow of words. Then Luke sat down next to Mar. "Paco was found, beaten, two days ago. His wife was in hysterics. Paco's in intensive care and she's in a ward for now. The doctors feared she might accidentally harm herself. Someone injected her with a strong drug. It was someone knowledgeable, too… enough to silence her, but not to kill her."

Luke continued. "We think they planned to kill her husband, but she walked in on it. He's barely holding on, but he's alive. But she keeps repeating your name, Mar. We think you're in grave danger. Jeb's been tracking someone who's been following you for weeks. It's always a different car, but they all have dark windows. Very elusive. I couldn't warn you without blowing both Jeb's and my covers. Did quite a bit of praying, though. I'm sorry… and so glad you're both okay."

Luke paused and drew in a breath. "Do you think you could come with us to visit Jasmine? It might help in her recovery. But after that we'll be moving you two into hiding. Jeb will be staying at your house with a female cop and continue to work as the church janitor while I'll be signing on as church security."

Mar and Mitch were speechless. After an uncomfortably long time, Mitch took it upon himself to move the conversation onward. "We might have evidence at our house," Mitch finally offered. "Our computers and the stuff I took from Mar's office."

Mar seemed to be close to shock, but in reality she was questioning how having Jeb stay at their house made any sense. Wouldn't that, in itself, expose him?

By Dianne J. Beale

The door swung open. "Change of plans," explained the Chief. "Jeb, I need you to live out where you've been living. It's too dangerous for you to risk bein' seen at that house. We need to keep you at that church since you're already there and no one suspects anything. Luke, their house will have to be part of your cover. You can say you volunteered to stay there with your partner. That way they'll believe the house is unprotected since you will have fed them this important misinformation. Margaret, Mitch, you'll be moved tonight to stay with Jeb. No one'd expect you to be there. Our receptionist has already arranged a 'family emergency' excuse for your employers. She'll call them in the morning to relay why you'll be gone. Got it?"

The room of people shook their heads in acknowledgment, and the Chief, after giving a quick, "Good," left the room. He motioned for Luke and Jeb to follow him.

Mar and Mitch fell into discussion. They still weren't sure that Luke could be trusted. They'd been told to contact close friends and let them all believe they'd be out of town due to a "family emergency." The couple staying at the house was to be explained away as house sitters. So Luke would be the one staying at their house with a female cop. Neither expected Trish to believe any of this, but they were instructed to feed her the story anyhow. They didn't like this plan yet realized they had no choice but to make the calls.

The time passed quickly. "Ready?" It was Jeb. Mar and Mitch nodded their heads. "You'll be driving a rental with tinted windows, following me. Keep you cells available in case we get separated, though. If this happens, we'll have to reconnect without it being obvious that this is what we're doing. Okay?"

Mar and Mitch nodded, and Jeb handed Mitch the keys. He then crossed the room to grab two of their bags. "Let's go then," he instructed. "Try not to lose me." With that out of the way, he strode out the door. Mitch and Mar followed mechanically. Five minutes later, they were traveling behind a gray Mitsubishi down one of the busier roads.

By Dianne J. Beale

Chapter 48

The tension was thick with silence as Mitch and Mar drove along. Mar decided to break the strain. "Are we there yet?" she joked, using her best child's voice.

Mitch laughed. "It does seem like we've been traveling forever. Where do you suppose he's leading us?"

"I'll bet we end up two or three miles from where we came," Mar suggested. "You know, traveling in circles."

Just then, Mitch's cell phone rang. He had Mar take the call as he'd left his hands-free device in his own car. "Hello?" Mar answered.

Jeb's voice sounded unsure of himself. "Um, yeah. Tell Mitch I'm going to turn right at the next light. He should drive on by and take the next right after that, though. Then he'll need to go two blocks–two more stop signs–and turn right again. He'll see the car on the left and should park next to it. We don't have a garage." Jeb hung up.

"Well?" asked Mitch. "I assume that was Jeb?"

Mar relayed the message and at the next light, Mitch drove on. He continued onward as directed, and soon they were parked next to Jeb in the driveway. He motioned for them to get out as he lifted their bags from his back seat. They then went into the house.

Jeb dropped the bags just beyond the entryway and headed toward his kitchen. Mar watched him as he crossed the room and then passed her eyes over the main room they were about to enter. A small, leather, love sofa was paired with an elegant coffee table, and a large easy chair was set off to the side. There was a reading lamp in the corner and a modern-looking fan on the ceiling. The rug was a deep ocean blue and very lush. On the wall were oil and water paintings, and the fireplace was a rich, gray marble. On the mantle were what appeared to be family pictures. Mar jumped at the sudden twinge of loneliness and loss.

"You okay?" Mitch asked. "Why don't we just sit for a bit? It's been quite a day." Mar aimlessly allowed herself to be led to the couch. Shortly after, Jeb handed her and Mitch each a cup of tea. He set a small dish of cheese and crackers on the coffee table. He then sat down in the easy chair and turned on the television to watch the news. This time, the silence was comfortable.

Jeb suddenly seemed agitated. "No. He's not supposed to be in the news. Don't these people have any scruples?" He picked up his cell phone.

"Hey. Did you see the news? Is he protected? Do you know? Ah. Hmm. Mm. So, he's been moved? Good. Good. Sweet. Okay, thanks. Oh, Caller ID. It's the Chief. Gotta go.

By Dianne J. Beale

Sure. Bye. Jeb here. Yeah. Luke said. Oh. Oh. Definitely, Sir. Okay. Bye."

Mitch and Mar looked at Jeb in expectation, but he didn't share the other end of the conversation. Mar was about to open her mouth but then seemed to think better of it and said nothing. One word stuck in her mind: Paco.

"Um, guess I should show you your rooms. Let me know if you need anything else." Jeb picked up two of their bags and headed toward a closed door. Mar and Mitch each picked up a bag and followed.

Mar's room was like a small suite, restroom included. Jeb assured her there were fresh towels, etc. waiting for her and wished her a good night. Then, he and Mitch moved further down the hall. Mar closed the door and unpacked what she needed from her stuff. She plugged in her cell and then went into the restroom to freshen up. Everything was of impeccable taste.

Wrapped in her oversized robe, Mar sat on the edge of her bed, reading her Bible. There was a knock on the door. She and Mitch prayed together, and then Mitch gave her directions to his room in case she needed him. Parting company, they each headed off to their beds.

Chapter 49

"Blood? Why am I standing in blood?" Mar could see splintered wood everywhere; the air was thick with termites and locusts that also covered the walls. She could hear bleating, as well. But where was it coming from?

She walked toward a group of people at the end of the hall, yet they appeared to be oblivious to her presence. Their faces were turned toward the adjoining hall as if mesmerized. As she merged into the assembly, the bleating grew louder. The crowd wore smiles–some were laughing while others jeered.

The now nearby spectacle caused Mar to catch her breath. A large, strangely beautiful lion stood amidst a herd of sheep. In its mouth laid the smallest, feeblest of lambs–its eyes were weeping.

The lion's eyes held an unfathomable void that was so dark that it extinguished any hope of warmth. As the animal targeted Mar as its next victim, she shivered. Holding her ground, she continued to meet the beast's odious glare, despite the trembling.

Just as the lion was about to drop its prey and lunge for her, another lion jumped between them. This lion lacked the

By Dianne J. Beale

majestic characteristics of the first lion; it was plain and unassuming. Yet such serenity filled the room; his eyes emitted a warmth so powerful that it overcame the chill that had previously stifled the atmosphere. As this lion roared, the building shook; the first lion dropped the lamb and bared its teeth. Thick blood dripped from its mouth and onto the snowy white coat below. "Spotless. Free. Mine," claimed the new arrival. "You have no business here. Leave."

The first lion no longer shone with beauty. As cold as sheer dampness, the dark shadow leaped over the sheep herd and headed away, down the deserted hall. The remaining lion motioned for Mar to join the sheep. His eyes were pure and filled with compassion. He brought order to the flock, cleaned the wounded lamb with his tongue, and then breathed into it a new life that left the lamb completely restored.

The lion turned toward Mar: "Do you love Me?"

Mar then saw the scars. Tears began to fall freely onto her cheeks. "Yes, Jesus. You know that I do."

"Then feed my sheep. They look to a shepherd that has forsaken Me. Prepare for the battle, for your enemy will return. He has been invited here by the very ones that build a kingdom in My name. But their kingdom is not My Kingdom. The devil masquerades as an angel of light. But do not be afraid. The battle is Mine."

Mar felt a flood of questions rise to her lips, but she could not find a voice. "It's not yet time," the lion assured her. "Wait."

Mar woke from her sleep, opened her eyes, and reached for her notebook. When her hand met the air, she remembered she was not at home. Moving to a bag, she removed the notebook and then took up its pen. After filling numerous pages, she used the restroom, returned to her bed, and then prayed herself to sleep.

By Dianne J. Beale

Chapter 50

Sun was streaming into the room when Mar awoke the next morning. The surroundings puzzled her at first, but then she remembered the events of the previous day. Bible teachings began to flood her mind: *when you are weak, then you are strong; His grace is sufficient; He will never leave or forsake me;* and *resist the devil and he will flee.* She felt rested and safe despite the circumstances she'd been subjected to.

She climbed out of bed and went to the restroom to ready herself for the day. There didn't appear to be a fan, so Mar cracked the window before getting into the shower. She began to sing quietly, humming whenever she'd forgotten the words. Closing off the water, she grabbed the large, fluffy bath sheet and began to dry off. She then wrapped herself in the softness, making a turban out of a smaller towel. She went back into the bedroom and scooped up her toothbrush and paste. Then she returned to the restroom to finish her morning routine.

Once dressed, she opened her Bible. She instinctively went to 1 Peter 5. It had been a reference point for her ever since her parents' deaths. Her father had read from this passage almost weekly while they were growing up. It served as a reminder to live in God's will, humbly and with reverence; it was her dad's understanding of their place within the whole picture.

After her prayers, she ventured out into the hallway and headed back to the part of the house she and Mitch had come from just the night before. What was actually only a matter of hours seemed so much longer. She felt a sadness fall down around her as she thought of what was once her parents' church. Nothing was the same; not even the name had survived.

Sighing, she entered the kitchen. To her surprise, Jeb sat at the table with a newspaper. She had expected him to have left hours ago for work.

Not wanting to disturb him, she opened the cupboard, took out a cup, and poured herself some coffee. The milk and cream were already on the table. She set down her cup and poured in cream. She decided to just drink it without sugar, so was pleasantly surprised when she tasted it. There was a pleasant semi-sweet chocolate flavor. She sat down across from Jeb and continued to sip.

"Are you going to eat something with that?" Jeb inquired, breaking the silence. His voice had a warm, teasing quality to it. Mar had never experienced this side to him. She decided, instantly, that she liked it.

"What's good?" She asked. "It'll be difficult to top this coffee."

By Dianne J. Beale

Jeb smiled. "Yeah, it will. My sis brings it to me whenever she visits. It's a Bavarian chocolate java blend. Just a tad of brown sugar in the pot makes it irresistible every time."

"Where's it from?"

"Not sure. Never thought about it. When you can get it for free from someone you trust, sometimes it's best to just accept the blessing. That way, you might never need to pay for it."

Mar laughed. "You and Mitch should get along just fine," she offered. "What types of cereal do you have?"

"And here I thought maybe I'd get an omelette out of it. Tough one, I guess."

"So how come you're not at work?"

"Got the day off. We need to return the rental so it's not obvious that I have company. Last night also finished off my hours for the week, unless I'm approved for overtime. I'm liking the hours much more than the job I'm really signed up for. More perks, too."

Mar caught a glance of Jeb's plate now that he'd set the paper down. "Ah. I guess I, I'll eat a biscuit thing, then. Can I have more coffee, too?"

Jeb rose, shaking his head, and poured her more coffee. Then he put a sausage biscuit on a plate and committed it to the microwave. He sat back down to the wait for the beep. "So, am I to assume I've gotta play host while you're here?" He got up again and then set her breakfast before her.

"I wouldn't complain," she countered, "but I'm sure I'll find my niche eventually." Just as she began eating, Mitch appeared.

"Good morning all."

"Good morning," they returned in unison.

Mitch couldn't help himself. "How long did it take you two to practice that?" he asked.

Mar blushed, concentrating on her food. Jeb just laughed. "We're naturals," he tossed back. "Who needs practice?" Then he excused himself so he could ready himself for the rest of the day.

By Dianne J. Beale

Chapter 51

Once she was sure that Jeb had left the house, Mar scolded her brother. "I wish you wouldn't do that. You know I can't stand it when you do."

"Do what?" Mitch seemed genuinely confused.

"Teasing me is bad enough, but when you see the need to pair the teasing with others… well, just stop it, okay? I'd like to be able to have some relationships progress normally, you know. Not every guy needs to feel as if you're trying to marry me off."

"Jeb was fine with it, Mar. You make too much of these things–really. Most guys would see that as a friendly gesture, and I'd rather spare you from those who make too much of things. It's better to know ahead of time which ones are psychotic."

Mar didn't seem convinced. "Whatever. Just don't do it with me around, then, okay?"

Mitch changed the subject. "How do you suppose that works?" he began. "I realize that Jeb really is employed with the police department, but the church doesn't know that. Or at least the church isn't supposed to know that. So how does he not go to work as the church janitor without raising suspicions? Wouldn't he have to work overtime in order to keep his cover?"

This comment made Mar wonder just how long her brother had been listening before he had actually entered the room. "I believe he was referring to the church when he said he can't work overtime," she suggested. "You might realize that if you'd made your presence obvious and hadn't insisted on lurking."

"Not lurking," Mitch answered, "just eavesdropping. You know, I don't like not having a car. I think maybe I'll call Luke."

Again, Mar pondered how long her brother had been listening, but realized it was actually a comfort to know she had someone watching out for her. She remembered to absentmindedly agree. "Yeah. Me too," she shared.

Directly after confirming how to block his number with customer service, Mitch dialed Luke. Just as Mar opened her mouth to question, she remembered the reason for the block and chose not to say anything. Besides, Mitch's call had been answered.

"Hi Luke," Mitch was saying. "Can you fill us in a little, or is this not a good time?"

Mar was watching her brother's face. She wanted to be sure she could tell if he later left any of their conversation out in its retelling.

"Hmm, hmm. Oh, okay. When?"

By Dianne J. Beale

Mar got up and rinsed their dishes and cups, all the while keeping her eyes on Mitch. She then moved the dishes from the sink into the dishwasher.

"Oh. Um, so you don't know where we're at, then. Do you at least have news on Jasmine and Paco? We never did stop by the hospital to see them. Oh, okay, later then. Bye."

"Well?" Mar questioned.

"I can't be positive, but…"

"Yeah?"

"I think he may have been with Jeb. I'm not liking this 'keeping us in the dark' bit. We'd better pray."

"Definitely. Did we really leave all the evidence in our house?"

"Not exactly. I took pictures and made photo copies and then put small samples of whatever I could into baggies. Then I also bought a memory stick and put most of your hard drive on it."

It's all now in a safety deposit box and a pastor friend in another state has backups of it all. He also has the second key to the box. And my laptop's at my new job since it belongs to them. My secretary is keeping it for me."

"Ah. Well that's good. At least something's safe," she faltered.

Mitch began to pray. "Father God, We put our trust in You. We believe that all things work together for good to those who love you. We are the creation and humbly submit ourselves to You, the Creator. Fill us with Your wisdom and give us discernment. We are nothing without You. Heal Jasmine and Paco. Protect them. Guard our friends and all of our homes. And give us strength and understanding–help us to overcome evil with good, and to not grow weary. In Your Son's name, Jesus — name above all names — we ask Your will to be done in our lives. Amen."

Mar rose and gave Mitch a hug. She felt better already. Mitch seemed more relaxed, as well. "So, brother," she smiled, "What now?"

Mitch decided they should watch some news. Neither was good at remaining idle. Mar suggested that later they could maybe bake cookies or something. Then they sat down, surfing channels for some news.

By Dianne J. Beale

Chapter 52

A little over an hour later, Mitch and Mar were sitting on the back patio, outside, despite Jeb's statement about returning the rental car. They were not people who enjoyed sitting still and refused to stay entirely indoors. Besides, the yard was fenced and they were seated, not standing.

I'm glad you thought to grab a couple games," Mitch stated. "Otherwise this waiting and staying put would be unbearable."

"I agree. I think it was more God's idea than mine, though. I'd gone into the computer room to grab a few of the more important disks and–*Voila!*–they were sitting on the nearby table."

She and Mitch were sipping lemonade, snacking on cheese and bread, and playing Scrabble. So far, they'd been mostly equally matched. This thought caused Mar to smile. So many people had asked their parents if they were twins. But Mitch was about two and a half years older than she and always slightly ahead in the world. The memory of their last family Christmas together brought tears to her eyes. It was just two days later that they'd been taken from them.

Mitch didn't seem to notice her sudden mood change. He was highly concentrating on what Mar assumed were his letters and the board. She began to watch his face. When the phone rang, they both jumped.

"Do we answer it, you think?" asked Mitch as they went inside. "I guess it's best to listen to the message first, right?"

They waited for the answering machine to finish its spiel and then for the caller to identify him or herself "after the tone." At first, there was a huge pause, but then "Jeb? You there? Um, I know we told you to take a day off, but… well you'll get paid for it. There's an emergency at the church. Call, okay? Oh, this is Jodi–the secretary. You've got the number. Okay. Um, bye then."

Mitch and Mar stood silently at first. Then Mitch grabbed his cell, blocked the number, and dialed Jeb.

"Yeah? Jeb here," he heard.

"The church just called you. We thought maybe you should know," said Mitch.

"Oh. Really? Who was it?"

"Jodi, the secretary. Said something about an emergency and that although they gave you the day off, you'd get paid."

"What kind of an emergency?"

"She didn't say. Just said to call."

"Oh. Did she give a number?"

By Dianne J. Beale

"Nope. Said you knew it. The caller ID didn't register anything except the time of her call–2:15 p.m."

"No number? Hmm. She musta used her cell. I'll call her with my cell and tell her I'm calling from the car as I'm on my way. Can you call and tell Luke where I'll be? I'll try to find my way back home soon. Sounds a little mysterious, though."

"Okay. Can do. Be careful."

Mitch hung up and, blocking his number, he immediately called Luke. He got the message center, and hung up.

Then he tried again. "Yes?" Luke sounded agitated.

"Jeb got called in to the church for an emergency. He asked us to let you know. He planned to call the secretary, Jodi, and go on in. No idea what the emergency is–she didn't say."

"Oh. Okay. Thanks." He hung up.

Mitch and Mar refilled their lemonades and went back out into the back yard. They packed up the Scrabble pieces and then put away the board. Setting it to the side, they then began to nibble at the cheese.

Mar spoke first, "I'm not liking this at all. Do you think we should call your friend and tell him what's going on?"

"We can't call him from any of these phones or his number will be monitored. I've used payphones before now, but now we're kind of stuck here."

"Would the *pay-as-you-go* phone we bought for Trish help? I packed it on the way out since we didn't get a chance to give it to her."

"You're a genius, Sis. No one knows that phone even exists since we paid cash and all. Go get it, and I'll call him."

Mar went back into the house and Mitch followed, carrying the tray of food and one glass of lemonade. He set them on the kitchen table and went back out to get the rest of the stuff.

Mar returned with the phone and the card, and they sat down together at the kitchen table. They said a short prayer and then dialed Mitch's friend.

"Jeff here," came the voice. "How can I be of service?"

Mitch explained everything to Jeff, including the status of the phone he was using to call. He explained that he'd blocked the number so that it wouldn't accidentally ring and give away their secret. He also expressed their nervousness and the feeling of being trapped inside the *X-files* and asked him to remember them in his prayers.

When he finished, Jeff answered, "Me and Maxie will definitely be praying with you. I've already copied all I could and put it, along with the key, into a separate box here. Maxie's sister's a cop, and she recommended we do that. She has our extra key. We put the tea sample, etc. into the box and made copies of the information to stay with us here. But it's merely a precaution since no one even knows of us."

By Dianne J. Beale

Mitch breathed a little easier and explained they'd not used this phone and would need to keep it off so it could remain a secret. He told him he'd try to call, but only if there was any new information to give. Then, they said their goodbyes and hung up. Mar took the phone, shut it off, and brought Mitch with her to reveal the hiding place. They were both soon sitting in the kitchen, eating, as if nothing had happened the entire day.

Chapter 53

After surfing the Internet, watching more TV, listening to music, and even doing a load of laundry, Mitch and Mar were in the kitchen again, discussing their boredom. Mar had raided the freezer and found a pound of ground turkey, some California vegetable mix, and a loaf of French or Italian bread. She set them on the table and began to search the fridge: cheese, garlic, tomatoes, iceberg lettuce, and carrots. Then, she went to the pantry: spaghetti pasta and sauce, and croutons. "He's gonna need to get us more food," she said absentmindedly.

"Yeah, I wonder if they'll compensate him. Do you think this is really his house?"

Mar didn't answer. She was programming the microwave to thaw the meat. She then began opening cupboards and setting out potential pans, etc. She placed some garlic into the blender, along with the sauce and then washed a couple carrots and two of the four tomatoes. She chopped these into the blender as well. Then she stuck on the lid and began the chopping and blending.

By Dianne J. Beale

Next, she read that the lettuce was already washed so began tearing it into a dish. "Could you check if he's got dressing? I forgot to look."

Mitch moved to the fridge and scanned its contents. "He's got ranch or Italian," he said.

"Good. You know, I hadn't thought of the possibility that it's not his house and that maybe he rents or even that it was all arranged for us. It's unsettling. I'd rather believe it's his. He seems comfortable and relaxed here–you know, kinda in his element."

"Yeah, I thought that, too. Is there something I can help with?" He was looking toward the running blender.

She smiled. "Yeah. Thanks. Just pour it all into that pan, and I'll season it if he's got spices. Otherwise, the store-bought sauce's spices will have to be enough. Um, set it to medium-low, I guess." She was now cleaning more carrots, and the last two tomatoes. When Mitch turned back to the table, she was adding the chopped pieces to the salad and then shook Parmesan over the top. She tossed it all with a fork, lidded it, and then handed it to him to put into the fridge. "Don't let me forget to add the croutons later," she commented.

She began to go through upper cupboards now and managed to find black pepper, cayenne, Italian herbs, and some cilantro. She added a little of each and then stirred the sauce, topping it with the lid. Next she took the meat from the microwave and tossed it into a skillet. She added only a dash of salt and pepper as she began to fry the contents. When the ground turkey was ready, she drained off the grease, enjoying the popping and sizzling sound as it hit the remaining water pockets that remained in the sink. Then she added it to the sauce, as well.

Now she filled a large pot with water, set it on a burner, and moved the spaghetti over to where it could sit nearby. She wiped up any spills with a sponge, returned any extra supplies to where they belonged, and then sat herself down across from Mitch. "I was going to make garlic bread but didn't see any foil," she stated. Mitch told her she should heat the bread anyhow, just at a very low temperature since it had been frozen. He got a knife, made partial cuts that would serve as slice markers, and then set it into a two-hundred-degree oven to warm. He took out a Pyrex measuring cup, added a stick of margarine, and popped in some freshly chopped garlic. He covered it with a paper towel and set it in the microwave for one minute. Then he stirred it all together, put a new paper towel over the top, and set it back into the fridge.

"There. Done," he smiled. "Now we just wait."

When the water was ready, steam rising off the rippling bubbles, she added the pasta. Then she sat back down. "I hate waiting," she sighed.

They each laughed. "Well, we could set the table instead," Mitch offered. They had just finished when the front door had opened. Jeb looked terrible. He was

By Dianne J. Beale

obviously wet and muddy, and also looked exhausted. He managed a smile before he went off to shower and change.

When the spaghetti was ready, Mar drained it and changed it to a bowl. She added the pasta tongs and set it onto the table. Then she got out a bread board and knife, set them onto the table, and added the warm bread. Mitch got out the salad, added the croutons, and then put out the dressings, Parmesan, and garlic butter. As he added utensils, Mar poured the sauce into a bowl and moved it to the table.

Then she filled a pitcher with water and poured it into the awaiting glasses. She refilled it and set it in the table's center.

Mitch checked for ice in the freezer, but there wasn't any. Everything was now ready, so Mar went to tell Jeb. Mitch sat down to wait.

She turned the corner that would lead to the bedrooms and collided. Jeb steadied her with his hand. He looked as if he wanted to laugh but feared concern should be the action he took. He didn't manage to do either. Mar was grateful for this.

"Sorry. Seems this happens more and more," she stammered. "Dinner's ready."

"I smelled it on my way in," he admitted. "Who else have you been knocking heads with?"

"Oh, don't worry. You're my favorite." She smiled. "Everyone else seems annoyed at best. At least you tried to show concern–you even stopped your laugh, which, by the way, would still have been far more acceptable than the other responses I've gotten," she answered.

Jeb suddenly wanted to know for real who all these others were. He suspected that he did know. He couldn't imagine being so cold to Mar. Of course they should've at least feigned concern, yet if they were those of the church–her coworkers–they long since had dropped any formalities unless it somehow was of benefit to them. Jeb just smiled: "Glad I'm your favorite. Lead the way," he said.

By Dianne J. Beale

Chapter 54

The first fifteen minutes of the dinner seemed much longer. After the initial acknowledgments between Jeb and Mitch, they had said a short prayer and then lapsed into silence. Even the tapping of utensils against plates was minimal. Mar felt as if the air was an invisible, thick mattress that hung in the midst of them. Finally, she could take it no longer: "Must have been quite the emergency," she offered. "You looked worn and exhausted when you arrived home."

Jeb lifted his eyes toward her as he responded. "Worn from the constant chatter of the office staff and exhausted from the overwhelming heat. I don't know how they managed to make such a mess of it. They claim the air conditioner burst into flames and that Jodi pulled the plug. Then Andres doused it all in water."

"Water? For an electrical fire?" interjected Mitch, scoffing. "It's a wonder that anyone survived." Mitch rolled his eyes, shook his head, and then added, "Water. How could anyone be so... unaware?"

Mar had to laugh. "Nice catch there. What were you going to say? Whatever it was, you still managed to work in the drama," she teased.

Mitch, ignoring her, continued. "Did anyone get hurt?"

"Someone did. The ambulance was leaving as I arrived. I'm not sure who it was, but no one in the office seemed to understand the gravity of the situation. Not even two people could agree on the circumstances of how it all happened."

"That's a first," Mar quipped. "They musta really been flustered. The norm is to all sound like parrots that've been coached to agree. They rarely have separate stories to tell. I've not seen much conflict, even if they're forced to lie. It seems they have the ability to convince themselves that reality is what they make it; they all live in a perpetual state of denial." In her mind, she was recalling the day her office had been moved. Before anyone could interrupt, she added, "Do you know what's happened with Paco and his wife? Are they safe? Are they doing okay?"

Jeb shook his head. "No. Luke's the one you'll have to ask about that. I've not been informed, either. Maybe we can call Luke later." Jeb's voice seemed to trail off in avoidance and the room fell silent once more.

Mar broke off a section of bread and mechanically applied garlic butter. She sensed there was something that Jeb was not sharing, and as she glanced sideways at her brother, she could tell that he seemed to agree with her.

Silence once again blanketed the room. She began to feel the accustomed uneasiness that often overcame her in such situations. Her palms were sweating, but she did conquer her urge to babble. Often silence, when combined

By Dianne J. Beale

with three or more people, would cause her to become nervous and then just spill out words as if she were an overfilled balloon that had burst. Too often she had emptied unintentional information in this way, sharing far more than she had planned and often causing others discomfort.

She drew in a breath, counted to ten, and then silently thanked God for the reminder. Grasping hold of the earlier words of Jeb, that he was "worn from the constant chatter," Mar managed to swallow the stream of consciousness that had threatened to make its way out. She literally bit down on her tongue so she would remain silent.

A nagging began to poke at her: she did not want Jeb to see her as a chatterbox. This realization almost made her choke on the bread she'd been chewing. She took a drink of water just in time to prevent this from happening.

The clattering of dishes pulled Mar back from her thoughts into her surroundings. Mitch was clearing away his place setting. "If you'll both excuse me," he gestured, "I need to go phone Trish. She might think I'm away on family business, but that won't excuse an absence of a call."

Mar suddenly felt panicked, but did not let it show on her face. Jeb had just refilled his plate with the remaining food, and she still had plenty to finish from the one serving she had taken. Both she and Jeb nodded, mouths full, and Mitch left the room.

The room fell still again. Jeb, sensing her discomfort, offered, "I'll need you to make me a shopping list. I'm not acquainted with the art of family groceries." He waved his hand around the kitchen. "But I'm sure you noticed that on your own." As his speech came to a close, he dropped his eyes, skin flushing. Mar had never seen him so unsure of himself.

"Um, okay. I can do that. Is there anything I should be avoiding? In preparing the meals, I mean? Mitch and I can basically eat anything, but he hates olives. So, unless you just gotta have them, that would be one less thing we'd need to purchase."

Jeb looked thoughtful. "I don't think I have any hang-ups–oh, um, not to say that Mitch does…" Jeb looked as if he wished he could kick himself. "Thanks for the meal," he quickly added, "It was nice coming home to such a pleasant aroma of food for a change."

Mar pretended not to notice his awkwardness since it had helped to put her at ease. "Well, Mitch helped. We've never been good at just taking it easy. I think we find it's more comfortable to keep ourselves busy. Whenever we do take the time to slow down, we usually get sick. Dad used to say that it was God's way of getting our attention." Mar's eyes softened at the mention of her dad. "He said that spending time with God needs to be our top priority and that some of his most profound thoughts were given to him when he had no choice but to slow down enough so that he had time to actually think. Maybe Mitch and I are just too aware of where our thoughts will take us."

By Dianne J. Beale

Jeb laughed. "Well, I would say that you two are far from thoughtless. In fact, you're two of the most thoughtful people I've ever had the pleasure to meet. It's obvious you're both well-read."

Mar blushed. "Wow. Thank you. That's a nice thing to say."

"I only speak the truth." Jeb winked, but then seemed to sober a little. "I'm really sorry," he began, "for… um… all the, um–for lack of a better word–junk, that is happening to you. But I'm not sorry it's forced you both to stay here with me. It's nice to have the company. This house has longed to hear the voice of a woman for some time now." Jeb's voice trailed off almost into a whisper.

Mar wasn't sure how to respond so forced a renewed interest in the food before her. When her cell phone rang, she let out an audible sigh of relief. "Excuse me a moment," she managed. She gingerly arose and moved out into the family room. She had never felt right about answering a phone while sitting at the dinner table.

"Hello? Um, no, I didn't call. Maybe Mitch did, though. Oh. Oh, okay. I don't know." She paused when she heard Jeb moving in the kitchen and became distracted. A sense of loss fell over her and she now regretted having answered the phone. But she knew she had done the right thing since it was Luke. She hadn't wanted to risk missing an opportunity to speak with him, but she now realized just how aware Jeb must have been of the relief she had felt. She would have answered regardless the caller, and Mar was sure that Jeb had sensed this.

Watching Jeb disappear through the door that led into the back rooms, she became even more distracted. She was glad that Luke was on the phone and not in the room with her. It appeared he had not noticed. She had been listening, just not attentively, so she was able to answer whenever it became necessary. When Luke finally hung up, he asked her to fill in Jeb and Mitch. She was privately glad he had asked her to do this because now she had an excuse to seek out Jeb.

As she cleared her dishes from the table and ran the garbage disposal, she realized she felt right at home. She finished loading the dishwasher, added soap, and then turned it on before heading off to find the men.

When she reached the back hallway, Mar suddenly recalled more of the conversation and was filled with the distinct impression that Luke had been flirting with her. He had hung up rather abruptly; maybe she had offended him by coming off as disinterested. Well, it was best to not lead him on. Shrugging this idea aside, she convinced herself that she had taken the call more out of the desire to hear about Paco and Jasmine than for any other reason. In the past she would have been flattered by Luke's advances. But now she wasn't even sure what he or she had said. But deep down she knew she had really answered the phone for an entirely different reason. She had wanted to see what effect it would have on Jeb.

By Dianne J. Beale

When she reached the room where her brother was staying, she could hear him talking so knew he must still be on the phone. She ventured onward and was soon in front of the door that she assumed was Jeb's, so she knocked.

"Coming," he said. The door opened shortly after. "Been on the phone this entire time?" he teased. But there was also a promising edge to his voice.

Mar decided to pretend she hadn't noticed. "Actually, no. I cleaned up in the kitchen and then stopped at Mitch's door. But I didn't knock because he was still talking on the phone. Luke wanted me to fill you both in. Why, did you need to talk with him?"

Jeb sighed. "Let's go out to the kitchen and have some coffee. I might even have some shortbread cookies in the pantry, if you like. Was Luke upset or something? You seem concerned."

"No. At least not that I noticed, anyhow. Is there something that I and my brother should know?" Again she received no answer.

When they reached the kitchen, Jeb busied himself preparing the coffee but there was no shortbread. So Mar took it upon herself to quickly mix up her mother's coffeecake recipe. When she turned from placing it into the oven, Jeb was watching her.

"If you keep this up," he said, "the house will never let you leave. It has a life of its own, you know. It'll lock you up, trapping you inside, forever."

Before she could stop herself, she replied, "Not a problem so long as you come with it." Embarrassed at her forwardness, she added, "Well, we'd need a handyman, you know, the house and I. And you can't be too careful when it comes to trust."

They sat at the table while the coffee brewed and the cake baked. Both were quiet. When the coffee finished, Jeb rose to get the cups. Mar crossed to the wall with the oven mitts and then opened the oven to look in on the cake. "Maybe another five minutes," she offered. She took off the mitts and then closed the door. The handle fell loose, pinching her finger, and she couldn't stifle the soft, short sound of pain.

Jeb crossed the room, catching her hand in his. He found the now bluing bruise and slowly brought it to his lips. Kissing it, he released her hand and quietly said, "There. All better." He then returned to the table as if nothing had happened.

Mar stood for a moment in quiet confusion; she began to question if maybe it had never happened and was all in her head. She sat down at the table, and he handed her a cup. She added cream to the coffee and began to stir, never taking her eyes from his. Although he appeared no different from usual, there was a challenging smile in his eyes. And Mar chose to challenge him back.

This is the way that Mitch found them as he entered the kitchen. He shook his head slowly and went over to the oven

By Dianne J. Beale

to remove the cake. The aroma had called to him and he had followed. He set the cake on the table, got small plates, filled a cup with coffee for himself, and then joined them.

Chapter 55

Mitch decided to break the spell. "I'd forgotten just how good life can be! Take away this woman's distractions, and, *voila*, hello baked goods!"

Jeb and Mar laughed in unison. Mitch poured the cream and stirred sugar into his coffee. Then he turned toward Mar. "Did you want something, Sis?"

Mar had to bite her tongue. She and Mitch often sparred in jest. The words were hanging on the tip, waiting for their release: *Yeah, and he's sitting right here.* Instead she answered, "Um, yeah. Luke called and wanted me to fill you both in."

"Oh, so I call him, but he calls you. Well, can't say I blame him. You sure are a lot more interesting. At least, to a man, you are." Mitch batted his eyes and blew Mar kisses. She threw him a dirty look.

"Yeah, well, I imagine he tried your phone, first, but couldn't get through. But you're right that he didn't seem to mind. Said he was glad to hear my voice. It kinda made me uncomfortable, actually."

Mitch seemed surprised. "Really? Why?"

"I don't know. Maybe it's because of how he behaved toward Amelia. He also seemed to be flirting with Trish, before he knew she was taken. I guess I'm just tired of games."

Mitch nodded. "I hear that! So what news did he have to pass along?"

"Well, Jasmine and Paco are together now, recovering nicely. They've been moved to a new location, but he can't say where. He hasn't seen Trish or Amelia, and he said to tell Jeb that the next time he should call the Chief, instead. Oh, and he liked your hat and wonders where he can get one."

Jeb and Mitch both responded, "Whose hat?"

Mar seemed puzzled. "You know? He didn't say. He just said 'tell him' and I guess neither of us realized he had just been talking about you both. At the time I was thinking he meant Jeb. I don't remember why I thought that, but I do remember thinking it." She did know why she thought that, but she was not going to share the reason. She'd been admiring Jeb as he had walked out of the kitchen and then passed her as he headed to his room.

Jeb frowned. "I wasn't wearing a hat when I saw Luke. I don't remember any hats hanging at the office, either. You, Mitch?"

"Hmm. Well, I was wearing a hat one time when we ran into each other, but that was quite some time ago. It was a hotdog hat that one of the youth had given to me."

"Well," interrupted Mar, "I don't wear hats very often, and I'm not *a him*. Maybe it was some sort of code? I don't remember his exact words, though." Mar blushed as she again recalled the reason for her distraction.

"I'll just call him and ask," Mitch reasoned. "It's really that simple."

Mar excused herself and moved to the couch in the other room. She had just switched on the news when Jeb joined her. They sat next to each other, silently watching the happenings of the day. Neither realized how tired they were. When Mitch sat down in the nearby chair, they both jumped, having nodded off a bit.

Mitch spoke. "Says he doesn't remember mentioning a hat. But I didn't quite believe him. Either there was someone in the room with him and he didn't want to draw attention to who had called him, or he's joined the gas lighters."

"Could be," responded Jeb. "Or maybe he's spent so much time with them that he's losing his own grasp on reality."

Laughing now, the three of them shut down the television and headed off to bed. Mitch had jokingly followed Jeb and made Mar walk in a single file behind him, insisting they needed a chaperone. Mar liked the thought behind her brother's teasing but also knew he was sending a mild message to Jeb. But she was too tired to care. Besides, Jeb had decided to just ignore him. She doubted he was even thinking of her in this way.

By Dianne J. Beale

Chapter 56

Mar awoke to knocking at her door. She climbed from the bed, pulled on her robe, and slipped her feet into her nearby sandals. The she went to the door, opening it only a crack.

Jeb stood in an empty, dark hall. He, too, was wearing a robe. He motioned her into the hall, prompting her not to speak. He then pointed her toward the room where her brother was sleeping; his door, too, was slightly cracked.

Mitch moved aside to let her enter and once she had, Jeb motioned for them to close the door and turn the latch. He then readied his gun and headed back down the hall toward the rest of the house.

Mitch and Mar sat, crouched, in the corner of the room, hidden by the bed. They could hear voices. Mitch began to whisper a prayer, and Mar joined in. A gun shot went off and then sirens could be heard nearing their destination.

The leaves outside crunched under the pressure of what sounded to be a scuffle. Then a nearby engine started, resulting in a high-pitch squealing of tires. At least one set of sirens changed direction, most likely to follow the fleeing vehicle.

All this occurred within no more than fifteen minutes, but when Jeb returned, it had seemed much more like hours had passed. He assured them that it was now safe and asked them to join him in the kitchen. They rose from the floor and followed him out of the room.

Once they were all seated, warm drink in their hands, Mar was overwhelmed by the complete hush of the surrounding neighborhood. She was visibly shaken and much paler than Jeb had ever seen her. He reached out to touch her hand, and offered her a weak smile.

As she rotated her position to acknowledge the gesture, she noticed his other hand was cut along the edge and still bleeding. She stopped herself from commenting and instead grasped the hand he had extended. She blushed as she suddenly had a vivid picture of his lips brushing against the bruise on her hand. Their eyes locked for a moment and then Jeb lowered his as if he feared she might understand the emotion she could possibly read in them.

Mitch had hoped that Jeb would volunteer information and wasn't really sure what to ask him. He looked pensive while Mar exuded insecurity. Looking over at his sister, he finally managed to pose a question to Jeb. "Was tonight just a random event? Or were you—we—targeted?"

Jeb ran his injured hand through his hair impatiently. But his voice did not match his appearance. With a polished, trained calm, he answered. His self-control was amazing.

By Dianne J. Beale

As Mar watched him steadily, she gained strength yet understood that his mind was actually racing beneath his composed facade. She listened quietly as he explained that it appeared to be random but that more would be known once forensics had completed their tests. He added that his neighborhood had always been a low-crime area and rarely saw these types of crime. He didn't, however, elaborate on what that type of crime might be. Finally he suggested that they all return to their beds.

Mitch watched the effect this last statement had on Mar. She had mostly settled when a new bout of trembling took hold. Jeb must have noticed it as well: he squeezed her hand. "You could sleep out here if you'd like. I have a pull-out cot, and Mitch could sleep on the couch. It also pulls out into a bed."

Mar wanted to disappear, to become paper thin and slide quietly into one of the kitchen drawers. She chided herself for being so ridiculous and searched her mind for a glimpse as to why she had melted into tremors. But just as she landed on a possible reason, the rug was pulled rudely from under her feet. She didn't have the strength to search again. "I'd like that," she stammered, "But only if it's agreeable to Mitch. I'd hate to put him out."

Within the next half-hour, she was snugly tucked into the couch with Mitch sitting on the nearby cot. She had taken the couch so the bed would not need to be pulled out and there would be more room to move about. Jeb dropped a kiss onto her forehead and then left to return to bed. Mar was glad to see he had left the adjoining door open for them. This was her last thought before she drifted off to sleep.

By Dianne J. Beale

Chapter 57

With the brightened effect of the livingroom blinds, Mar was the first to rise. She could hear birds chirping outside and was instantly comforted with the thought that she was worth more than many birds. She went to the door and let herself out into the back yard.

She sat down in one of the chairs and watched the birds interact. Noticing that the gate was swinging, she walked across the yard to latch it. But as she turned to go back to the chair, her eyes locked onto a bald patch of dark soil. Paw prints stared up at her, mocking her. She became mesmerized–as if frozen–and her steps seemed to halt in mid-air.

Falling to the damp grass, she found herself reaching for her phone. But instead of the pocket in her jeans, her hands encountered a towel-like texture. Looking away from the dirt, she remembered she was still wearing her pajamas. She forced herself to stand to her feet, and willed her legs to move back toward the safety found behind the house's door.

Just as she reached the entrance, Mitch opened it and she let out a scream. He whisked her inside and locked the latch. She shook herself off as if freeing herself from a spider's sticky, hidden web. Words poured from her mouth. "They know we're here. We were the targets, Mitch. They know."

Jeb entered the room, dripping wet, robe clinging closely around him. He had his gun in his hand and a determined expression on his face. He turned on the safety and lowered the gun once he saw only the two of them. "I thought I heard Mar scream," he simply stated. "Is everyone okay?"

Mitch admitted it had been Mar but assured him that he could return to his shower. Mar, after indulging in the knowledge that he had used the familiar form of her name, apologized for the interruption. Once he had left, Mitch turned to address her. "How can you know that? And what were you doing outside?"

"I heard birds. But that's not important. Paw prints. It had to be that same creepy cat."

"Mar, you're not making any sense. The same cat? We're miles from our house."

"Mitch, I just know, okay? Call it discernment or women's intuition, or whatever you want. I know they know we're here." Her voice was filled with conviction and she had never before been so insistent.

As the paw prints he had seen in their kitchen surfaced in his mind, he recalled the short conversation where Amelia had also spoken of a cat. "Look," he sighed, "We'll talk

By Dianne J. Beale

about it later, okay? You're muddy, wet, and covered in leaves. Go take a shower and relax."

Mar shook her head, but Mitch guided her toward the back hall anyhow. Once he had pushed her through the door, he closed it. Mar, exasperated, moved to the door where she could enter her room.

She was about to turn the knob when arms slid around her waist and drew her backward. She maneuvered her position so she could face Jeb instead. He pulled her closely to him, holding her against him. When he loosened his grip, Mar let her hands slide down off his neck. It seemed he would kiss her when he reached and opened her door, instead. "I believe you were on your way to shower," he offered. "I'm glad you and your brother aren't hurt." Then he gently pushed her into the room and closed the door.

She stood motionless until she heard the hall door open and close. Then she went to her suitcases, chose what she would wear for the day, and headed for the shower. A short while later, she appeared again in the living room. She had smelled coffee and had been heading for the kitchen, but the back door was open. Jeb was standing over the patch of dirt, so she decided to join him, instead.

She was about to greet him and then give him her thoughts when he swiftly rose to his feet and insisted that they go back in. As he gently touched her elbow and guided her back across the yard, Mar found herself growing angry. She broke away from him as if she'd been manhandled.

With deliberate attitude, she then returned herself to the house.

Once inside, Mar ignored Mitch and poured herself a cup of coffee. She added creamer and then took the cup with her as she returned to her room. She sat down at the desk, unsuccessfully concentrating on the devotions that were before her. As she read the first sentence for the fourth time, a knock came at the door.

Intent on ignoring it, and hoping that the person would just assume she was in the restroom, she set aside her devotional materials and drew out her Bible, instead. She had planned to read the daily Scripture passage but was interrupted by Jeb's voice. "Mar," he implored, "I thought you didn't like to play games. Open the door so we can talk this through."

Mar wanted nothing more than to lock the door loudly, but she grudgingly admitted that such behavior would appear rather childish. She opened the door and faced Jeb, defiantly. "I am not playing. I'm trying to do the right thing. I've found that if I'm upset then it is rarely a good time for me to talk. I don't want to…" her voice was stopped by his kiss.

At first it was no more than the basic kiss a father might give to his daughter; she had friends whose families would drop such kisses. But hers had not taught her to kiss lip to lip. Besides, the kiss also had a determinedness that caused

By Dianne J. Beale

her to fight against it. Yet she found herself being inched into the room with him blocking any way of escape.

He lifted his head and placed his hand on her chin. "I've asked you both to keep a low profile. How many other times have you been outside? Why were you out there today?"

Mar moved to push past him, but he blocked her way. Frustrated, she pushed her hands against his chest. "Move out of my way!" she ordered.

"No. I will not. I want answers, Mar. Why must you be so stubborn? Why do you not listen to me? You and Mitch are here for your own safety."

"Well, I don't like it here!" she seethed. "Mitch, alone, is bad enough. Dealing with Andres, far worse. And now I have to deal with you, as well. I don't need three masters."

Jeb was growing impatient. "Masters? Are you now grouping us with Andres? Mitch and I are not striving to be masters, Mar. Friends, yes. Brothers in Christ? Definitely. We're people who care about you. But that's the problem, isn't it? We care? You've taken quite a different tune from yesterday," he scoffed.

"Yeah, well," she stammered.

"Yes?"

Mar sighed and tried again to leave. But he refused to let her by. "Stop that," she insisted.

"No."

"Just leave me alone, okay?"

"I can't."

Mar slumped against him in defeat. "I don't know what to say."

"I do," he comforted. "We only want to protect you. We want you to be safe." He gently kissed her cheek.

She cautiously raised her eyes to meet his. "We? You've been spending too much time with Mitch."

"Maybe," he answered, "But my reasons are far less noble, I assure you."

Mar lowered her eyes, blushing. She was staring at his top shirt button when he lifted her chin. She was positive that he must be reading her every thought and learning her innermost secrets. Scanning her face, his eyes then locked onto hers. "May I kiss you?" he asked.

She wished she had the confidence to tease him–to say that it was a little late to ask, wasn't it? But she knew the other kisses had been nearly platonic. His eyes were now asking for much more than that.

She heard herself answer as if from a distance. She had answered yes. And now she was kissing him back, her arms raised around his neck, her fingers playing with his hair.

Time seemed at a standstill. She wanted this moment to never end: when he was about to raise his head, she drew him back, kissing him again. And time obliged by freezing them as if a painted portrait that had just been framed. Mar knew she had spoken the truth: if she had to stay in the house, she'd relent if it came with him.

By Dianne J. Beale

Chapter 58

The catcall whistling caught them both by surprise. Jeb, slightly flustered, planted a final kiss on Mar's forehead, smiled, and then meandered down the hall, disappearing into his room. Mar made a much more difficult recovery.

Mitch had no intention of easing her discomfort, either. "What was that?" he badgered. "I thought you had something going with Luke. I guess maybe I should have put my foot down last night when we had the coffeecake."

"I don't want to talk about it," Mar managed.

"Really, I never would have guessed. That was not just your average, nonchalant kiss. What are you thinking? We hardly know him."

Mar went to the desk, picked up her coffee, and then stated that she was going to the kitchen and that he could do whatever he liked. But Mitch just followed. "It's a good thing I was here to break you two apart. Kissing a man like that is risky enough, but kissing a man like that with a bed nearby…" Mitch's voice trailed off. After a short pause, he added, "I think maybe we need to request a different safe house… and a different body guard, as well."

"Drop it, Mitch. I'm a big girl now and you have no right. I can't believe you think I'd sleep with him. I don't think he'd have me even if I offered. But thank you for your vote of confidence."

"You're still not making any sense. I'm not saying that you would intend for it to happen. You must realize that you've only kissed one other man in the way that you just kissed Jeb. Mar, please listen to me. He broke your very substance, remember? I can't go through that again."

Mar just stopped walking and turned toward her brother. "I'm not asking you to. Forget it. I'll not let it happen again. Okay? How dare you remind me of my past! We agreed we'd never talk of it again. I was young and stupid. Now I'm older, and still stupid, is that it? You have Trish and I have no one and now I'm not sure I ever want someone. Happy?"

Mitch sputtered, "You didn't even kiss Anthony that way, Mar. I now know you were engaged, but it was an innocent romance with Anthony. Don't let Jeb become another Jack."

Mar began her walk back toward the kitchen and expected her brother would follow. But Mitch had decided to have a chat with Jeb. Not realizing this was his plan, Mar had a momentary feeling of relief. She dumped her cold coffee and poured herself a new cup. She set it on the table, along with a bowl of cereal, and then sat down.

By Dianne J. Beale

Her prayer was not for the food. And she didn't dare voice it aloud: *God, please fix this. I can't stay angry at Mitch. I'm not strong enough to face Jeb. Help Mitch to not be angry with Jeb. And help me. I need Your strength. I'm falling and I don't see the ledge. I'm trusting You to catch me.*

Chapter 59

Throughout the next few weeks there were no signs of Jeb. Mar began to wish she could just slip away. She knew nothing of Mitch's confrontation so assumed that Jeb was never really interested. He just knew how to play the part.

She would stop throughout the days and chide herself for believing he was different. She just needed to get away-to leave this house-and find a quiet, lonely place where she could think.

More than a month had passed since her last devotions, and she hadn't read even the short Scripture passages. Her Bible still sat on the desk in the same place it had the day that Jeb had kissed her. She thought about the friend that had given her that Bible. She was Jack's sister-one of her oldest and dearest friends. But it had been this friend's brother who had ripped out Mar's soul.

Yet they remained as close as sisters, even with the less frequent visits. They talked regularly, but never about the past. Tears came to her eyes as she remembered the perceived warmth of Jeb's eyes. How stupid could one person be?

By Dianne J. Beale

Mar dug out the *pay-as-you-go* cell and then locked herself in the restroom. Then she dialed.

"Hello?" came the deep, sultry voice.

"Norma Mae?" queried Mar.

"Yes, this is Norma. Is that you, Marge?" Her voice seemed to perk up a little at this possible realization.

"Yeah. How've you been?"

"Better now that I've heard from you. Did you know that your church is all over the news?"

"Yeah, it's been pretty weird. I wondered if you might have room for a temporary roommate."

"Really? Are you coming to visit? I would love to see ya! When ya coming?"

"I thought maybe I'd take the bus down tomorrow morning, if that's okay."

"The early one?"

"Yeah. If that's okay."

"Okay? No, Honey, it's not okay." There was a long pause, but when Mar didn't speak, Norma continued. "It's grand, I mean. I can't wait to see ya!"

"Me too. See you tomorrow, then. I gotta go get ready. Bye."

Mar hung up the phone and then sifted through the menus until she had erased all evidence of the call. Then she turned it off and returned the phone to the agreed hiding place. Next, she pulled out a small backpack and began to shift things around, taking only what she deemed was absolutely necessary.

Once the back pack was ready, she slid it under the bed. Then she took her cell phone out from her pocket and pushed it into one of the bags she would leave behind.

When Mitch disappeared into his room later that day, Mar slipped on a few of his dirty clothes, shoved her hair under a baseball cap, donned sunglasses, and slipped out the back door and then out through the gate. She walked to the corner drug store and went inside.

Casually, she made her way to the back left corner and then took two hundred dollars from the ATM. She put the money and receipt into a zippered compartment in the jeans she was wearing and then pulled out a five from the pocket above in order to buy some gum. Then she left.

Returning to the back yard, she latched the gate, and crept into the living room. Once back inside her room, she removed her brother's things, transferred the money and gum to the front of her back pack, and then returned Mitch's clothes to their proper place. Then she went back to hide in her room.

Breathing a little easier, she sat down at the desk and began to read her Bible. She was about to go make lunch when Mitch knocked to tell her he'd made enough for two and asked if she'd like to join him. Mar acknowledged with a quick "Okay" and then said a short prayer, asking for

By Dianne J. Beale

strength. She went out to the table and sat down while Mitch served them.

Misinterpreting his sister's wan appearance, Mitch found himself confessing. "Look, Mar," he began, "About Jeb. Um, I'm sorry. I didn't expect him to stop talking to you."

"What did you do, Mitch? He's not only been not talking to me, but I haven't even seen him." She said this even though she had convinced herself that she really didn't care. If Jeb had truly been as interested as it had seemed, wouldn't he have defied her brother? As she recalled the interest that had shone in his eyes, and the kiss that had seemed to seal it, she began to feel shame at having believed.

Mitch, watching her, continued. "All I did was ask him to slow down. I told him that he needed to be sure of what it was he wanted and convinced that he could deliver. I said that if he couldn't guarantee that you'd not be left with a broken heart then I wanted him to stay away. But I didn't expect him to ignore you completely. I thought he would at least explain."

"Well, I guess that's it then. He's decided he's not sure. I don't see how he could be, actually. It's probably for the best. I don't know what's gotten into me. Don't worry about it, okay?"

Although this is what she said, and with an uncommon, calm conviction, her heart was screaming at her. She coldly ignored it, using the calculated ease that she had trained herself to use after having lost Jack. "The heart is deceitfully wicked above all things." Ignore it. When her mind rebelled by conjuring up Jeb's sincere, determined face with his searching, smiling eyes, she shook the image off.

"What's wrong?" Mitch asked.

Mar suddenly realized that she had been actually shaking her head while clearing her thoughts. "Nothing," she lied. "Just a mild headache."

Mitch saw that her smile never reached her eyes but knew better than to question it. He now regretted his interference and made a decision to fix things the next time he saw Jeb.

The rest of the meal passed in silence. Mitch excused himself, forgetting even to rinse off his dishes. Mar mechanically cleaned up and ran the dishwasher. Then she turned on the television in hopes of burying any sudden bursts of rational thought that might try to break in.

Hours later, Jeb snuck past her as she slept. He, too, appeared edgy, sleepless–almost gray. He entered his room before Mitch even had the chance to emerge from his. When he did, he went to close the hall door. Seeing Mar asleep, he swore softly, left the door open, and returned to his room.

By Dianne J. Beale

Chapter 60

Mar awoke to the hissing of the television as it went off the air. She grabbed the remote and shut it down. Slightly disoriented, she realized she was hungry. She went into the kitchen, mixed up a breakfast shake, and then drank it slowly, as if dazed. She then programmed the coffee to come on at 5:00 a.m. and headed back toward her room. The bus left early and she would need to be ready.

As she headed for her room, she heard moaning. Despite herself, she walked down the hall, past Mitch's and on to Jeb's. As the moaning continued, she knocked loudly on his door. At last it opened. "Yes?" Jeb snapped.

"I heard you moaning. Are you okay?"

"Peachy. I'm sorry I woke you. Go back to bed."

The sarcasm and coldness fed Mar's defiance. She raised her wrist to his head and then nonchalantly answered him. "You are not 'peachy.' You're burning up." Looking past him, she added, "Your bed is drenched."

"Mar, please, just go to bed. I've been taking care of myself for a long time now. I do not need your help."

"I never said you did. In fact, I'm glad you don't. I don't want anyone to need me. People need God, not people. I admit I've been stupid enough to believe that you might want me, but don't worry, I'm over that now." She turned away, but he stopped her by placing his hand on her shoulder. She tried to shake it off, refusing to turn back.

"I do want you," he admitted. "But your brother's right. I'm a cop. I have no business involving myself in a relationship, especially not with you. I risk my life daily. Haven't you experienced enough loss already? I want only to be with you, share with you, love with you. But I can't promise I won't break your heart. I would never leave you by choice, Mar, but look how I live." As Jeb trailed off, his hand dropped from her shoulder. "Just go, okay?"

Mar instead turned to face him. "I guess I don't even get a say. Okay, I'll go. At least let me fix your bed and get you some medicine. Sit there." Mar pointed at the small couch he had in his room and then went to the linen closet. She pulled out crisp, clean bedding, including an extra blanket. She then returned to his room.

She stripped the bed and changed the pillow cases. Then she made his bed and helped him into it. "I'll get you some medicine, now. I know I have flu tablets somewhere. Mitch and I each get sick at least once during this season so I try to keep it on hand."

She dragged the removed bedding into the hall and then went into her room. She pulled the hidden phone from hiding and found she had a voice message. She'd forgotten to block her number when she'd called her friend.

By Dianne J. Beale

Sorry Hon. I hope you get this. Jack's in town. So don't come, okay? I hate it when he does this. I didn't know he was coming. Sorry. I'll assume you got this unless I get a call from the station tomorrow. If you call me then, we'll just have to somehow work it out so Jack doesn't see you. Okay. Sorry. Bye.

Mar erased the message and then the menus. Then she put it back away. Taking medicine from a bag, she returned to Jeb. As she passed the restroom, she got some water for him to take it with.

He swallowed the medicine and water without a fight. Mar set the remaining medicine on the night stand and then wrote down the dosage and time on a notepad nearby. As she got up to leave, he reached for her.

"So cold," he pleaded. "Please…"

"Let go and I'll get you more blankets," she answered. She went back to the linen closet, took the two remaining blankets, and returned to cover him with them. Despite this effort, he was still shivering. "I'll be right back," she assured him.

She went into her room and pulled the warmer comforter from off her bed. This left one blanket for herself. Adding this blanket to the pile, she turned to walk away from Jeb.

But he continued to shiver, so she made a snap decision to lie down next to him, but on the top most blanket. She was still dressed in her daytime clothes, and planned to move as soon as he warmed a bit, so wasn't worried about how it might look.

Jeb immediately moved close to her, pulling one arm out from the covers and wrapping it around her as if in protection. The rest of his body remained encased in blankets and pillows.

She took his hand in hers, hugging it to her. And this is how Mitch found them when he rose at seven. Jeb's door was open, bedding was piled high in the hallway, and the night stand was cluttered with papers and medicine. Mar was snuggled next to a buried mummy that he assumed to be Jeb.

Although far from happy, he left them this way. He was done meddling. He went on to the kitchen to get coffee and breakfast. Besides, he needed to touch base with Trish.

By Dianne J. Beale

Chapter 61

Mar awoke to a groaning Jeb. She shifted carefully off the bed, took his glass, and went into the restroom. She set his glass down on the sink and then closed and locked the door as she freshened herself. Filling the glass with water, she then returned to Jeb's side.

"Jeb?" she whispered. "Jeb, it's time for more medicine."

Jeb turned slowly and then opened his eyes. "Hi," he mouthed. His throat was dry from the moaning. He tried to clear it.

Mar handed him the water and the medicine. The fever had left his eyes, but he was still sweating quite a bit. He took the medicine and drank the water thankfully. "Do I have any more clean sheets?" he asked.

"I'll check." Mar set the glass back onto the night stand and headed out into the hall. She found another sheet set and returned to his side. "Can you sit in the chair while I fix your bed?" she asked.

"I'll go use the restroom instead," he answered. He slid himself out of bed and pulled on his robe.

Mar pulled off the bedding as she heard the shower come on. She made up the bed, changed the pillowcases, gave him her last blanket from her bed, and then carried everything she considered to be tainted out to the laundry room. Just in time, she remembered he was showering so did not turn on the machine. Instead she returned to his room.

"I hate to ask," he voiced a few minutes later. "But can I get a short second of privacy?"

Mar unconsciously ran her eyes over his body as she answered. The robe was loosely fitted but could not hide his muscular frame. She smiled. "I'll just go start the washer," she said.

When she returned, he was back in bed. She asked if he needed anything, and he said he just wanted to sleep. When she had acknowledged this, she went out into the hall.

Just as she was about to close the door, he stopped her with a question. "Did someone call in for me?" She shook her head. "Could you? Would you mind?" he asked. She told him she would, and he thanked her. Then, he added "for everything." She nodded, reminded him to write the time he took his medicine on the notebook, and then left, closing the door.

She made the call to his employer, apologizing that it was late, and then entered the kitchen. Mitch was on the phone with Trish. She poured herself some coffee and then,

By Dianne J. Beale

at the shock of tasting cold, she put it into the microwave, trying not to listen.

"Well, I don't know what to tell you. I'm sorry, okay? I have no idea when I'll be able to see you." There was a pause as he listened. "Right. Okay. Obviously, I was wrong to assume that you … What? Why? Trish, I can't marry a woman who doesn't trust me. Marriage is all about trust." He stoically ended the call.

He turned to look at Mar as she removed her coffee. "Shut up! Okay? You know nothing about anything! You dated Jack for three years, and the whole time he was engaged to SOMEONE ELSE! Now, you're making it with a man you hardly know. What? One month, maybe?"

Mar was startled. He had never spoken to her this way. Although angry, she decided not to show it. She knew he didn't really mean it. He was frustrated and hurt. "I was a lot younger then," she calmly began. "And actually, if you include the time that I worked with Jeb prior to our move-in, I've known him a bit longer than you have. We weren't 'making it,' either, as you so delicately put it. He's got a fever of a hundred and four."

Mitch didn't even apologize. He just threw his dishes dramatically into the sink, breaking a plate, and left the room. *I hope that didn't go into the disposal*, she thought as she quietly followed to be sure he didn't plan to bother Jeb. But he went directly to his room and slammed the door.

She returned to the kitchen and ate, and then unloaded the dishwasher. Then, she put all of the new dishes in, but turned the sign to say "dirty" as it was not yet full enough to run. She had taken it upon herself to add the sign after she'd almost accidentally used dirty dishes the second day she was there.

Next, she went into the laundry room and moved the sheets from the washer to the dryer. Then, she put the three blankets into the washer, set it, and left. Jeb still had almost four hours left before he'd need more meds. She decided to slip into her room and take a nap. With the alarm set, she slowly slipped off to sleep.

By Dianne J. Beale

Chapter 62

Vines were choking her. Why couldn't she break them? Where was she?

Looking at her surroundings, she saw she was again at the church. The vines suddenly fell away, and she was dressed in an elaborate, lacy, satiny, wedding gown. Luke was standing next to her, smiling down, eyes shining. Panic began to grip her, and the dress again appeared as binding, merciless vines. She was being pulled down the aisle, and Mitch was nowhere to be seen. She struggled, but Luke pulled at her all the more.

The end of the aisle placed her between Jack and Luke. Each was smiling almost groggily. She began to struggle again, and the vines became the gorgeous dress once more. On her finger was a dark, almost black emerald. It seemed to speak to her in hisses.

"Mar, darling," she heard. She looked up to see Andres beaming down at her. "You've never looked more stunning," he said.

She felt something moving on her hand. The ring had become a miniature serpent. It was golden with a green head, ready to strike. She screamed!

Mar awoke to Mitch pleading with her gently. "Mar," he coaxed. "Mar, it's me. Wake up. It's just a bad dream. Mar?"

Mar slowly opened her eyes. Tears fell off her lashes and slid down her cheeks. She grabbed her brother, burying her face in his shoulder.

"It was just a dream," he repeated. "You're safe with me. We're together. You're safe."

She began to cry. His voice threw her into another time. "But no, Mitch," she heard herself say. "Momma's gone. Daddy's dying. It's not okay. We're not safe."

Mitch was jarred at these words. Mar hadn't had dreams about their parents for a number of years. He was startled and had pulled away.

Mar snapped out of it. "I'm sorry, Mitch. I didn't know what I was saying," she pleaded. "Your assurance–I think it triggered–please. Mitch!"

Mitch had gotten up from the edge of the bed and moved away. He seemed to almost be sleepwalking, he was so unaware. Mar had used the exact same sentence she had once spoken before; this engulfed him in a grief that he thought he had finished experiencing long before. Didn't she know how hard he had tried to protect her? Tried to make her life happy, maybe even normal? Well, obviously he had failed. "No, Mar," he wrenched away, "I can't." Then he left.

Mar pulled herself up from the bed and tried knocking on her brother's door. But he refused to answer. A twist at

By Dianne J. Beale

the knob revealed that he had locked it. Overcome with helplessness, she instead returned to the laundry room. She folded the sheets and then moved the blankets to the dryer. Placing the comforter into the washer, she again adjusted the settings, and carried the sheets to the linen closet. She jumped when she turned and Jeb was closing in on her.

"I heard a scream," he was saying. "Then you weren't in your room and Mitch's door is locked, and he's not answering. You guys okay?"

Mar was determined to be strong. She could see that the fever still gripped him. "You should be in bed," she chided.

"Acknowledged," he managed, although impatiently. "But didn't you scream?" he insisted.

"Yes," she admitted. "I had a nightmare in the middle of the day."

Jeb lifted her face so he could probe her eyes. "You're not okay," he said. "Come with me."

He pulled her with him toward the couch and sat down with her. Then, he took her hand, encouraging her to confide in him. "Please, Mar. Speak to me."

Mar stopped resisting him and nuzzled her face into his shoulder. At first she could only cry. Then finally, "I had a bad dream, and then Mitch woke me, to comfort me. But he used the same words he had used when our parents…" she stumbled, "the night our parents died."

She fell silent for a moment. Jeb took in breath as if he were in pain. She continued, "We had words earlier in the kitchen. And we both were angry. I think he might have thought I said what I did just to be spiteful. But I didn't mean... the words just came out. It was as if I was again sixteen; he was just about to turn nineteen. He was being strong for me. He fought for the will to be honored with him as guardian. He gave up his hopes, his dreams, everything for me. But the dream had nothing to do with any of this. It was just his voice–the comforting, and his protection from the pain. I didn't intend..."

"Of course you didn't," Jeb consoled. "What happened in the dream?"

Mar raised her eyes to his. "I'm sorry, Jeb. I'd rather not say. I..."

Jeb, although feeling as if he'd been slapped, loosened his hold slowly so as not to convey this. "Maybe you should try calling your brother's cell," he suggested. "I think maybe you two need each other right now." He then reminded her that he needed to refresh his medicine, and he moved to leave.

Mar wasn't fooled. She saw in his face the pain she had caused. But she agreed he should go. She waited for him to disappear and returned to the laundry room. But it was too soon for anything to have finished cycling.

As she headed back to her room, she was relieved to see Mitch's door was open. She went to him in hopes that he would se she'd been as disturbed as he. But he wasn't alone. He and Jeb were involved in what appeared to be a lengthy

By Dianne J. Beale

and in-depth conversation. She backed away before they had seen her and went back into her room, closing and locking the door. Throwing herself on the bed, she cried uncontrollably into her pillow. It wasn't long before she was again asleep.

Chapter 63

Darkness concealed the room when Mar finally awoke. She opened her eyes, waited for them to adjust, and then went into the adjoining restroom.

Returning to her room, she heard the doorbell ring. She went to her cloaked window, moved aside the curtain, and used her fingers to separate her blinds. Luke's car was parked in the driveway.

She quickly moved back to her bed, ready to lie back down if it became necessary. She sat quietly, listening for voices. The doorbell rang again.

Why wasn't anyone getting the door? She got up from her bed and slipped out into the hall. Mitch had just done the same from his room. Both turned toward Jeb's room. Mar was the first to move. Then Mitch joined her. They knocked on his door. Finally, there was motion. Jeb opened the door and joined them in the hall.

"It's almost midnight," Jeb complained. "Who'd be here at this time of night?"

Mar answered, "I took a peek, and although I didn't see the person, the car looks quite a bit like Luke's. Why would he be here?"

"Why indeed?" repeated Mitch. "Are you sure it's his car?"

"Not totally, but it sure looked like it. I was trying to be discreet, though."

"Well, since they're not leaving, I'd better go take a look. You two stay back here, okay?" Jeb went toward the adjoining rooms as Mitch and Mar waited quietly in the hallway.

Then they heard argumentative voices. Mar tensed as she heard her name. She wondered if Mitch was hearing things better than she could. He was closer to the wall. But they soon backed away into the hall's center once more as the door opened. In stepped Luke and Jeb.

"They're moving you two to a safer location. It seems that Mar snuck out to use her ATM card the other day, and they're convinced your safety's been compromised."

Mar trembled as she realized how stupid she'd been. Jeb wouldn't even look at her.

"When? I was here the entire time," countered Mitch. He looked directly at Mar. "Mar?" he queried.

Mar looked down at her feet. "Yes, it's true. I did it. But our position isn't compromised. I wore your clothes with my hair stuffed up under a baseball cap, and I had on Jeb's sunglasses." Even as she said it, she realized it wasn't true. She'd called the church just this morning to call in sick for Jeb. She'd given no thought to their safety. She'd felt happy and safe and forgot they were in hiding. She should have called in to the station, not the church.

Luke's voice cut into hers scathingly, "You can't let your feelings rule your actions," he said. "Not only did you take out the money, but then you called in sick for Jeb. What were you thinking?" Then, he turned to Jeb. "You of ALL people should know enough not to involve yourself with a client. You've given her a false sense of security."

Jeb's eyes burned dangerously, but he didn't say anything. He turned to look at Mitch.

"We're not going anywhere, not at this hour, anyway," determined Mitch.

"Then you're no longer guaranteed our protection," shot Luke. "Oh, and Jeb? The chief says you're off the force 'til further notice. He doesn't like you seducing clients, either."

"You know where the door is, Luke," Jeb said. "I suggest you use it." Luke turned and walked back out to the other part of the house. When they heard the door slam, they followed.

As Jeb locked up, Mar slumped to the floor. Mitch moved toward her, thinking she had fainted. But she was sitting on her knees, crying.

"What was I thinking? Well I wasn't thinking. He's right. I let my emotions get the best of me. I was angry and hurt and frustrated. Then I was happily playing the unwed housewife. I'm such a fool."

By Dianne J. Beale

"Must you always be so hard on yourself? We've suspected Luke of being on the wrong side for practically forever. I wasn't about to go anywhere with him, and I wasn't going to let him take you, either."

"But I wasn't talking about that. I was talking about my trip to the ATM. And then today I called the very people we think we're hiding from. I gave Luke the ammunition he was looking for."

Jeb spoke up, "You suspected Luke? Why haven't you mentioned this before?"

"We thought his being a double agent had explained it away. But how did he know about you and Mar?"

"He didn't, unless he's been spying on us. Or, I suppose he might have assumed since she made the mistake of calling in for me…"

Mar stopped crying. "There's an us?" She looked at Jeb.

Jeb reached down to help her to her feet. "I thought we were clear here. We agreed not to play games. What am I missing?"

Mar looked from Jeb to Mitch and then back to Jeb. "I thought. Oh, never mind what I thought. Do you think we should move ourselves somewhere else anyway? Just to be safe?"

Jeb smiled. "Women," he said. Then he added, "What they don't realize is that we already have a plan."

He motioned them into his back yard. Then he lowered his voice to a whisper once they were there. "We need to quietly get ready to leave. I actually *am* a double agent. I really work for the FBI. We've been tracking these guys for awhile now. At first we thought drugs. But now we suspect it might not be any more than a crazed power-hungry man running a basic cult. Either way, we need to quietly pack up and leave. My partner will get a car ready. We'll leave by the gate."

They went back into the house and were ready shortly after. Mar and Mitch had already adjusted to living from bags, and Jeb had even set aside a few packed bags, just in case. Soon, they were all seated in a bulletproof, dark-windowed SUV that was taking them to a country cottage somewhere in Canada. And Jeb, his position at the church compromised, and having been fired from the police force, was going to join them.

By Dianne J. Beale

Chapter 64

As the days in the cottage increased to weeks and then months, Mitch seemed to become a caged animal. They had everything they needed. The FBI had removed their phones completely, but they replaced them with non-traceable, disposable cells similar to the one they had originally purchased for Trish. Each had about five hours of talk time.

Jeb and Mar had been swimming together almost daily, and were growing closer all the time. Mar tried to unsuccessfully convince Mitch that he should try again with Trish. Eventually, he angrily told her to drop it in a manner which made her do just that. She now understood that Trish was Mitch's Jack.

Mar, tired of the mood swings, took a phone out by the lake. As she dialed Amelia, she cautiously watched over her shoulder. Jeb was sleeping on the outdoor hammock, and Mitch was taking an afternoon shower. As a precaution, she blocked her outgoing number.

"Hello?"

"Hi Amelia, it's Mar. How are things going for you?"

Amelia gasped, "Mar! Oh, it's so good to hear from you!"

"You, too. Have you worked out the name problem yet?"

"Yes, I have. I'm finally a free woman. I even feel free. And with Andres arrested… oh, you don't know that. Well, he'll be on trial in just a few days. Luke's the main witness, and he's engaged to Trish now. Can you believe it? She's so excited. I'm sorry about Mitch, though. But Trish didn't treat him right. She didn't deserve him. She doesn't understand real love. She's gotta have a physical body she can see and touch. I'm not sure she deserves Luke, either, but they seem happy enough."

"Wow. That's quite a bit to take in. Do you know what's happened with our house?"

"Oh, Mar, I'm sorry. I thought you knew. It burned to the ground a few days ago. And the church, well, with the scandal and all, has been permanently closed down. Will you and Mitch be coming back soon?"

Mar was shocked, but she knew she couldn't show it. "Well, I'm not sure. At least not now. I don't have a job, or a house, there now. I had planned to return. Well I gotta go. I'm happy for you and we're both praying for you. Bye."

"Oh. Okay. Call me again. Bye then."

Mar decided to call Betsy. Kyle answered. "No, Betsy's on a woman's retreat," he said. "I think she gets back next Wednesday," he added. When Mar asked about Liza, she found that she had gone on the retreat with her mother. Mar thanked Kyle and hung up. Returning to the cottage, she

By Dianne J. Beale

found Mitch and Jeb talking. Neither noticed as she slipped back inside. Her entire life outlook had changed with just two phone calls. And her good friend, Betsy, was unavailable for comment.

She made her way into the kitchen and began to cook. Soon, the aroma had both men coming inside.

"What spurred this?" Jeb inquired.

"She's either sad or bored," offered Mitch. "Which is it?"

"Maybe a little of both," she shared. "Or maybe neither," she added.

Mitch spotted the phone. "Who'd you call?" he guessed correctly.

"People," she retorted.

Jeb walked over to where she was stirring the sauce. He took the spoon from her hand and then pulled her toward him. "Your mysteriousness is not funny," he said, "What's wrong?"

Mar pulled away from him and moved nearer her brother. Then, she turned to Jeb, "Why didn't you tell us? Is your house still standing?"

"What are you talking about?" Jeb replied. "Who did you talk to?"

She turned toward Mitch. "Amelia said our house burned down, that Trish is engaged to Luke, that Andres is about to be tried, and that Luke is the main witness."

The Uninvited

Turning toward Jeb, she shot out, "When were you going to share all this?"

Jeb stared at Mar in disbelief. "You think I knew all this? You think I'd mislead you? I can't believe I ever thought of asking you to marry me. I'm glad I found out, now, how you really feel."

Jeb walked out of the cottage, slamming the door. Mar just burst into tears and ran to her room. Mitch shut down the burners and oven and went out into the next room. Their lives were in ruins. Well, if Amelia was telling the truth, they were. He decided to call his friend from the other state to see if he could get some help with determining the truth from fiction. He'd see what Jeff made of it all. He could trust Jeff.

By Dianne J. Beale

Chapter 65

When Mar exited her room about an hour later, Mitch had moved everything to storage containers and fridged it. It appeared that he had retreated to his room, and that Jeb had not yet returned.

She poured herself a glass of water and then determinedly returned to her room. She pulled out the outfit she'd worn the first time she and Jeb had kissed, and then went to shower.

After her shower, she sprayed her body with the rose petal spray she'd worn, as well. Then, she dressed quickly and went back to her room. She dug out her makeup. He'd never seen her in makeup. She hardly ever wore it. Then, once ready, she ran her brush repeatedly through her hair, and then left to find Jeb.

She saw him almost immediately. He was sitting at the edge of the lake, throwing in stones. She walked right up to him. The sun was setting, casting a beautiful orange glow all around. She slid her arms around him.

"I'm sorry, Jeb. I know you've been just as much in the dark as us. I also know I can't fix how I reacted. I can't take back what I said. I can tell you I'm scared, though. The only person, who really knows me besides Mitch, is you. And you're amazing, and I'm just a nobody. Eventually, when you realize this, I'll have to say goodbye again. But my heart won't let you go."

She paused, took in some air, and then continued. "So my defenses finally found a way to sabotage it all. I don't deserve you, I know you're better off without me, yet I still selfishly want you. What I didn't realize is that I want whatever I can have, even if it's just friendship. I'll take what I can get for whatever period of time, regardless of the future pain and loss I'll have to face."

Mar felt as if her heart were melting. Tears seemed to be filling her very essence, and yet her eyes remained dry. "Yet at the same time, I've been on the defensive for so long… well, never mind. I just wanted you to know that I love you more than life itself. God will always be first in my life, but no matter what, I will always love you. And I'm sorry… sorry for everything."

Jeb remained motionless. He didn't shake her off, but he didn't respond either. He had stopped tossing the rocks, but as soon as Mar released him, the stones again began to hit the water. He hadn't even acknowledged her. She felt defeated. Her preparations had been pointless.

It's better this way, she thought. *Mitch was right. I knew Jack for three years. He knew Trish for more, and dated her for the last two. And Anthony was actually a complete stranger. Do Jeb and I really know each other? The answer is obviously "no."*

By Dianne J. Beale

Mar walked slowly back up to the cottage. She laid down in the hammock, regretting it almost at once. Jeb's cologne filled her senses. She closed her eyes and begged the tears not to come. But they didn't listen. She didn't have the energy to sob, but the tears still fell, one by one. She just laid there silently, not feeling anything; she was once again empty, and this time, completely alone. She no longer cared about her house. She only wished she had the ability to dissolve with her tears.

When he spoke, she heard him as if from a long way off. She didn't even open her eyes. It was as if he wasn't even really there, as if she'd imagined him. "I need time, Mar. You say you didn't mean it, but it feels as if each word, each accusation, was a poison dart that was meant to kill. I want badly to pretend everything's okay, but I can't. I've gone completely numb and will have to wait for our love to either grow again, or to die. I can't pretend that nothing has changed. I can't even say that I'm sorry. I'm not the one who did or said anything wrong. I just need time to sort it all out. There are things I've not shared; things I know you've not shared with me. And that doesn't work. Not in a marriage, anyway. We've both been hiding, revealing only a fraction of who we are." Mar opened her eyes because she had to know he had really come. When she saw the pain, she wished she hadn't. She took his hand and kissed the scar. He showed no noticeable response. She ignored the ice as it slowly encased her heart. But this time she deserved it. This time it was all her fault.

Mar stayed still long after Jeb had finished talking and even after he'd gone inside. She felt her last tear fall. She was completely dried up. When Mitch arrived and asked her to please come inside, she watched herself from the safety of her newly formed glacier. It was as if she had completely died and was watching her body respond. She forced a smile and followed him in.

Mitch asked if she was okay. Although she knew it was hollow, she calmly replied with a "yes" and gave him another empty smile. He accepted it as her being tired. He knew he was.

By Dianne J. Beale

Chapter 66

Mitch was talking on the phone when Mar surfaced the next afternoon. She had stayed in her room for as long as she felt she could without bringing on Mitch's inquiry.

She could tell that Jeb was in the kitchen, so she waved to Mitch and went outside instead. She walked down to the lake and then back up to the cottage. Then, she saw a bike path that appeared to cut through the trees. Why hadn't she noticed it before? She went over to it and was soon walking under a canopy of trees.

She wasn't sure how long she'd been hiking but was beginning to wish she'd returned to the cottage to pack a backpack. She was both thirsty and hungry. She was about to turn back when she saw there was a clearing ahead. So, she continued onward, hoping she'd find a spring.

But when she arrived, the clearing appeared to only be a round space of no trees. She turned to go back but heard voices. Something told her that she needed to hide, so she climbed off the path into an especially thick area of trees. She watched as about twenty young men arrived in the circle. She couldn't hear what they were saying, but it appeared to be some sort of meeting. She stayed hidden even after they'd all biked away. Finally, she found her way back onto the path and hurried back toward the cottage. Once she reached the porch, she nearly collapsed. Her arms and legs were badly scratched, and there were twigs stuck in her hair. She willed herself to enter and managed to make it to the kitchen.

"Mar?" she heard Mitch call. But her throat was too dry to respond. She bumped a spoon off the table instead. When he turned and saw her, his face went white. "Are you okay? What happened?"

She signaled that she'd like water and he got it for her. Then, she finally was able to speak. "I followed a bike trail but then came to a clearing where I heard voices. Something told me I should hide, so I did. About a good twenty or so college-age boys arrived on bikes. I couldn't hear what they were saying, but it looked like some kind of meeting. Once they left, I waited to be sure they were gone, and then hightailed it back to here. Anyway, I'm not going in there again. I'm exhausted."

"Wait here, okay? I'm gonna see if Jeb's got a medical kit."

"No, Mitch. Please don't bother Jeb. A medical kit? Why?"

"Look at your arms and legs, Mar. Did you not even realize you were bleeding?"

"I guess I was too afraid. I was running on adrenaline."

By Dianne J. Beale

Mitch disappeared but soon returned with both a medical kit and Jeb. She lowered her eyes before he had a chance to notice she had seen him.

"Do you think this is enough, or should we take her to a clinic or something?" Mitch asked.

Jeb took her hand in his and analyzed the scratches. "They're just surface cuts. The worst we'll have to watch for is infection."

Although infuriated, Mar held her tongue. They were talking about her as if she either didn't exist or couldn't comprehend. But when Jeb began to gently work on her wounds, she found herself savoring even this artificial form of contact. She closed her eyes and stifled any cries of pain.

"Can you get me some warm water?" she heard him ask Mitch. "Some stickers have lodged themselves into her shoulder. Are there any tweezers in there? That might help, as well."

She bit her lip as he pulled the stickers. Then he was rubbing down her arm with a disinfectant. He and Mitch switched places. Mitch began to wash the arm that Jeb had just finished.

It took about an hour for them to finish both of her arms and legs, and she still had twigs and stickers in her hair. She listened as Jeb dismissed himself. Mitch thanked him for his help. Then he tackled the task of combing out Mar's hair.

"Mitch, can I eat something first? I'm so hungry," she pleaded.

Mitch heated her some food and then sat with her as she ate. She was grateful that no one had scolded her or asked her what she was thinking. But she was exhausted. She allowed Mitch to fix her hair and then immediately went off to bed, thanking him.

When she went out to the kitchen later that night to get another drink, she walked directly into Jeb. She dropped her cup, and it broke onto the floor. Thankful for the diversion, she apologized, mumbling something about not seeing him, and then dropped to the floor to clean up the mess. Jeb hesitated but then moved on. Mar breathed a sigh of relief, finished cleaning the mess, then took two bottled waters from the refrigerator instead. She went back to her room.

"We need to talk," came a voice from her bed. Startled, she dropped yet another item. Well, at least this time it was plastic. She swooped it up and then set them both on the table near the bed.

"Okay," she answered, not wanting to assume anything. "I'm listening."

"Do you listen? I had difficulty discerning if you were while you were on the hammock the other day."

"I heard everything you said, Jeb. I hurt you and only time will determine if your love has died or if it will grow again. And do we really know each other, anyhow? But it doesn't matter; my heart can't let yours choose life. I can't ever be allowed the chance to hurt you again. I'm sorry, but I just can't do it. You deserve better."

By Dianne J. Beale

"So now you're assuming I came here to declare my love? Mar, you don't listen. You might hear, but you don't listen. I wanted us to do our best to get along. That's all. We're making Mitch uncomfortable. Oh, and I think you need to tell the FBI about the bike trail. It might be connected to one of our investigations." Jeb then got up and left.

Chapter 67

When Mar woke up the next morning, she was in immense pain. The scratches had scabbed over and resulted in stiffness and tearing whenever she moved. She decided to use this to her advantage and opted to just stay in bed.

After a while, she realized she'd at least have to venture out to use the restroom. This made her long for the room she had used while they were staying at the house with Jeb. As she made her way to the door, tears pushed at her eyes. She wanted to be strong but didn't seem to have control over this ridiculous leakage.

Finally, she made it out of the room and into the restroom. Then she washed up and headed back. She pretended she didn't see him when Jeb passed by. Instead, she hyper-concentrated on getting back to her bed.

"Oh, for goodness' sake!" Jeb exclaimed. She had barely the time to acknowledge this when she found herself lifted into his arms and carried into her room. "And you have the nerve to tell Mitch not to be dramatic!" He was gone as soon as he had appeared.

Mar was seething with anger. How dare he! Where was Mitch? Jeb hadn't even bothered to close her door. She yanked her night shirt and robe back down around her knees. What was even more maddening was that she could still feel where his arms and fingers had been. This realization only made her all the more livid.

When he waltzed back into her room with a phone and handed it to her, pre-dialed to the FBI, Mar lost it. "Just go away! Get out of my room! Leave me alone!" she shouted, throwing the phone back at him.

Jeb began to laugh. "I thought you didn't want to hurt me anymore." he mocked. She turned her back to him, and he laughed even more heartily than before. Mar just broke down and cried, sobbing uncontrollably.

Jeb softened. "If God has forgiven us, who are we to build up walls and withhold forgiveness? Can you really continue to punish yourself? To punish me? Wouldn't you say that His love is stronger?"

Mar just continued to cry. Jeb rose, crossed the room, and shut the door. She had assumed he had gone when instead she felt his arms lifting her to him. "He sent you to teach me. Now let Him teach you, too."

Mar buried her face into his neck. She stopped crying but refused to look up, even when he gently stroked her face. "Do you deny that you love me?" he asked.

She remained silent. She feared he would twist whatever she chose to say. He smiled. "Okay, let me find out how you feel then," he stated. Gently, he kissed her forehead and then moved to her cheeks and nose. When he finally closed his mouth over her lips, she responded with the same. Once more he tried to raise her eyes to his face. "Mar, do you love me?" he asked.

"More than life itself," Mar responded.

"But you don't want to love me?"

"It scares me to love you, Jeb. I've never trusted anyone in the way my love for you is asking me to trust. If I love you, you can hurt me. If you love me, I can hurt you. And if we choose to share pieces of our lives, what happens if we decide to go our separate ways? Will the pieces no longer fit the separate puzzles? If not, what could we do? How could we forget?"

"Ah, but do you want to hurt me?"

"No, never. But if you love me, I will. Ask Mitch. That's all I do."

Jeb laughed. "So you would leave me to burn for you? Is that better? Do you plan to punish me because of your fears?"

Mar's breath caught in a gasp. "You burn for me?"

"More than a lifetime can show," he answered. "Will you deny your love? Or will you declare it to me forever in marriage?"

Mar flushed in confusion. Would he laugh and then deride her if she agreed to marriage? Or was he truly desiring of it. Her heart felt as if it was maintaining a delicate balance. *Help me, God,* she silently prayer.

By Dianne J. Beale

"If you truly want me, Jeb, then I give myself forever to be yours," she managed.

Jeb smiled, "See? You *can* do it," he quipped. And before she could misread him, he kissed her once more. "And now I think you should rest a bit. When Mitch gets up, I'll have him help me moisten your scratches. Olive oil should help immensely." Then he was gone.

Chapter 68

Had she dreamt it? If it was a dream, then she never wanted to wake up. But the knocking at her door wasn't going away.

She finally realized the knocking was real. She sat up, pulling the blankets around her, and called for whoever it was to come in. Mitch and Jeb entered with a dish of oil and a dry cloth.

Mitch coated her scratches with oil and Jeb patted the area with a dry cloth. Soon they were finished and she realized that it really had helped immensely. She thanked them and then asked if she could join them out in the kitchen for dinner. They readily agreed.

Sensing that peace had been made, Mitch remembered Jeff. He decided it was now safe to fill in the spaces. "Um, a friend I called has helped to shed some light on some of the dark places." he began. "Luke is not being hailed as a hero, at least not by most. He traded knowledge–his secrets–for his own freedom. He is the main witness, though. Turns out that he is supporting Amelia's claims and testifying with her. She hasn't been willing to press charges prior to this. Luke was blackmailing Andres; they're related somehow."

"What was he blackmailing him to do?" asked Mar.

"That remains a mystery. But you hadn't imagined Andres' advances toward you. I thought he stopped because of me, but it seems now that Luke also had something to do with it. Anyway, our house did burn to the ground, and Trish tried to collect on it. That's why she was so burned when I didn't come back. I wasn't calling her often enough to convince the insurance company that I was the one who gave her the ring. They wanted either my notarized signature or me in the flesh."

"I'm sorry I ever approved of her," apologized Mar. "I had no idea."

"Yeah. Well, forget it. There's more. The church closed, not because Andres was arrested but because the deed to the church was discovered, and it belonged to Dad, not the congregation. So, since no one knew where we were, the church was seized until a certain period could pass. It won't be released to the congregation unless we're not found within two years. This might be why Luke showed up that fateful night—or early morning, to be exact. He hadn't counted on us not agreeing to go with him and he needed Andres to think he was still on his side."

"Yeah." interrupted Jeb. "Well, he also didn't realize I called the Chief as soon as I heard the doorbell and was told not to let either of you out of my sight. The Chief and I agreed he would fire me so that Luke wouldn't know he'd lost our trust."

Mar glanced over at Jeb, "You did? I guess we really are lucky you're on our side. We had no idea our escape had already been planned."

"I'll have to remember to enlighten Jeff on that one. He thought it seemed to go far too smoothly for not having been premeditated. Oh, and Trish appears to only be pretending that she and Luke are engaged until he gives his testimony. Andres is using Trish in hopes of discrediting Luke's word by saying he's protecting future family. I guess they don't realize that everything is either on tape or had witnesses. But Jeff didn't know why Trish agreed to help Andres or why Luke seems to be playing along. Amelia stands to inherit everything that is Andres'. Their divorce was never official. She just managed to make it official when she was finally able to change back her name."

"Well, if anyone deserves it, she does," stated Mar. "I hope it works out for her."

Mitch continued, "Um, oh yeah, and Jeb's gorgeous little house is still standing."

Mar looked down at the floor and didn't say anything. Jeb reached under the table and squeezed her hand. She covered his hand with her other one and met his gaze from across the table. "Well, I told her that the house would eventually trap her and never let her leave, didn't I? It would have to remain standing for it to do that," Jeb teased.

By Dianne J. Beale

Mitch was pleased to see that his fishing statement had worked. He now knew for sure that they had patched things up.

"I'm sorry I called you dramatic the other day, Mitch," offered Mar as she considered how hurt her feelings had been when she'd been accused of the same. "I thought I was only being silly. But I can see how you might have taken it the wrong way. It won't happen again."

"That's okay, Sis." he said cheerily. "We've called each other a lot worse."

"That we have," she readily agreed.

Soon, everything had been covered, and the three of them headed off to their beds. Jeb paused for only a second, but his eyes relayed an entire message. Mar, blushing, entered her room.

Chapter 69

Mar awoke to a maddening itch, so decided to shower. She dug through her bags, searching for the baby oil she packed. She also took out her toiletries and then proceeded to the restroom.

As Mar finished drying off, she suddenly realized she had forgotten her robe. She slipped on her nightshirt, gathered her things, and returned to her room.

Once fully dressed, she headed to the kitchen. As she hunted through the cupboards for pancake ingredients, she discovered all that was missing was some syrup. She quickly gathered the necessary ingredients, created the sugary mixture, and set the pan to simmer on the stove.

Then she mixed up the pancake dough, greased a skillet, and began to cook one pancake at a time. As each cake finished, she would place it on a plate to stay warm in the oven. Just as she was cleaning up, Mitch appeared. He excused himself to go notify Jeb, and then returned alone.

"How long you been up?" he asked.

Mar calculated the minutes in her head, estimated ninety if she counted the shower, and then answered him while she poured the syrup into a nearby liquid measuring

By Dianne J. Beale

cup that had a pouring spout. Since she was concentrating on this, she failed to see the concern etched into her brother's face. When he didn't respond, though, she turned to look at him. "Why?"

"Well, I just wondered if you'd seen Jeb today. He's not in his room and I'm not sure where he's gone. I thought maybe you'd know how long he's been gone."

Mar set the syrup on the table, returned the pancakes to the oven, making sure it was off, and then suggested they look for him. "He might just be out by the lake. He likes to skip stones–seems to help him relax." But Jeb was nowhere in sight. Mar began to feel uneasy.

"What time were you out on that trail the other day?" Mitch suggested. "You don't suppose he…"

Mar interrupted as her face went white. "He wouldn't. Would he? I mean, wouldn't he wait for instructions or backup? He's never seemed impulsive, or at least not the type to play the hero."

"I wouldn't think so," Mitch assured her. "Why don't we check the phones to see if he spoke to anyone?"

They returned together to the cottage. Once inside, they began to check the phones for messages, call logs, whatever they could think of. They even checked the trash. But all seemed normal.

Then Mar remembered the phone that Jeb had tried to give her the other day. She went to her room, picked it up from the dresser, and handed it to Mitch. Trembling, she explained how he had dialed the phone but then they had decided not to use it. Mitch found a number in the memory, so called it.

At the mere mention of Jeb's name, Mitch's call was transferred. Then it was transferred again. Next, when he finally found a person who asked to take a message, he tried instead to get some answers but was resolutely told that Jeb was not available but that he would receive a message to call as soon as possible if they could just have his name and phone number. Mitch realized he could not give either, especially since no one had identified what organization it was he had rang. So he hung up the phone.

Mar and Mitch sat down and began to run through some possible plans. But none panned out upon further reflection. Finally they came to the conclusion that they should pray. Why hadn't they thought of this first? Why was it that people turned to prayer as a last, rather than first, resort?

Mitch prayed aloud first, then Mar. Then they alternated between silent and verbalized prayer. When they finished, Mar began the chorus to a traditional hymn and Mitch joined her. Then they again began to discuss options.

"Yesterday I got the impression that Jeb was trying to say that the Chief of Police where Luke works can be trusted. Do you think we should call him?"

Mitch was shaking his head. "No, Mar, that won't work. We're in Canada, remember?"

By Dianne J. Beale

"Well maybe we could pack a small backpack of water, food, and other items that a person takes when planning a hike and go walk the trail ourselves. We're sure to be thought of as tourists, aren't we?"

"We can't leave the cottage alone. Jeb has the only key, remember? He could also lose his job if it looks like we've been placed in jeopardy."

"Okay. I know you're right, but I don't have to like it. He could just be in town buying supplies for all we know. And we've been told to stay here. So I guess we might as well go eat."

"My thoughts exactly. All we can do is wait, anyway. Why starve, too? You know I don't like you involved with him, right? I mean what kind of life can you build with someone like him? He's a good person, Mar, but… well, you know how I feel. I think you understand my concerns."

Mar did understand but didn't want to hear it. She decided to ignore the building fear and got up, instead. They walked to the kitchen together.

Just as they sat down, a phone began to ring. Mitch quickly rose, crossed the room, and grabbed the ringing phone. Despite a fumble, he answered just in time. It was Jeb.

Chapter 70

"How long do you suppose it would take for you two to pack up our things?" Jeb was saying. "We'd need to clean up and return the key, too."

"We're leaving the cottage? Let me ask Mar. She's better at determining these sorts of things." He turned to his sister; she had already moved next to him shortly after he'd answered the call. "We need to pack up all our things, clean up, and be ready to return the key when Jeb arrives. How much time do we need?"

An inward sigh relaxed her almost immediately. *Jeb was okay.* "Give me a second to check the rooms," she responded. Glancing around the main room, she then poked her head into the kitchen and quickly assessed each of the bedrooms. "We need to be ready to leave? His things too?"

"Yes."

"Um, so he won't be helping. Maybe an hour to pack and another to clean?"

"Did you hear that, Jeb?" Mitch questioned.

"Yeah. That long? We were hoping to pick you up within the hour. Aren't most of our things already in bags?"

Mitch turned again to Mar. "He thought our packing was mostly done. It's not?"

"I think we all sort of relaxed some here. We actually used the dressers. But the clothes are all clean and most have been folded. It might be possible to get done sooner. I'd say at least an hour, though. We haven't even finished eating."

Mitch again spoke to Jeb. "Well, it all seems a little overwhelming, but we'll do our best. What time are we aiming for?"

"We'll leave here in about fifteen minutes and then you'll have half an hour to forty-five minutes after that. If you're not ready, we'll just have to grab everything else and sort it out later." Jeb hung up.

"Well, Sis, we might have forty-five minutes if we're lucky. I still think we should eat first." They returned to the kitchen, ate, and then washed up the dishes.

Mar, putting the last cup into the cupboard, looked over at the fridge. "How about you go pack your things while I pack up the food? Then I'll work on my stuff while you begin Jeb's once yours is finished. Then I'll help with Jeb's once I've finished mine and have checked the restroom and outside porches. Okay?"

Mitch smiled. "You make it sound almost do-able. I guess we'll meet at Jeb's then."

Mar gave Mitch a weak smile in return and then opened the freezer to get the cooler's ice packs. She then dragged the cooler out from a closet next to the restroom and wheeled it across the main room and into the kitchen. She arranged the ice inside the cooler and then began filling it with the frozen foods. Once the freezer was empty, she packed up the refrigerator contents, as well. Then she threw a thermal hot/cold bag on top, closed and latched the cooler, dragged it out to the center of the main room, and ducked into her room to work on her stuff.

She began pulling bags from the closet and filling them. Once filled, each bag was dragged out to the main room. Then she went back into the room where she had stayed and pulled out all drawers, opened closets, ran her hand across shelves, and looked under the bed and other furniture. Satisfied she was finished, she then went out onto the porches; there was nothing to gather, so she went on to Jeb's.

Mitch wasn't there yet, and she suddenly felt shy. So, before beginning, she went to ask her brother if he wanted her to help him finish up and then they could work on Jeb's room. But he assured her he was almost done and she should just keep working, sticking to the plan.

She remembered the restroom, so gave it the once over. Having just cleaned it the day before, she wasn't worried about its appearance. Finding only one toothbrush, she popped in to ask if it was Mitch's. When he assured her that it was not, she went back to tackle the room that had belonged to Jeb.

The room was very clean and organized. She took out the larger bag first and moved all the clothes from the

By Dianne J. Beale

dresser. Then she moved all of his toiletries into the pockets. Next she filled the smaller bag with his shoes and sneakers. She discovered a small pile of slightly hidden dirty clothes, as well, so she put these here as well. Then she was done. She pulled it all to the main room and then went back to give the room one last once over just as she had done for hers. Mitch popped up just as she was finishing and asked if she could double-check his room now that it was done. He would recheck the others, as well. Mar agreed and soon all their stuff was sitting on the porch next to Mitch. She returned inside to finish the cleaning while he watched the luggage.

    Once done, Mar joined Mitch and asked him to do one more check before locking the doors. Jeb would be turning in the key. She sat on the porch, waiting, and two vehicles pulled up. Jeb hopped out from the SUV and began to load up the trunk. Mitch came out and locked the cottage door. Jeb, continuing to load, instructed Mar to please go return the key. As she passed the car, a man got out and escorted her to the office. He paid the bill, took the receipt, and then, together, they walked back to the cottage. The man gave Jeb the receipt, they spoke briefly, and then the car drove off. Jeb motioned that they were ready to leave as well.

Chapter 71

Mar watched out the back window as they drove away. Tears threatened to fall, but she held them back. Mitch reached over and placed his hand on her shoulder to give it a squeeze. She reached up, squeezing his hand in acknowledgment.

Although they were dying to ask questions, they remained silent. They saw that Jeb's face was etched with concern and dragged with exhaustion. So no one spoke the entire ride. They passed through the Canadian border, stopped for food and a restroom break, and then drove and drove. Finally they arrived at a tall, gray office building located inside their small town of Mayhaw.

"We'll leave the luggage here for now," Jeb explained. "You'll need to follow me because they don't let you wander our buildings alone." He used his head to motion to Mar's purse. "They'll have you open your purse for them and it will also be scanned." He stopped in front of the door. "Welcome to the FBI."

Jeb opened the door and ushered them inside. As they followed him, it was disconcerting for them both. Nothing of significance had yet been explained and Jeb came off as cold

By Dianne J. Beale

and indifferent. Mar tried to picture him as the FBI agent he was and to ignore that they knew each other. This seemed to help.

Jeb began to talk again. "Okay. I don't like this plan but it is the best plan to follow and I can't allow personal feelings to interfere. My boss wants you prepared as witnesses in case we need your testimonies. No one believes it will be necessary, but since we must legally provide an exit interview for your health report anyhow, it is best to get statements and to make sure you understand any dangers you might encounter. The trial's not been as smooth as was expected and my boss wants you each prepared in case we have to call you to the stand. So, you'll be brought up to speed, asked to relate whatever you know, and asked to put it all into writing, which you will then sign. I had hoped this wouldn't be necessary. Sorry."

Neither Mitch nor Mar responded. They appeared to be pondering what had been said. But it made Jeb a little nervous.

"On the upside, the Canadian government stopped the gang you discovered on the trail; they were involved in drug trafficking. Since no one saw you on the trail, and enough incriminating evidence was found, that is one trial you'll not need to attend." Jeb tried to smile in hopes of relieving some of the strain.

"Why didn't you wake us or at least leave a note for us this morning?" Mar inquired, softly.

Jeb was taken by surprise. He was not accustomed to switching between his personal and professional lives. "I don't know. I guess I'm used to living alone, so didn't think to leave a note. I also left very early so did not want to wake you. Besides, I expected to be back before you'd even known I was gone. Things took longer than expected. Sorry if you worried." He looked sheepish as he answered.

"Oh," said Mar. Mitch didn't say anything.

"Well, here we are. I'll be sitting in with you, so try not to be nervous. Just tell what you know. It's easier when you are used to telling the truth and have nothing to hide, so you two should do just fine. You might feel as if you are being interrogated or that they think you are lying, but this is not the reality. They're here to prepare you to defend yourselves against the defense lawyers who will use this tactic in hopes of flustering you so that the jury doubts your testimony. This will give you the practice you need to remain firm and to just calmly repeat the truth. Okay. In we go." Jeb turned the knob and they entered the room.

The questioning seemed to go on forever. Questions were often asked repeatedly; sometimes they were rephrased or reworded. The questions also would at times be altered to include a small, incorrect phrase and Mar and Mitch would repeat the truth of how it all happened, emphasizing that this alteration was incorrect.

After what seemed like hours, another worker was called in to work with them. She had file folders, a laptop, notebooks, pens and pencils, and some CDs. She explained that she was to go over the case with them and that they were to share whatever they felt was important.

When the lady had finished speaking and was about to open the first folder, Mitch broke in before she could continue. "Ma'am, we really are more than glad to help, but we've not used the restroom since we arrived. Do you think maybe we could have a five minute restroom break?"

Mar added, "Yes, I really could use a small break as well. And could we maybe have something to eat while we go over this with you? I'm just a little thirsty, and a bit hungry, too."

The woman agent smiled. "Of course you should have a break and eat something. I'm sorry we didn't think of it. Jeb can go purchase you something at the cafeteria while I take you to the restrooms." She asked the others who had just completed the questioning to watch the room and the evidence until they got back.

The man who appeared to be in charge called out after them. "No more than five minutes, Jeb, Jen, well no more than ten."

"Okay then, let's get a move on," Jen said.

When they arrived back at the room, those who had stayed rapidly departed. Jeb placed subs and water in front of them and then sat down.

"All set then," said Jen. And she began to chronologically go over all the information that the FBI had collected.

By Dianne J. Beale

Chapter 72

When Jen came to the analysis of different computers, Mitch and Mar made her aware that they were hearing this information for the first time and asked if she could slow down. She smiled, thanked them, and then continued. "We were able to trace multiple keyloggers to your employer, Miss Zeiler. It appears that your printer output was also being logged. Was the computer in your home a company computer?"

"No. It belongs to me and Mitch. We often bring work home with us, but the computer is ours. What are keyloggers, exactly? And what would the printer logs contain? Could that be what caused my printer to begin streaking?"

"Keyloggers are tiny programs that monitor the keys of your keyboard and record everything that you type. They are used most often to collect passwords but would also record any letters or other personal information that you might have typed. And yes, it is possible that the program monitoring your printer could have affected the driver enough to cause your printer to streak. But the computer was purchased by you, for yourselves? It wasn't a gift or loaner from the church?"

Mitch answered this time. "No. It belongs to us. We've been planning to upgrade it. So you're saying that they were monitoring us. That brings clarity to many things."

"Care to elaborate?" Jen requested.

"Well, it sometimes seemed they knew stuff that I was sure we hadn't shared with them. But Mar and I decided that at least one of us must have let it slip or that maybe my girlfriend had said something. We knew it couldn't be prophecy." Mitch smiled as he added that last sentence.

Jen returned to the reports. "It appears that the keyloggers and extra printer driver program were sending all information to the main church computer every time you connected to the Internet to pick up your mail. It went in a roundabout route to get there, but this is where it eventually all collected. The only computer we analyzed that showed no problems was the laptop that was loaned to you, Mr. Zeiler. It is the only computer that could have had the legal right to monitor since it didn't belong to you, but even then you would have had to sign something that made it clear you were aware of the monitoring. The other, since it is yours, could not. This is good news for our case."

"Wait," Mar insisted, "You didn't analyze my work computer? I used a desktop computer daily and it was always having conniptions. That's why I brought so much of my work home. They erased it all the time and would give

By Dianne J. Beale

me no warning. So I would back up my documents on a CD every night before leaving the church."

Jen looked pleased. "Do you have any of those CDs? They might have some hidden evidence on them. The church staff insisted that only the secretary and receptionist used computers and by the time we had the legal means to go in and check it out, those were the only computers we found. And these computers seem to have been reformatted a number of times. Why would they do that if there was nothing to hide? We also found a root kit embedded in one of the Word documents that you received from the church. If this had been activated, they might have been able to control your computer. Can we go back to the church now that we have proof that your parents were the owners? It might help to have you there so we can check if there's anything we missed."

"I do have a key unless they changed the locks," offered Mar. "Is there anyone we need to check with before we go?"

Mitch then spoke up. "You're not considering us suspects, are you? We have a friend who repairs our home computer sometimes when it freezes up. That isn't going to make it look as if we've tampered with evidence, is it?"

"No. But can we get the name of this friend? She might have a record of what she cleaned up. That could be helpful."

Mar answered this time. "She's not going to get into trouble, right? She's a good person and was trying to help.

She never charges, either. Anything on our computers was there when she came. I know she wouldn't do something to harm us. She wouldn't give us bad programs. And she's tried to teach me but I'm not good at this kind of stuff and I think I get it while I'm listening and then when I read over the notes I didn't get it at all. But she only ever helps. I know she said she removed spy something and that she gave me a firewall. She even tried to give me programs that would run the scans themselves."

Jen could see that Mar trusted this friend and it did sound as if Mitch trusted her as well. So Jen assured them that she just wanted to ask their friend if she kept a list of the programs she installed and the ones she removed. Mar seemed to calm down.

Then Mar's eyes widened as she seemed to remember something else. "What does it mean when you are working on a computer and the mouse pointer starts to move around on the screen all by itself? Could that be a root kit? Folders were opening themselves, too. This never happened at home, but it did happen to me a couple of times at work. I remember having to turn off the computer manually to get it to stop. One time it was as if someone were even planning to play a game of solitaire."

Mitch raised his eyebrows. "How come you never mentioned this to me?"

Mar gave him a guilty look. "It kinda creeped me out at the time and since they had no problem with changing my

By Dianne J. Beale

office location and then stating that it had always been where it is now, I assumed they'd say I was crazy about this, as well. So, with you no longer at the church, and with me still needing the job until I found a new one, I guess I shoved it out of my mind. Sorry."

Jen seemed troubled. "I just don't see why you stayed so long in that environment. But that's neither here nor there at this point in time. I would guess they had remote access set up on your work computer. That way they could copy, move, or delete files without ever going near your machine. But it would only work when the computer was on. We need to find this computer. Let me make a few calls and then we'll make our way on over."

Chapter 73

As they traveled in the car, Mar felt as if her stomach were dough being churned in a large factory machine. She had gladly stayed away from this building. Yet now she found it was necessary for she and it to reunite. Her dreams began to surface and she closed her eyes. Silently she called out to Jesus. It seemed that now was the time, so she asked for strength.

Her key unlocked the door with ease, and the three of them entered the now-empty building. Mar led the way, ready to climb the familiar stairs, but the area was blocked off as a wall. Both Mitch and Mar gasped in surprise. She turned left, instead, to head for the other stairway.

Mitch couldn't help but comment. The quietness was maddening. "That's unusual. We should have been able to climb stairs here. The offices are right at the top. When did they remove those stairs?"

Jen turned to scan his face and he bumped into her. Mar stopped as well. Jen seemed puzzled. "You mean there were stairs there? Where the wall is now?"

By Dianne J. Beale

Mar shook her head, holding a sadness in her eyes. "They were there on my last day here. We can check it out more closely once we get up there, though."

Jen sighed. "I think maybe you should have been with us the first time we came around. I hope we can still find what we need."

When Mar turned left, Jen veered right; she appeared to be following the signs that had been posted to re-direct people. "It's shorter this way," Mar offered. "At least it used to be." Jen and Mitch followed.

Once upstairs, Mar began to open rooms, naming the use they had while she'd been working there. When she came to the office that she had been moved to, the door said "storage" and was locked.

As she took out her keys, she explained how it appeared they had returned the original nameplate but that this room was where she had worked from during her final weeks. As the door opened, a computer could be seen sitting in a corner. All the cords had been removed, to make it appear that it was being stored and was not in use. Boxes and stacks of paper had also been set around it.

Mar moved in for a closer look. "Well, it's not the one I used, but it might have something worth analyzing. Should we set it up or take it with us?"

Jen was writing in a notebook. She had drawn a quick map of the hallway they were in and had labeled the doors with Mar's explanations. She looked up from her work. "Oh, for now let's leave it here. I'm making a list in case we have more than we three can manage. But we'll leave the doors unlocked, if that's okay. If this is all we find, we'll take everything that's here with us. But if we find more, we may need to call in a team. We did lock the main door on the way in, right?"

Mitch and Mar both said that they had, but Mar reminded her that if her key still worked than a multitude of others did as well. Jen didn't think that it would be a problem since it was broad daylight and they were in the building themselves. So, Mar motioned them along to continue the search. Jen's decision seemed careless to Mar and she began to wonder why the FBI had kept Jeb there. She put the thought out of her head and continued to just lead the way.

At the end of the hall, Mar paused. There was now a wall at the top of where the first stairwell should be, as well. A painting hung in the center as if it had always been this way. Mitch's expression matched her thoughts, but her face gave nothing away. She was too busy noticing that the new painting was of a majestic lion standing over a flock of sheep. There was more to this new wall than just blocking off stairs, but what? Her dream surfaced, then dispersed, and she suddenly recalled a small saw that Jeb had kept in the janitor's closet next to her isolated new office.

As Jen and Mitch discussed the wall in a technical fashion, Mar returned to get the saw and then began to cut a

By Dianne J. Beale

hole directly next to the painting. She made it just large enough for a person to climb through and was about to go in when Jen stopped her. "I should go first, just in case," she said.

Once they all had entered the newly found space, they saw that the stairs appeared undamaged. And there was a room to the right of them. Mar, recognizing it as the old break room, went in first this time. Jen was recovering from having made such a discovery. How could an entire FBI team miss this?

The room no longer had the warmth it had had when she was employed and often ate there. The original furniture was no longer present and instead there was only one long, cold, rectangular table that had been altered. The usual table top had been replaced by a counter top material that resembled clear, smooth quartz crystal. It was layered under dust, but in the center of the table, a design could be seen. After checking with Jen, she went back out to the janitor's closet and got a clean, unused dusting cloth. When she returned, she began to dust only the area of design. A swastika inside a pentagram appeared. All three of them gasped. Under the design, in what looked to be blood, was inscribed, "I Will Follow You."

Mar dropped the cloth next to this discovery and Jen picked up her cell phone to make a call. But there was no signal. So Mar explained that cell phones had never worked well in this building. She had Jen follow her back out to the hall where she then opened a window. "Try standing here," she told her. "It's the only place my phone would work."

Mitch remained frozen, staring at the table. Mar and Jen waited in the hall. And soon the entire place was swarming with FBI. But Jeb was again not among them.

Once the FBI had safely acquired the new computer and its surrounding evidence, they began to collect pictures and take samples to go to forensics. Mitch told them that the cloth had been used by Mar to wipe off the dust so the symbol could be seen and that it in no way indicated she was involved. Then he rejoined Mar and Jen as they continued down the remaining hall.

Jen wrote down what the rooms had been, but they found no further evidence. Mar's work computer was nowhere to be found. Jen assured them that every detail could lead to discoveries and to not give up hope. She encouraged them to try remembering what members attended so they could be interviewed. They then returned to the FBI building.

Once inside, Jen returned them to the room where they had spent most the day. It was growing dark now, and Mar just wanted to go home. She was trying to determine where that might be, when Jeb re-appeared. Jen thanked them and left. They were left to follow Jeb back down to the SUV. They were going home with him once more.

By Dianne J. Beale

Chapter 74

The house was just as they had left it. Jeb turned the water and water heater back on and then set the thermostat back to its "people live here" profile. They unloaded the SUV and then locked up. Apologizing for his lack of hospitality, Jeb then headed directly to bed. Mitch, although anxious to discuss everything with Mar, followed suit. But Mar, despite the day's events, was too wound up to sleep. She went to her room, wanting a nice, warm shower. Realizing she needed to wait for the water to heat, she dug out her Bible and sat down on the edge of the bed.

The image from the church's false wall had burned into her mind. The lion, floating above the sheep, seemed to haunt her. Why was the lion placed above the sheep as if it were a predator? Or was it meant to be a shepherd? Regardless, her dream was beginning to make a little more sense.

Looking though her concordance, Mar found it to be insufficient. The lamb was grouped with a wolf, not a lion. And it seemed the references listed for lion did not even mention a lamb. But she had always heard the lion grouped with the lamb and knew she had seen pictures portraying it this way. She knew that Christ was referred to as both.

Finally she decided it didn't really matter. She'd helped to find the hidden room and the time had come and gone. But she wanted to remember the verses she'd been taught, so turned to the two passages that seemed closest to the teachings she remembered.

And the wolf will dwell with the lamb, And the leopard will lie down with the young goat, And the calf and the young lion and the fatling together; And a little boy will lead them. Also the cow and the bear will graze, Their young will lie down together, And the lion will eat straw like the ox. The nursing child will play by the hole of the cobra, And the weaned child will put his hand on the viper's den. They will not hurt or destroy in all My holy mountain, For the earth will be full of the knowledge of the LORD As the waters cover the sea (Isaiah 11:6-9).

Well, a fatling could refer to a lamb, right? She was sure that she had learned that it could. And besides, the animals did appear to be grouped all together. The confusion began to clear.

"The wolf and the lamb will graze together, and the lion will eat straw like the ox; and dust will be the serpent's food They will do no evil or harm in all My holy mountain," says the LORD (Isaiah 65:25).

Mar took great comfort in this second passage. She'd been so frightened by the dreamed marriage to Andres. But

By Dianne J. Beale

now she felt it fall away. "Dust will be the serpent's food and they will do no evil or harm." She'd wiped a good measure of dust off that table today. Yawning, she cleared her bed, turned off her light, and had soon fallen asleep.

She was standing beneath an enormous cobra that was talking with her. It was gloriously beautiful, with huge, mesmerizing eyes. And she understood all that he and she were discussing and felt safe and happy.

The air was thick around them, almost impermeable to the eyes. A black form seemed to pass her, but she couldn't be sure what it was or even if she'd actually seen anything.

The serpent's voice drew her back to him. "Ah, you like my eyes," it hissed. "I've not seen yours this color before–intriguing–so misty. I'm sorry that Adolph tripped you. He sometimes has a mind of his own. But he watches over me, informs me, and keeps me one step ahead in the game. I'm sure you understand he was just looking out for me."

As Mar looked over to where the snake's eyes had traveled, she saw that Adolph, a black cat, shared the Cobra's eyes. They were the same in every way. Realization began to surface. Where had she experienced this? She had the distinct feeling of déjà vu.

As she turned her eyes back on the cobra, she remembered. Suddenly she was in the parking lot with Andres. She had tripped over an animal–one that Andres insisted was only in her imagination. He changed back into the snake.

"Why must you resist, me, Child? I've taken the form of your salvation. Eve was enchanted with me. She so wanted to be like God. She was eating the fruit in her mind long before she had ever taken a bite. I had her convinced that eating the fruit in her mind was no different than eating it in reality, so she took it and ate of it. Adam was there. He could tell you. He stood and watched as she ate. He was lost in her beauty just as you are in mine. He didn't stop her, and then he ate with her. And they became as gods."

"No," Mar heard herself argue. "They introduced sin into the world. You are not my salvation. Their spirits died that day. You were—are—death."

The snake leaned in as if about to strike. But instead she was again standing next to Andres. The fog was so thick around them. "Oh, Garnet, Garnet," he was saying. "So beautiful… so naive. Why do you resist me? We belong together. Together we…"

His voice trailed away as she dug deep within her depths to gather strength. Her "No" was weak and unconvincing. Andres reached out to touch her. She squeezed her eyes tightly shut, willing him to go away, and compressed her lips. "Jesus," she pleaded, "Help me."

Suddenly she was looking up from what appeared to be the church floor. A majestic lion, with fire in his eyes, was breathing down on her. She opened her mouth to thank him and realized she was bleating. She was the lamb from her dream. Jesus had rescued her. He promised to rescue His

By Dianne J. Beale

sheep. Mar woke up. She could hear voices, but thought maybe they were only in her head. But then, realizing that they were real, she climbed out from her bed.

Opening the door to the hall, she wandered out into the corridor. Both Mitch's and Jeb's doors were closed. She listened for the voices and was about to return to her room when they started up again. They were in the front section of the house.

She pressed her ear against the door. What was Luke doing here? And why would Mitch be talking to him? She wandered down the hall to Jeb's room and turned the knob. His bed was empty. She found the same to be true for Mitch. She knew the voices to be Mitch's and Luke's. She was sure of it. But Jeb must be out there as well. She opened the adjoining door and walked into the room. All the voices instantly stopped as if children who'd been caught in an act of disobedience.

Then Luke stepped toward her. "Mar, please, tell me you didn't believe Amelia. Tell Mitch I'm not that way. Trish used Amelia to spread false rumors. Please. I know you've chosen Jeb, but I need you to believe in me. We were friends once, right? Mar, I'm not with Trish. I'm not. I've sacrificed everything for my cousin Jeb, even my love for you. I knew you'd choose him. All women do. It's always been Jeb or Andres. Not me… I'm the boy next door. But Andres trusted me. I was in his wedding. He's my half-brother. Mar, please."

Mar looked from Jeb to Luke, and then back to Jeb. "You're cousins? When did you plan to enlighten me with this information? Are you related to Andres too, or was his parent the wrong half?"

When Jeb ignored her, she turned toward Luke. "And you. When did you ever love me? You weren't very open with it. I know I'm a mess, but at least I try to make that clear up front. And just how do you figure you've done anything for Jeb?"

Luke had a toxic answer. "I sure underestimated you. What you hear is what you believe. I never would have guessed that of you. No matter. You've chosen Jeb and I say you two deserve each other. With you, I'm good. But without you, I'm better."

Mar couldn't help herself. "You can be sure of that," she answered. "I'm not the right woman for you. I never could be."

Jeb finally spoke up: "Mar, let us handle this, okay? Yes, he is my cousin and I think I know him a tad better than you think you do. And no, I'm not tainted with anything even remotely to do with Andres. But Luke? He is. It's in the blood. Just be a good girl and do as you're told, okay? Go back to bed."

Mar turned toward Mitch, pleading with him. "I do believe Luke if he says he's not with Trish. I think you should listen to him. Maybe it was Trish who was flirting with Luke, and I just assumed the worst of him. Amelia

By Dianne J. Beale

wouldn't lie for anyone; she had to believe that Trish and Luke were together or she wouldn't have told me that. Besides, someone else already told us that the engagement was nothing more than a sham, remember? Maybe we should at least give Luke a chance to explain."

Mitch countered: "Do you not even realize that you are contradicting yourself? If Amelia believes they're together, don't you think he managed to be rather convincing then?"

Mar opened her mouth to answer, but Mitch and Jeb interrupted before she could even get one word out. They insisted that Luke had to be lying. He wasn't even supposed to be there.

When she tried again to get them to listen, they stubbornly repeated that she just needed to go back to her room. But Mar recalled how Luke had warned her more than once. She also remembered his interest in, and concern for, Jodi. And she wasn't convinced he was as bad as he'd been painted.

She attempted one last time to encourage Mitch and Jeb to at least hear him out. She even appealed to Jeb's own need for secrecy and insisted that maybe there was more that could not yet be revealed. But Jeb ordered her to stop being naive and gently pointed her in the direction of her room.

So she left. She slammed shut the adjoining door, went in to her room, and began to pack. She decided that Mitch could provide a list of members to the FBI if they needed one. When she finished rearranging her bags, she had her backpack ready once again and took up her phone to call Norma Mae. She was going to be on the morning bus.

By Dianne J. Beale

Chapter 75

Mar knew she was supposed to still be in protective custody, but she just couldn't stay at Jeb's any longer. She scratched out a note for her brother to find, laid it in the center of the bed, but then instead scooped it back up. Quietly, as she tore it to pieces, she went to the kitchen and dropped the pieces into the trash. She didn't notice the small piece that had fallen to the floor. Tears slowly slid from her eyes as she determinedly left the house.

She purchased her ticket and then went to the corner of the station where there was a small café. She bought two fresh bottles of water, a small box of doughnuts, and a box of orange juice. Then she boarded the bus and waited for the trip to begin.

As the bus rolled along the roads, Mar remembered how she had deliberately left behind her Bible. She pondered this decision and recognized it was related to the possibility of encountering Jack. The number one reason that he had given her for the breakup was that she was obsessed with God. She knew this was just an excuse since Norma Mae had admitted he'd been engaged to another woman the entire romance.

But Norma and this woman did not get along and she had remained quiet in hopes that Jack would dump the other woman and keep Mar. Neither of them had ever called her Mar, though–it was always Marge. And now Jack was divorced and Norma said she couldn't promise he wouldn't pop in.

But Mar no longer wanted Jack. In fact, she was now in the process of sealing her heart against the idea of marriage, completely. She'd even picked up some brochures that were advertising working with nuns. And what better place to be if you want to avoid marriage?

The bus only had one destination, and Mar, having only one bag, fastened it tightly to herself. She placed her hands over the zippers and arranged herself so she could nap. She fell into a restless sleep.

Mar found herself in the church kitchen. She was baking bread, but the leaven had failed. She tried again and again to make bread that would rise. The yeast mixed beautifully with the warm milk and sugar, it foamed excitedly as it anticipated being added to the dough, but then the bread would fail to rise.

But the bread needs to rise; it's not the time for unleavened bread. She places yet another failed loaf on the counter and marvels at the fresh, active leaven that is bubbling nearby. Why does the leaven fail?

The members of the church begin to file in; they are complaining and grumbling. Some of the pastors and staff

By Dianne J. Beale

members join them. They, too, are murmuring. They brag of how their bread always bakes into perfect loaves and flatter those who say the same.

But when the building begins to rock, the pastors and staff are suddenly shepherds. They lead the members to hide under tables. As they comply, each member becomes a helpless sheep. They tell Mar that she must join them if she is to live.

But God tells her that she must leave. The rocking is not because of an earthquake. The building will sink, instead. All who remain in the building will die.

She frantically begins to warn those around her. But no one listens. When she opens the door to leave, they all jeer at her and call her a stupid girl.

But as soon as she leaves the building and is a safe distance away, the church begins to sink into quicksand. She pulls out her cell phone and calls for emergency help. But the judgment of God has come too quickly. Who will save the sheep?

Mar woke up with a start. She shifted in her seat so she could look out the bus window. Estimating she still had about an hour to go, she took out the box of doughnuts. As she nibbled each doughnut, thoughts of last night flooded her mind. She pondered the idea that Luke claimed to love her and still could not come to any logical explanation. Why would he have said such a thing?

As she continued to search the past, she began to think of her parents. She then thought of how much Mitch had sacrificed for her. As the bus pulled into the station, Mar decided she wasn't going to return home. Mitch's testimony should suffice if they need one. After all, they had her signed statement, didn't they? She just knew it would be better for everyone if she just disappeared. She wouldn't be able to stay at Norma Mae's for long.

The bus finally arrived and Mar began to look for her friend. When she didn't find her, she went into the station to wait. But Norma was already there. And beside her, sat Jeb and Mitch.

By Dianne J. Beale

Chapter 76

Once the hellos and goodbyes had been said to Norma, Mar was forced to leave. She fell completely silent in the car and opted to sit alone on the back seat. Mitch decided to ignore her obvious attitude and filled her in on the events she had missed, starting with how he had found her. A piece of the note had been found on the kitchen floor. Fortunately for him, it contained the word *Mae*. He had easily made the connection from there.

The computer that they had found in Mar's second office had been instrumental to the case. It was all over. Jodi came forward and admitted that she had been the one who traded out Mar's computer for the one they had found that day. She had discovered early on that there were encrypted files that she had not been able to access, so when Mar went missing, she had taken the opportunity to exchange the computers then. She had provided Mar's computer, but insisted the one they found was the one of importance.

Jodi's parents had wanted her to marry Pastor Andres but she was appalled at the idea; the man was older than her own dad. Yet when the church had needed help, her parents insisted that she go. So, when Luke approached her, she was only too glad to help. She provided a statement that Luke had never been in league with Andres. He had merely pretended so he could protect Mar, and later because of his love for her. She had been one of his secret agents all along.

The new paint samples had clenched the deal. The red paint had indeed turned out to be blood. The lab had been able to decipher a minimum of five DNAs. One of the five proved a match to that of Andres.

So, Mitch and Mar were free to return to their lives. The trial was over. Andres had been convicted, and Luke was pardoned.

Mar suddenly felt completely alone. She forced a smile and feigned happiness. She even brightly suggested that she could house shop for them. Did he want to lease for now or should they buy? Her falseness was totally missed as he told her that he thought it would be a great project for her.

Mar didn't mention that they'd picked her up under false pretenses. Why couldn't she visit with Norma if they were now free? They wasted her bus fare, ushered her away from her friend, barely allowed even a hug, and now they were headed back to a life that no longer existed for her. They had totally treated her as a child when she had tried to defend Luke, and now she hadn't even received an apology. So what was the hurry?

Jeb reminded Mitch that before they could go anywhere they would need to return to the FBI to sign off on the case. Mar's eyes clouded over at the thought of it. So they had a legitimate reason after all. But she again forced a smile and tried to feign happiness.

Once inside the building, Mitch read through the report with enthusiasm. He was ready to go just after ten minutes. Jen offered to give him a ride and Mitch accepted. No one noticed that a civilian had just been left alone in the FBI. Mar smiled and silently thought, "She likes my brother, a lot."

As Mar read the report, things became even clearer. Paco and Jasmine had been key witnesses in the trial and were the missing link to the involvement of the church counselor, who had not only broken Jasmine's arm but also led the attempt on her and Paco's lives. Luke had made sure that these two would be entered into the Witness Protection Program. They were given new names, new jobs, a savings account, and moved to a new, hidden location. By signing the report, Mar would be agreeing to never try to locate them. She was happy to comply and found herself smiling at the knowledge of their new life together.

The report also told how it had been the praise minister who had burned down her and Mitch's house. He had signed a statement of how he and Andres were lovers until Mar had entered the scene. Then Andres had moved their relationship to the closet and focused on obtaining Mar. The praise minister had grown increasingly livid that Mar had not returned Andres' advances and was one step away from lunacy. He had wanted to harm Mitch and Mar but had not been able to locate them. So he took it upon himself to destroy the last surviving remnant of Zeiler heritage. Known as a practical joker while in college, this was not much further than he had gone before. Yet this time the evidence was overwhelming and there was no possible way for his wealthy parents to cover it up. Mar felt pity well up inside of her. The house held memories and mementos, but the Zeiler legacy was far more than just material or human sentiment.

As Mar read on, it became clear that Luke had done all he did in order to remain in Andres' confidence. He had only done as was required of him as a cop. She began to smile as she thought about the relationship between Jodi and Luke. She had seen the way Jodi looked at him. That was one of the reasons Mar had dismissed any interest she might have thought he had shown to her. She was happy for them. He deserved to find the life that he so desperately craved.

Next she thought of the dreams where she had dreamt of Andres. How could she have even thought she was interested in him at one time? It seemed eons ago. Just thinking about Andres was bad enough, but the dreams were making her ill.

Mar finished looking through the report, added a few notes to the bottom, and then signed it as she'd been instructed. She walked to the phone and read the available numbers that she could call. She finally opted for the front desk and punched in the numbers. The guard who answered told her that Jen had said she'd left her locked in the room and that someone should already be on the way.

By Dianne J. Beale

As she waited for the new escort to arrive, she nervously put her hands into her pockets. The escort turned out to be Jeb. She supposed that Jen had just assumed that she'd feel most comfortable with him. But she had guessed incorrectly.

"So, I'll bet you were glad to hear that Luke's been exonerated," he fished.

"Yes. Especially since he wasn't guilty," she answered.

He ignored this jab. "Did you finish the report? Is it signed?"

"Yes. Here it is. Will Jen get into trouble for leaving me here alone?"

"No. She locked you in." Jeb skimmed through the report, read her slight additions, and then noted the signature. "Okay, I guess you're ready to go then." Mar just nodded.

As they walked down to the first floor and then out the front door, neither spoke. The tension was excruciating, but she refused to let it be seen. Once on the street, Mar headed for the bus stop.

Jeb followed. "Why are you running from me?" he asked.

Mar just threw him a look of frustration. Jeb became impatient. "I thought you said that you don't like to play games. I can't read your mind, you know." When she refused to answer, he turned and walked away.

As she began to read through the schedules, Mar realized she had left behind her bag. She walked back to the building and went inside to the front desk. The guard laughed at her predicament but then called someone who could retrieve it for her. Again it was Jeb.

As he handed her the bag, their eyes met for a second. Mar dropped her gaze immediately. She apologized for being so much trouble and then thanked him for all the help. But he had already begun to walk away.

Mar went back to the bus stop and sat down to wait. She planned to go to the police station to get back her car and original phone. Then she could drive out to Jeb's, collect her stuff, and get out of his way. When the Police Chief saw her, he offered her a ride. She accepted immediately and soon they were on the way to the station to fill out more paper work so she could claim back her stuff.

When the Chief asked if she'd been out to see the remains of her house yet, Mar became acutely aware of her situation. She had bills to pay, no house to live in, and no job. But she answered in a normal voice. "No, Sir. We've practically been nowhere since getting back. I'm not sure we even know where to begin. I do, however, plan to start looking for a place to stay."

"What's wrong with Jeb's? He kicking you out?"

"No. Nothing like that. We Zeilers are a proud stock. Now that we've been told to get on with our lives we don't

By Dianne J. Beale

feel right. I mean we don't want to impose or wear out our welcome. You know?"

The chief rubbed his chin. "I see. Why was I under the impression that you two have something special?"

"I'm not sure, really. I suppose maybe because Luke thinks we do? But we don't. Not really. At least not anymore."

"I see," was all he said.

They pulled into the station and the Chief directed her to where she needed to be. But once she filled out the paper work it became clear she'd forgotten her I.D. She was just about to make a call to some friends when Luke walked up. "Hi Mar," he said.

Mar smiled wanly and said a hello in return. Then she got out her address book so she could call a few friends. Luke was walking away when the guy with her car called out to him. "Hey, Luke. You busy? Could you maybe give this little lady a ride to her I.D.? I can't give her back her car without it."

Luke walked back. "Sure can," he answered. "I just got off duty."

Mar went with Luke despite her reservations. She wanted to be friends again. She decided to try lightening the mood. "Hey. I hear you're Luke. Well, I'm Margaret. Most people call me Marge."

Luke seemed to be playing along. "Good to meet you. I'm Luke." But then he decided to have a little fun. "I believe you're *living* with my cousin." He laughed. He'd deliberately accented the word "living" just to get a response.

Mar stopped in her tracks. She wasn't going to do this anymore. She turned and began to walk toward the bus stop. But Luke stopped her. "Mar, I'm sorry. Please. Just let me take you to your stuff. You need your car, right?"

Mar turned to look at him. "You know, Luke, this morning I was wishing you the best. I was thinking about how pretty Jodi is and how much she likes you. And I remembered her saying once how she was helping you but that no one was supposed to know. I wanted you to find happiness and really wondered if she might be the one for you. But you've said some very hurtful and mean things since I've known you. And Jodi doesn't deserve that. And I don't really feel that I do, either. I didn't plan to love Jeb, I just do."

Luke was watching Mar's face. When she finished, he reacted, "I'm sorry. You're right. I wasn't trying to be mean, really. I just thought I'd have a little fun. Come on, I know you're not that kind of girl. And Jeb's a good guy."

Mar let a tear fall but wiped it quickly away. "Well I'm not sure… never mind. It's okay. I just don't think either of you know how it feels to be undermined so often that you begin to doubt your own sanity, your own judgments. Because that's who I've been for some time now. And now I'm finally allowing myself to experience the loss and pain

By Dianne J. Beale

that Mitch protected me from. For the first time I feel completely alone."

Luke apologized, giving her a hug. He ushered her to a nearby table with chairs. "Mar," he sighed. "I did at one time think that I might love you." He paused, but Mar didn't say anything, so he rushed on. "Anyway, I wanted you to know that most of what you may have heard was deliberate rumors to keep my cover safe. I wasn't doing the blackmailing–Trish and Andres have that corner of the market, not me. Will you promise not to tell anyone what I'm about to share?"

Mar agreed and Luke continued. "Trish was being blackmailed by Andres. This is why she agreed to be the daycare lady even though she'd be working for him. She was told to do whatever it took to get Mitch out of the way. There was no ex-boyfriend. It was just supposed to look that way. And Trish blackmailed me. She was terrified of Andres so wanted me nearby as insurance. Trish was, and had continued to be, Andres' mistress, even while he was wooing, and then married, to Amelia. But Amelia doesn't, hasn't ever, known. She can't find out, either. She and Trish need to work that out on their own; they need each other."

Luke paused to scan Mar's face. "Anyway, remember the day I text-messaged your phone, telling you not to go home? Andres had planned to kidnap you that day. Well, Trish knew I warned you, but kept her mouth shut until she decided to blackmail me into an engagement. I took a gamble and agreed. I couldn't risk Andres finding out that I was not acting in his best interest. I feared that Jodi might think that she'd been scorned, but I decided to confide in her, and she consented to help. I just want you to think well of me again. I want us to stay friends."

Luke then stood, held a hand out for Mar, and ushered her into his car. "Please think about it. Okay?" Mar nodded, saying that she would. They traveled in silence to Jeb's house. She went inside to grab her I.D. and checkbook and then returned to the car. Once in, she buckled her belt and they headed back to the police station. Neither noticed the car that passed them. It was a gray Mitsubishi. And Jeb was the driver.

Back at the station, she and Luke went their separate ways. She filled out all the forms and her car was returned to her. She gathered all the information that her brother would also need and then headed toward the empty lot of charcoal that she once called home.

Once there, she couldn't even bring herself to exit the car. She sat crying, through memory after memory. When she realized it had grown dark, she finally tried to pull herself together. She climbed out from the car and kneeled in the ashes. And she prayed.

When she finished, she began to stand and her knee uncovered a ring. She picked it up and put it on her finger. Crying, she thanked God for the special reminder. It had belonged to her mother.

By Dianne J. Beale

Chapter 77

As she drove back toward what she now considered her prison, she became more and more like stone. When she saw the familiar sign, she pulled into the drive and went in to rent a room. She just couldn't be in that house another night. Jeb couldn't possibly want her if he didn't understand what he did. How could he not know how much he had hurt her by just dismissing her on the night that Luke had come out to the house and spoken of Trish?

She decided to call Mitch from her cell and make arrangements to meet him somewhere so she could give him the information about his car and phone. Then he could just bring her things once he was again driving around on his own.

She moved the car to in front of the rented room and then got out from behind the wheel. Not having any luggage, she suddenly realized that she was still wearing yesterday's clothes. After tonight, these clothes would be three days old. Well, she could buy a cheap outfit in the morning, but she'd still need to eventually get her things from the house. She picked up her phone to call Mitch but wasn't sure how to reach him. What if Jeb answered? She put the phone into her pocket and went back to the front desk.

"Can I help you with something?" the lady asked, recognizing her.

"Do you think you could ask for a Mitch Zeiler for me? I don't want his house mates to know it's me who's calling," Mar lied.

"Sure thing, hon. Got yourself a rendezvous?" she twinkled.

Something like that. Actually, he's my brother, but I've dated some of his friends," she stammered.

The lady took the phone, hit the *send* button, and then asked for Mitch.

"Hang on, I'll get him," she was told.

"Mitch Zeiler here; who's calling?" The lady handed Mar the phone.

"Hi Mitch, it's me. I didn't want Jeb to know. I'm at a hotel for the night. I've got information I need to give you about your car and phone and wondered where I should meet you tomorrow."

She waved a thank you to the lady, mouthing the words as she walked back toward the door. She went into her room once she'd arrived.

"This is ridiculous. He's brooding, and you're avoiding. What's going on?"

"I can't believe you don't know. You both treated me like a child last night. I won't live like a mindless drone

By Dianne J. Beale

anymore. I know you've always tried to protect me, Mitch, and I can understand that. But I can't live with a new someone who treats me like a child and doesn't value what I have to say. If the relationship were real, then he would have listened to me."

"Mar, then come and talk to him. Our relationship is real, and I didn't listen, either. We're human, Mar. We make mistakes. How come it's so easy for you to forgive me and not him? How can he treat you like a woman when you act like a little girl?"

When Mitch finished his sentence, she hung up the phone. She went to the computer in the corner that was advertised as providing free Internet and began an apartment search. But soon she was hopelessly weeping. What was she doing? She couldn't live with Mitch forever. He was the one with a job. And she had nothing. She looked down at her mother's ring. "God, I need a mother now," she muttered.

Her phone rang. She planned to ignore it but found herself answering instead.

"Hello, Mar," said Luke. "Has he called you yet?"

"Who?" asked Mar.

"Jeb, of course. He left me a rather colorful message. Something about my immoral behavior with his woman at his house. Then he uttered a bunch of expletives that I didn't even know he knew. He told me to keep you; he isn't interested in buying used goods."

The Uninvited

"What? Nice to know what he really thinks of me, isn't it?"

"Actually I think it was meant as a strike against me."

"Nice way to strike at you. Society is rarely as hard on the man. What's he going to do now, woo Jodi? I think I just decided to stay blissfully single."

"Doesn't sound much fun to me. Aren't you going to fight for him? What a pair you two are. Neither of you believe in your love."

"Good night, Luke. I think maybe he's decided it died." Mar hung up the phone, shut off the computer, then stripped down to her underclothes and crawled into bed. She'd just drive over to Jeb's in the morning, collect her stuff, leave a note with the key, and disappear out of his life. She fell asleep as miserable as ever.

By Dianne J. Beale

Chapter 78

She woke to a phone ringing. "Wake up call," the voiced claimed.

"Okay, thanks," said Mar. She dressed quickly and then went to the front desk to check out. She then got into her car and stopped off to eat. After a full meal, she filled her tank with gas and headed out to Jeb's. She felt smug in her plan and had a sense of satisfaction when there were no cars in the driveway.

She unlocked the door and went into the house. She was glad that she hadn't unpacked. She carried her cases to the car and was closing the trunk when she heard him.

"After all my hospitality, I don't even get a goodbye? Where are you running? To Luke's?"

Mar felt her face flush. She was livid. How dare he! She decided to ignore him. She had no reason not to. She'd left his key on the dresser, along with a thank-you note.

She moved to get into the car, but he was faster. "I asked you a question, Sweetheart," he grated. "Don't I deserve an answer?"

Mar moved to make her way around the car to enter on the other side. Again, he blocked her. Tears began to sear her face.

"Tears? A woman's answer to everything. Just squeeze out some water. Make the man falter. He will if he has a heart, right? I suppose that's true. So what does that say about me?"

Then he saw the ring. He grabbed her hand. Mar wanted to hit him. He knew she was inexperienced. He had to know. But how many women had he kissed before her? Probably more than she could count.

He was only her third boyfriend. And she'd only kissed one other. And he, Jack, had betrayed her, too. She and Anthony had barely even held hands. He had insisted that everything, even kissing, had to wait for the marriage bed.

She was shocked to hear herself say, "I love you, Jeb. But that doesn't matter. I need to go now. Please move aside. Mitch should be waiting for me."

Jeb scanned her face. "He was here with you yesterday. You drove right by me and didn't even notice. Don't try to lie to me."

"No, I didn't notice you. And yes, Luke drove me here yesterday. But he stayed in the car. I'm sick to know what you believe I'm capable of. And yet I still love you. But don't worry. No need to trouble yourself. It's not your problem anymore. I'm going to ask God to change that. I want to be free again. Free to desire only Him."

By Dianne J. Beale

He moved away from the car as if stunned and she got in and drove away. It wasn't until much later that she realized he'd worn a look of pained horror at her words. She suddenly realized that he still thought she was referring to Luke. He had no way of knowing that her "Him" had been capitalized and had chosen to believe the worst. She could tell because he had obsessed over the ring. He hadn't taken his eyes off it. Yet, fearing the answer, the question had not been voiced. It hung between them.

Mar finished off her errands and then helped Mitch to get his car. Once the car was released, Mar followed Mitch as they drove to Jeb's so Mitch could return Jeb's car. But when asked to come in, Mar declined. So Mitch reluctantly climbed into Mar's passenger seat and they drove off together; she dropped him by his car.

Leaving him behind, she drove away. She had then traveled aimlessly and it was growing dark outside. She decided she should eat since she hadn't eaten anything since breakfast. As she paid for her meal, the business card she'd taken from the cottage fell to her lap.

She went to a table to wait for her number to be called. Picking up her cell, she phoned the Canadian cottages. They had the very same cottage available for only fifty dollars per night since it was now off season. They told her that it would be ready whenever she got there; it was part of their twenty-four-hour, guaranteed services. Mar thanked them, picked up her meal, and went back to her car. She got in, after checking the back seat, and was again on the open road.

When she arrived, the clerk behind the desk insisted she didn't need a key. "The Mister picked it up," he had said. She was too tired to work it out so decided that as long as the cabin was open, the mix-up could wait.

The cottage smelled of burning pine and fresh Italian bread when she entered. She turned to go back out to her car so she could drive again to the check-in area. There had to be some mistake.

But a deep voice stopped her. "I hoped this would be where you sought refuge." Mar stopped in her tracks.

Jeb crossed the room and placed his hands on her shoulders. He gently turned her to face him. "I love you, Mar. I begged for God to give me a second chance. And here you are." Mar still hadn't moved. She was just staring, blankly.

"Later tonight, Mitch will arrive to kick me out for the night. He and I will stay at a hotel down the road. Then tomorrow, we'll take that wedding license we bought while I was making sense, and we'll tie the knot down at the town hall. We can plan a public wedding for a later date."

Mar, at last, looked up into his earnest face. "You still want to marry me? But do you really understand?"

Jeb flinched. "I lost one fiancée, Mar. She's the reason I joined the FBI. I needed to feel that I was making a difference. But I've been offered a consulting job at the

By Dianne J. Beale

offices where your brother now works, and I've agreed to take it. I want a family, Mar. I want you. We'll have a lifetime to build our understanding."

Mar looked down at her trembling hands. "The ring belonged to my mother. I'd forgotten I put it on," she whispered. "I hadn't meant to deceive…"

Jeb kissed her lips to silence her. "I know" was all he said.

Mar buried her face in his neck, kissing him. Then she looked up at his face. "Yes, Jeb, I will marry you," she whispered. Gaining confidence, she added, "Without you, I'm good. But with you, I'm better."

Jeb recognized his cousin's phrase and smiled at the twist she had given it. He beamed down at her; "I know exactly what you mean."

Made in the USA
Middletown, DE
23 July 2017